Hollingsworth

To my wife, Angela.
Thank you for allowing me to indulge in this, my latest whim.

And to the *lupis* who almost got me...
Tag, you're it!

Tom Bont

Angela took the lead and crept to the right across the dusty, wooden floor. Danny stalked left. They stayed hidden behind the control consoles should the alien, or monster, or whatever Task Force W called these things, chose to swivel around. As she got to her side of the console, she chanced a peek around the corner. One stretcher contained a woman, the second one, a man. The third one held one of those chupacabras…chupacabri…

What the hell is plural for chupacabra?

All three were restrained. Danny crouched below the other end of the console, one eye on her and the other on the alien. She nodded once and stood up.

"Freeze! FBI!" she yelled, "Cease all…cross-universe experiments and put your hands behind your head." Considering the FBI refused to train her on how to arrest cross-dimensional beings, she was quite pleased with herself and her ad-lib adjustments.

Hollingsworth

By
Tom Bont

Tom Bont

First Printing: 2019

Paperback ISBN 978-0-9962417-7-9

Table30PressBooks@gmail.com

Season 1

Tom Bont

Hollingsworth

Lagniappe

The first episode of *Hollingsworth*, "Redstick, Texas," appeared in *Road Kill: Texas Horror by Texas Writers* as the short story, "Redstick." Fans who read it strongly suggested that it would make for an exciting start to a whole new adventure.

Voila!

I want to thank Beverly, Jan, Kate, and Kathy for their help with editing and crawling inside a woman's mind. They are now part of Angela Hollingsworth.

I would also like to thank the DFW Writers' Workshop for their assistance and critiques. They have helped me refine my craft. Any errors or mistakes are only because I failed, not them.

Tom Bont

Episode 1: Redstick, Texas

"Hollingsworth," Angela mumbled into the phone. Moonlight shimmered through her window, and a blurry 5:02 AM glowed on the digital clock face.

"Agent Hollingsworth," a frantic voice babbled, "I...I need yer help and raht now!"

She sat up in bed. The voice... "Ambrose?"

"Yeah! I—"

"How the hell did you get this number?" She jumped up from the bed, and the wisps of a beach vacation dream evaporated.

"Yer business card."

Trick! grumbled through her head. "What do you want?"

"To confess...to everything! But you hafta' get me outta here!"

Angela's blood pressure spiked. She started the recording app on her phone. The conversation wouldn't hold up in court, but it would certainly go a long way toward helping her case. "Daryl, I'm recording this conversation. Is that okay?"

"Yes. Fuckin', yes! Just come 'n get me!"

"Okay, repeat what you just said."

She recognized the sounds of fear as they crowded her ear, heavy breathing, smacking lips. "I said I wanna confess to everything, but you gotta help me! They're comin' for me!"

"Settle down, Daryl. Who's coming for you?"

"Crazies, I think." His voice faded as if he turned to look over his shoulder, away from the handset. "Hell, I don't know! I just know they got really big-assed dogs."

A tractor-trailer roared through the call's background. "Where are you?" She tapped the speaker button on her phone and set it next to her laptop.

"Outside Redstick, Texas."

She brought up a mapping site but kept talking. "Okay, Daryl, go to the local police station. If you can't find that, there's a diner on the main strip. Should be open this time of morning."

"Okay, but yer comin' to get me though, raht?"

"Yes." She looked at the caller ID. "This number good to call you back?"

"No, it's a pay phone."

"A pay phone?"

"Yeah. It's an old gas station. North of town, I think."

"Okay, Daryl. Repeat what I want you to do."

"Go to the police and if they're closed, go to the diner."

"Good, Daryl. Good. We're coming." She hung up and called her boss. He was a good man. He'd take care of this.

"Angela?" She could almost smell the second cup of coffee in his voice. She hated morning people.

"Evan, listen to this." While the recording played back, she glanced at her sleep-mangled black hair in the mirror and decided with a grimace she didn't have time for a shower. Makeup either. She kicked her nightgown to the corner, put her hair into a ponytail, and took a "Marine Shower" as her brother used to say…lots of deodorant.

When the recording finished, Evan whistled lowly. "Why would he do that?"

"Something spooked him," she mumbled around her toothbrush. "Maybe his conscience woke up. Don't really care, though." Spit. "We got the bastard!"

"Ang, don't go off half-cocked. The U.S. Attorney got a black eye last time because the evidence was so weak. We need a good confession or good evidence this time, or we'll both be reading fertilizer invoices for the rest of our careers."

"Afraid of a little bad publicity?" she teased.

"Damn right, I am. My wife likes that supervisor paycheck I bring home. Keeps her in satin sheets and that Audi. Says it makes up for me not being there all the time."

"Don't worry, Evan. I want this twisted fuck nailed to the wall this time. If all I wanted were to see him off the streets, I'd have shot him in front of the courthouse." When the judge dismissed all charges against him, they bumped into each other on the front steps of the courthouse. He didn't say anything to her, but his laughing eyes spoke plenty. Her hands still shook at the memory of his smirk.

Her own blue eyes stared back at her from the mirror. "Teenagers, Evan. Those three girls were teenagers, for Christ's sake." She trailed off as the bloody scenes flashed before her. "I can't believe we can't find one damn witness."

"I know. But if you look up 'Average American Male' in the dictionary, his picture is listed next to the definition. On top of that, no credit, lives in his truck, collects a disability check once a month. He's well-nigh invisible in a crowd. Hell, the only reason I knew he was in the courtroom last week was because he smelled bad."

"Smelled bad? Damn, you've got a sensitive nose."

He chuckled. "You even know where Redstick's at?"

"North of Caddo Lake. Texas side of the border across from Fouke, Arkansas."

"You want me to send someone from Shreveport? They're closer than Fort Worth."

"Hell, no! This is my case."

3

"All right. Besides, if anyone knows their way around a small town, it's you."

"You trying to make me quit?"

"Sorry. I forgot how much you like to hide your roots." He took a long, deep breath. "All right. I'll call local law enforcement and have them hold Ambrose on a vagrancy charge until the U.S. Attorney okays his arrest. In the meantime, you go get that confession."

The lanky, wizened police chief walked up the sidewalk and stuck his hand out. "You must be Agent Hollingsworth. I'm Chief Wilcox."

He had a friendly enough look on his face but considering she was there to take custody of a child killer, he seemed too pleasant in her opinion. She figured Evan hadn't filled him in on the particulars of the case.

"Thanks for your help." They shook hands, and through unspoken agreement, strode into his office, her legs taking two strides to his one.

"Aw, think nothing of it! And call me Jim. How was your drive?" he asked.

"Long. But fine, thanks. And call me Angela. My apologies for sounding impatient, but I need to see Ambrose. Where are you keeping him?"

Jim took his hat off and scratched a balding pate. "We don't have him. He didn't show up here. An officer has been sitting at the diner since, um—" He pulled out a small notebook and flipped through a couple of pages. "Since Agent Evan Welch called this morning at 5:30."

Angela clenched her fists, turned in a slow circle, and made a beeline for the women's bathroom. "I'll be back in a minute."

Five minutes away, and no one went to get him! Maybe they should change the town's name to Redneck.

The thought brought a sarcastic snicker and turned the heat down on her boiling temper. She crammed a piece of gum into her mouth and chewed at it as if she was trying to gnaw through saddle leather, a habit she learned at the academy; it was better than opening her mouth when she shouldn't have. She stopped flexing her hands long enough to relieve her bladder and went back out into the main office. "Can you take me to the diner?"

"Sure," Jim said, "Not sure what you're looking for. My officer would have called if your suspect had shown up."

"I just want to look around, ask a few questions."

Jim rubbed his clean-shaven chin. "Yes, ma'am." He turned to an older woman sitting by a bank of telephones and an antiquated dispatch radio. She had a thick book in her hands, Stephen King's *Silver Bullet*. "Helen, I'll be at the Lucky Star."

"Surprise. Surprise." She never looked up from her book.

Redstick obviously didn't know how to petition the federal government for law enforcement cash because Jim led her out to an older model Ford Expedition. It had seen better days, but Angela had to admit it was still comfortable. There was a child seat, a plushy snake, and a primary reader in the backseat. "You do much cop-type work out of your personal vehicle?"

Jim glanced over his shoulder as he snapped on his seat belt. "All of it when I don't have the grandkids with me." A crooked grin crossed his face. "Don't see much trouble around here." He twisted the key in the ignition. "Occasional out of town hunter with a little too much beer in his belly and not enough brains in his head. And any of the kids who get in trouble, we just call their parents at the scene. Folks around here respect each other. And the law."

Idyllic, 1950s Americana. That was Redstick.

Three old men sat in front of the barbershop. The man pumping gas at the service station wore an attendant's uniform. Main Street was spotless, and the local postman walked with a spring in his step like he enjoyed every minute of his job. When Angela and Chief Wilcox pulled up in front of the diner, Angela swore she smelled homemade apple pie.

The diner was full of an early lunch crowd. When the little bell mounted over the wood frame and glass door announced their arrival with a ting-a-ling-a-ling, most everyone turned from their meals and either waved or shouted a friendly greeting. To the left ran a long counter fronting the steamy kitchen behind it.

An officer in a steam-pressed uniform with creases so sharp they seemed aerodynamic met them right inside the doorway. Jim said, "Special Agent Angela Hollingsworth, this is Officer Danny McIver."

The officer grabbed her hand and shook it. "A real-life FBI agent, here in Redstick? Heck, I ain't never woulda' guessed it!"

"Settle down, Danny. Don't shake her shootin' hand off."

"Well, that ain't my shootin' hand, but let's leave it there anyway, okay?" she said as she tested all of her fingers. She chastised herself; *did I really just say ain't?*

"Oh, sorry, ma'am." Danny spun around and quick-stepped over to a table. "Here, I been holdin' these seats for y'all in case you showed up."

Angela smiled. "Thanks, but I'd like to talk to everyone if I may."

Jim lifted his hands into the air and raised his voice, "Can I have everyone's attention, please? This is Special Agent Hollingsworth with the FBI. She'd like to ask y'all a few questions."

As soon as all eyes were on her, she pulled a picture of Daryl Ambrose out of her briefcase and held it up. "I am looking for this man. He called me this morning from a gas station north of town. I need to know if anyone knows where he is or if anyone's seen him." She handed the picture to a young woman sitting near her. "Please pass it around, ma'am."

A man from the back of the room spoke up. "What did he do?"

"I'm not at liberty to say. This is an ongoing investigation, but I can assure you it is imperative we get him off the streets. He's driving a '97 Chevy, supercab pickup. Red, but one of the passenger side doors is blue."

An old woman sitting in the back spoke up in a voice reminiscent of rusty nails being pulled from an old windowsill. "Bad folk don't last long 'round here," she cackled as she returned to her plate of food.

"Why's that, ma'am?"

Danny grimaced, and Jim stepped up. "Thanks, Mrs. Haster." He leaned in and whispered in Angela's ear. "That's Ma Haster. She lost her marbles well over twenty years ago."

Angela stepped back and waited while everyone passed the picture around. She watched for reactions, trying to glean if anyone was hiding anything or not. Small, jerky movements. Lip biting. Itchy noses. Avoiding looking at the picture. Bouncing knees. Popping knuckles. *Nothing.* There was one cowboy in tight-fitting jeans. *No more cowboys!*

When the picture made its way back, Jim stood up next to

her. "Thanks, everyone. If you see him, please call the police." He turned to Angela. "You might as well eat while you're here. We can stop by the 47 afterwards."

"The 47?"

"The gas station north of town. That's when old man Henshaw built it, 1947, after the war. Lived in the back until he died about twenty years ago. His son owns it now."

"I don't suppose it's got a security camera, does it?"

Danny sputtered, "Oh, crap!" He snatched his cell phone off his belt and pulled up some pictures before handing it across the table to Angela. "I forgot with all the excitement of actually meeting you. There's a cash machine there. I called the bank, and they sent the pictures to me. That there's his truck!" Jim looked at Danny with surprise on his face.

As she was forwarding the pictures to her email account, Jim's radio squawked to life. "Chief, I got a report of a 10-45 David out on Hobart Road with that early model, red Chevy pickup."

Jim looked over at Angela and keyed his microphone. "Definitely 45 David?"

"Affirmative. That's what Hobe said."

"Thanks, Helen. We're Code 3, lights only."

Code 10-45 David meant a dead body. Code 3 indicated lights and siren, but Jim modified it to lights-only. If the body was at the same scene as Ambrose's truck, it might be Ambrose. She hoped not. She wanted him to answer for his crimes. Death was too easy for him. "Any ID on the body?"

Jim radioed Helen. "Helen, any ID on the 45 David?"

"Negative, Chief."

They climbed into the Expedition, and everyone in the diner watched them through the windows. Exciting day in Redstick.

Angela and Jim drove out to the south of town and into a large thicket. The road they used had changed from asphalt to gravel a couple of miles back. They traveled deeper and deeper into the forest. "How long before we get there, you think?" she asked.

"Pretty soon."

"How do you know that?"

"This is Hobart Road," he said, pointing ahead. "We've been on ol' Hobe's land for about 10 minutes now. Any farther, and we'll be off his land."

Sure enough, they rounded a bend, and up ahead two trucks were parked by the side of the road. One was a large, four-wheel drive, painted camouflage, with two men in hunter's orange standing near it. The other was a burned-out husk, little wisps of smoke still curling around it. Angela sat as far forward as her seatbelt would allow and peered through the windshield. "What the hell happened?"

"I'm not sure…"

Angela made a phone call. "Evan, I might need an Evidence Response Team in Redstick."

"Why?" he asked.

"I think we've found Ambrose's truck, and we've got a body."

"I can't authorize an ERT, Angela. The U.S. Attorney is waiting on the results of your interview. If he's dead, it's a local matter. Case closed for us. Sorry."

"You serious?"

"I'm afraid so. I've been on the phone with them all morning."

There was no way she was going to let that stand. If Ambrose was dead, she wanted to know why. "I'll be in touch," she said, hanging up and turning her phone off before Evan had a chance to order her back.

Before the wheels stopped rolling, Angela hopped out and rushed up to the burned-out vehicle. She took note the cab was empty and pulled a napkin from her pocket to wipe the char from the license plate. She slowly stood up. "It's his truck." She turned to the hunters. "Where's the body?"

The older of the two—she guessed the father of the younger one—looked at Jim as if he needed permission to speak.

"She's with the FBI, Hobe."

"Oh," Hobe grunted, scratching his salt and pepper beard. "About a hundred yards in, ma'am. Just follow that small trail next to the fence."

"Can you show me?"

"Yes, ma'am."

The muddy trail brought her up short. She had her street shoes on, black with thick, rubber soles. They were as comfortable as tennis shoes, but they also suited the FBI's dress code. Unfortunately, they weren't designed to slog through the woods.

Jim dropped a pair of big-man-sized hunting boots at her feet. "These should do the trick."

"Thanks," she said. "My field kit includes a pair, but it's all in the trunk of my car." As she put them on, she glanced at Hobe and his son's feet. Their boots were mud-free.

They came upon the body right where Hobe said it was. What they hadn't mentioned was the condition of the corpse. Angela wasn't a forensic pathologist, but it was clear to her large carnivores had chewed on the body. She crouched down next to it for a closer look. "Chief," she continued, "y'all got critter problems around these parts?"

Critter problems? Ugh!

Her country roots were sneaking back into her speech the longer she spent in Hicksville.

The chief looked up from writing in his notebook. "Not that I've heard."

"Looks like you got one now," she mumbled as she scanned the landscape of the surrounding woods.

"This Ambrose?" He took his hat off and wiped his brow with his shirtsleeve. "Face looks kinda tore up."

"It's him. I recognize the tattoos on his arms. Three little, pink hearts. One for each of his victims."

Angela leaned back against a rather old, but still functional autopsy table. At the request of the FBI—well, she's in the FBI, right? —and in the spirit of interagency cooperation—she really needed their cooperation—the local coroner, Dr. Albert Monroe, moved the Ambrose autopsy to the top of the stack—a stack of one. He'd called her and Chief Wilcox to his office to discuss his findings the next day.

When they'd first brought the body to the coroner's office, the chief had suggested she head back to Fort Worth. "I'll forward the results to you once we've got 'em," he said, flashing a wide, white smile at her.

"I appreciate that, Chief, but if it's all the same to you, I'd like to hang around and see it to its end."

He'd bristled. "Suit yourself. Mary-Beth's there next to the diner usually has a room available."

She'd taken his advice, but the room was barely two-star, and she was glad she only had to spend one night there. The air conditioner rattled, and the shower mold looked like it needed a proper, wire brushing. She didn't consider herself

Susie Homemaker, but she did like a clean bathroom.

"Without getting into the medical details," Dr. Monroe began, "he died from an acute myocardial infarction brought on by severe cardiorespiratory exertion." At hers and Jim's confused looks, he translated. "He died from a heart attack due to long-term exertion."

"What about the mutilations?" she asked.

"Sharp tooth trauma. Ha! Get it? Sharp tooth trauma?" Neither she nor Jim laughed. "Ahem. Pack of dogs got him after he died. It's all in the file. Here's your copy. I've already forwarded one to your office."

She looked at Jim. "Dogs."

"I guess you were right," he said. "Sounds like we do have an animal problem. Al, any idea how many, breeds, anything?"

"At least three. Probably the size of German Shepherds."

Jim rubbed his chin. "So, Ambrose ditches his truck, runs into the woods, panics about something, either gets lost or is chased by dogs, and dies from a heart attack. Then some dogs, maybe the ones chasing him, chew on his body."

"That's the only explanation I can come up with," Albert said.

Angela tensed up. "I don't buy it. He was ready to turn himself in! And he was only thirty-five years old. A little young for a heart attack."

Jim shrugged. "Maybe he changed his mind."

"And his truck," she said. "Why burn his truck?"

"Setup?" he offered.

"Setup? How?"

"He calls you and says someone's after him. Then, lo and behold, his truck is found torched, and he's gone. You stop looking because you think whoever was chasing him, got him. Only instead of being gone on his terms, he stumbles on a pack of wild dogs. I have an official category for those types of situations."

"Yeah? What's that?"

"A win!" He shined his wide smile again. "This is a win, Angela. Take it and run."

Angela shook her head. "Eaten by dogs." She thumbed the coroner's report. "Thanks, gentlemen. I guess I'm done here. Could you ship the body to Fort Worth for burial? COD."

"We can cremate it here," the doctor offered. "It'd be easier."

"No, it's our responsibility," Angela replied. "Thanks anyway."

She called Evan as soon as she got on the road and filled him in. "It's all bullshit. I ran deerhounds with my older brothers. I've seen what meat looks like after large breed dogs have had their way with it. The teeth marks on Ambrose were twice that size. The hunters didn't have mud on their boots. What, did they change boots before I got to the scene? Something's not right here."

"Does it matter?" he asked. "We've got a child killer off the streets. The chief's right. This is a win, case closed. You've earned a notch in your belt even if you didn't personally collar him."

"Maybe you're right," she conceded. To her eyes in the mirror, she argued, *"No fuckin' way."*

As soon as she pulled onto Interstate 20, her mother called. "How are you doing, Angela?"

"Great! How are you, Mom?"

"Lonely. You know. What are you doing right now?"

Angela set the cruise control. "Driving back to Fort Worth. Working a case in East Texas." She refused to take the 'lonely' bait.

"Oh. Never mind."

Sigh. Hook, line, and sinker. "What's the problem, Mom?"

"Have you visited Chris this week?"

"Yes. You know I have. We always get there at the same time. Is everything okay?"

"I was supposed to get a call from him today but didn't."

"Maybe he didn't earn the privilege." It started to rain, so she turned the wipers on.

"Since when does a boy have to earn the privilege to call his mother?"

Here we go.

"Since he went to prison, Mom."

"You mean since you sent him there," she cried. "Can't you do something about this? You're the responsible one. They'll listen to you."

Angela wanted to tell her that Chris was getting the help he needed but knew her mother didn't want to hear that. "I'll see what I can do."

"Thank you." Sniff. "You coming over for dinner Wednesday night?"

"Yes, ma'am."

"Okay. Bye. Love you."

"I love you, too, Mom. Tell Dad hi for me."

Angela dreaded dinners with her parents these days. No matter how well she behaved herself, they always ended up giving her the Look. Betrayal. Remorse. Disbelief. Hate.

The first time she got it was the day she stepped down from the witness stand. Expecting heart-broken, she got

14

shattered instead. Her mother's face had been the worst. Testifying against her twin brother had been the hardest thing Angela ever had to do. And the jury saw it. The prosecutor crowed about her tears being magical deal-closers, but they might as well have been battery acid for the sting still ripping through her soul. Chris wouldn't be able to hurt their dad again, though, at least for the next year. After that? Who knows? You can't trust a junkie. They'd sell their own kid for a fix.

Their whole life, Chris had always been the one scratching up trouble where there shouldn't have been any. And it had always been her getting him out of it. Like their seven-year-old Christmas. She'd caught him standing on the TV trying to reach the lighted Rudolph on the wall. He wanted the blinking nose.

"I'm scared, Kis!" she hissed, using her toddler name for him because she'd had a hard time with 'r's when they were kids. "I won't be able to catch you if you fall!"

He ignored her. He tumbled off the side. She tried to catch him. She broke her arm when they hit the floor. She'd convinced her parents she was the one who'd wanted the nose, and Chris had gone after it for her.

Angela cursed the wipers for not doing their job until she realized it was her eyes that were blurry and not the windshield.

Angela pulled a stick of gum from her pocket and shoved it into her mouth. The Tarrant County Chief Medical Examiner, Dr. Fred Sherman, was laughing at Dr. Monroe's report. "Oh, yeah, Ambrose was definitely chewed on by something, but he was alive when it happened. Dr. Monroe is either incompetent, or he's blind. Every test shows

Ambrose died from blood loss. And my professional opinion is it was not a dog. I don't even think it was a wolf."

Around a stream of nervous gum chewing, Angela asked, "What was it then?"

"I have absolutely no clue. DNA says Canidae, though.

"Cana-what?"

"Canids. Dog, wolf, fox. You know. Can't narrow it down further than that."

"Why not?"

"Either the DNA has degraded too much to get a decent reading, or we have a prehistoric proto-wolf roaming around East Texas."

Angela stopped chewing. "Proto-wolf? What kind of critt...animal is that?"

"Something that was around before modern wolves evolved." He threw the pictures on his desk next to comparisons from other wolf and large dog attacks. "You were right about one thing; the fangs and claws that cut up Ambrose were larger than those on a large breed dog. In fact, they're larger than those found on the wolf skeletons from the La Brea Tar Pits in Los Angeles. That's what I'm saying. I'm not sure what killed him, but it wasn't anything in my taxonomical textbooks, and it damned sure wasn't a heart attack."

"I can't believe you managed to get time off tonight," Angela said as she swirled a large mass of spaghetti noodles onto her fork. She put the noodle ball into her mouth and sliced a giant meatball in half. The meatballs at Don Genti's were works of art.

"Got a new resident," Heather said. "He's taking Thursdays."

"Cute?"

"Yeah, in a kid brother kinda way." Heather stabbed a chicken piece with her fork and swished it around in the tomato sauce. "The nurses are all fawning over him." She chewed on the chicken and looked at Angela's bowl of noodles. "It doesn't even look like you've taken a bite yet."

"I know, right?" Angela said. "The noodles seem to multiply the more I eat." She raised her fork to her mouth, stopped, and put it back down. She tilted her head to the side, stared at her bowl, and whispered, "Noodles."

"Huh?" Heather asked, interrupting her.

Angela shook her head. "It's nothing."

"You sure?"

"Yeah." But she continued to gaze at the noodles. They reminded her of the old woman from the Lucky Star. Ma Haster.

She'd said, "*Bad folk don't last long 'round here,*" before turning back to her lunch—a large plate of spaghetti and meat sauce.

And the look on Danny's face when she'd spoken. In her mind's eye, he…grimaced? No. Wrong word.

Wince? Yes. He winced.

What am I missing?

Sticks and stones break bones, but words reveal secrets. *Angela's Interrogation Tome, page 1.*

With an inward groan and an outward sigh, she sat back in her chair.

"What's up?" Heather asked.

"Nothing. Really!"

"Angela, I've known you since college. You aren't going to be good company tonight until you solve that puzzle. I got the check, now get!"

Angela stood up and hugged her friend. "Thanks, Heather. I'll call you tomorrow."

It was past ten by the time Angela got to the federal building. She went straight downstairs to Archives. The hallways were empty. The only people left were guards and workaholics like her. She sat down at one of the terminals and typed "Redstick, Texas."

The results appeared on her screen. *Three pages of events around that half-horse town?* It was going to be a long night.

Most of the references on the screen were for boxes of files not yet digitized. She sent it all to the printer and spent the next three hours roaming the Lumber Yard, the Bureau's slang for the non-digitized warehouse of paper files. By 4:00 am and three large, unsweet teas later, she'd put together a brief history of the town based on newspaper articles, Texas Ranger archives, and FBI reports.

Jeremiah McIver, a preacher from New England and immigrant from Scotland, founded Redstick, Texas in 1843. *An ancestor of Officer Danny, I bet.*

The population doubled when the railroad put a train stop there about ten years later.

She could have put together a thorough history of the town, but she was more interested in the crime reports. For instance, back in the 1800s, a Texas Ranger chased a gang of train robbers into the area. No one heard from the gang again. The Rangers surmised they'd had a run in with the Baker Gang and lost. It wasn't until after the turn of the century the reports increased in frequency. She suspected there were more in the 19th century, but not reported.

The more interesting ones were the disappearances. In 1905, a snake oil salesman on the run from authorities in Shreveport was last seen headed into the woods to the east of town. No one heard from him again, either. Part of the Bonnie and Clyde Gang hid out in the area. When Clyde Barrow went to join them, they were nowhere to be found. According to one James Carter, a pianist at a downtown Dallas speakeasy, Mr. Barrow said, "That town scared the willies out of me, and I ain't going back."

During World War II, the Korean War, and the Vietnam War, most of the draftees from the area skipped out. The government never found them. A couple of oil and gas companies tried to drill in the area, and most of their crews quit within days of arriving. They said the townsfolk scared the bejesus out of them. Those who didn't formally quit, skipped town, and never picked up their last paycheck. The companies finally gave up.

And the latest: Ambrose turns up chewed to death in the woods outside of town by a prehistoric proto-wolf, the only victim she can find in the area who didn't disappear outright.

She sat back in her chair and reviewed the different reports. Disappearances happen all the time, especially during the time frames they were reported. *I'm missing something.*

She decided to look through the reports, not as individual events, but as incidents in a larger pattern. She sat up in her chair as she read the name of the police chief during two of the instances. The name pulled at her.

Conrad Welch. As in Evan Welch?

Her trance broke at the sound of a door closing and the lights going out.

"Hello? I'm still here," she yelled.

No one answered back.

She used her cell phone light to make her way through the aisles of shelved cardboard boxes to the door to turn the lights back on. When she got back to her terminal, someone had rifled through her notes and the neat pile of ancient records she'd collected. She twisted her head and looked around. "Hello? Who's here?"

Evan's voice echoed back at her from her left. "You should've taken my advice, Ang! Should've taken the win!"

"Evan?" She drew her Glock and gripped it in the two-handed style she'd been trained to use. "You're from Redstick?"

"Yes." This time his voice was from behind.

Keep him talking. "Why didn't you tell me?" No answer. She pulled her phone from her pocket, set it on the table, and pushed record. "Did you have anything to do with Ambrose's death, Evan?"

"Does it matter how he died?"

Angela spun around. His voice was close. To her right.

"Right to a trial, Evan. We arrest them. We don't try them." She crept down the aisles closest to her terminal. "We're not vigilantes."

"He was a child killer!" His voice sounded like he was back on her left again.

He's traveling in a circle around the room. He's stalking me!

"Why don't you come out? Let's talk." She peeked over her shoulder. "Maybe you have a point. You did save the courts a bunch of time." That last sentence sat on her tongue like sour milk.

He laughed with a low grumble. The laughter turned into a growl. "Don't patronize me!" he yelled. His voice changed timbre. It now sounded like he was talking through an empty paper towel tube. But there was something else there. Pain. He whimpered in pain. But it was deep, guttural. *Primal.*

The logical part of her mind told her she was in danger,

and the other part confirmed it by telling her to hide. She turned to make a mad dash for the door, but her feet rooted to the floor in primitive fear as a howl pierced the air. It grabbed hold of her soul and made her wish for daylight, warmth and peaceful ignorance.

She stood in a shooter's pose, afraid to move, and continued to stare down the aisle.

Be small. Be insignificant. Hide!

A shadow stretched around the corner, and a monster from forgotten nightmares followed it.

The creature crouched but was rangy. No clothing, though coarse, short, brown fur covered it. Huge teeth protruded down the sides of its blunt snout.

It rose to its full height when it finished rounding the corner and casually walked towards her, as if coming to ask for directions.

It dragged its paw along the boxes on the shelves. When the claws scraped across the metal framings, they dug in, leaving furrows as if they'd plowed through warm butter. She risked a look into its eyes.

Inhuman and pale blue, they glared back. The word "werewolf" jumped into her mind.

This is what killed Daryl Ambrose.

And it was coming for her.

She wanted to yell, "Freeze! FBI! You're under arrest," but her training and self-discipline failed her. She tilted the barrel of her Glock upwards a smidgen. The monster's eyes caught the movement and widened in surprise as she pulled the trigger.

Although she was going for a center mass shot, through luck, the grace of God, or errant FBI training, the bullet found its mark in the center of the creature's forehead. The werewolf fell to the floor, and Angela took a deep breath. She kept her weapon trained on it as it transformed into her boss, Evan Welch.

You don't like headshots, do you?

Deputy Assistant Director Stan Stevenson read from a stack of papers. "The conclusions of the Department of Justice's Office of the Inspector General are as follows:

Article One: Special Agent Angela Hollingsworth, acting on instinct and in the best interest of the American people, took it upon herself to question the official findings of the cause of death of Daryl Ambrose.

Article Two: Special Agent Angela Hollingsworth discovered a link between Supervisory Special Agent Evan Welch and Daryl Ambrose in Redstick, Texas.

Article Three: When Supervisory Special Agent Evan Welch discovered Special Agent Angela Hollingsworth had found the relationship between the two men, he portrayed the link as if he was responsible for a vigilante-style murder.

Article Four: It is assumed Supervisory Special Agent Evan Welch had unlawful and nefarious purposes planned for Special Agent Angela Hollingsworth. This is evident from the recordings made by Special Agent Hollingsworth, the condition of the surveillance cameras in Archives, and the state of Supervisory Special Agent Evan Welch's body; to wit, he was naked. This attack was staged to cover up his involvement, and any other as yet unknown facts.

Article Five: Special Agent Hollingsworth acted properly in self-defense against Supervisory Special Agent Evan Welch.

Therefore, it is the decision of this board, Special Agent

Hollingsworth, you be returned to active status and promoted in grade to Senior Special Agent, effective retroactively six weeks back from today to the night of the incident in question.

"And may I say," Deputy Assistant Director Stevenson continued, "Senior Special Agent, the American people and the Federal Bureau of Investigation owe you a great debt of gratitude for weeding out this cancer in our midst."

Angela continued to stand before the three-member board while their decision sank in. Not only did she stay out of prison, she kept her job. She never mentioned the werewolf, of course, and with the video cameras disabled, there would have been no one to believe her if she had. Indeed, she'd pushed the whole werewolf thought to the back of her mind, refusing to dwell on it until she'd had the time to evaluate in detail. That helped in the beginning; her shooting review psychologist insisted he wasn't getting the whole story, though. Over the weeks, the details turned fuzzy even for her.

Wait, Senior Special… did he say promotion?

It made no sense. Promotions were highly coveted and extremely competitive. *Hush money?*

She broke out of her reverie only when her lawyer leaned in close. "Angela, forget about the—"

"Sir, I have one question," she said.

Stevenson looked up from his papers. "Yes?"

"The research I was performing in Archives, the coroner reports. Was any of it ever recovered?"

"No, I'm afraid not. The investigating agents have been reprimanded for failing to properly tag all evidence. Unfortunately, no one knows where it's been placed." His smile was as sweet as Sunday ice cream. "I'm sure it will turn up eventually. And, as you know, Ambrose's body was cremated by mistake, a bureaucratic oversight, I'm told."

Angela paused for a few moments while her lawyer shifted from one foot to the other. "Yes, sir," she said.

"Good!" Stevenson said. "Now, what are we to do with you? Although you have been cleared, we here on the board are not so naïve as to believe you'll be able to find a comfortable working environment. You did, after all, shoot a fellow agent. Based on your experiences in this matter, and the initiative you've shown, I've decided to assign you to Task Force W."

An administrative assistant appeared at her side with a fingerprint-secured thumb drive. If plugged into a computer by a finger not containing the keyed print, a memory chip holding the decryption key would be destroyed.

"Task Force W, sir? I've never heard of it."

"Everything you need to know is on that thumb drive."

She put the drive in her pocket. "Yes, sir."

"Excellent. This hearing is adjourned. Congratulations, Senior Special Agent Hollingsworth."

Angela stood on the sidewalk across the street from the Lucky Star Diner for close to fifteen minutes before she decided to go in. No one showed any signs of recognizing her, so she chose a table near the front window and ordered a chicken Caesar salad. Chief Wilcox came in and sat down at her table as she finished eating. The waitress met him there with a cup of coffee.

"Good afternoon, Senior Special Agent Hollingsworth. Is there anything I can help you with?"

"You know my new rank." She pushed her empty salad

bowl to the side of the table and took a sip of her tea. "You're well-informed for someone so far from civilization."

He sat back in his chair, crossed his legs, and placed a toothpick in the side of his mouth. "We like to keep up with current events. We even have this new-fangled thing called an internet that helps us with that."

"Hmm. I didn't think vigilantes cared about what happened in real law enforcement circles."

Jim chuckled. "Vigilantes?"

She put her tea down on the table. "Tell me, Chief, how many people know what he was?"

"What do you mean? He was an FBI agent."

"Don't insult me. I've learned over the years to trust my instincts over unconnected facts. Yeah, he was an FBI agent, but he also grew fur and howled at the moon, right?"

All conversation in the diner ceased, and everyone looked over at her table. The chief's eyes had turned to pale blue—exactly like Evan's on the night she'd shot him in the head. She dropped her hand to her pistol.

"Don't," the chief said. "You aren't fast enough."

She froze as a chill settled on her forehead, and the hair on the nape of her neck stood up. "You're a werewolf…?" Everyone else's eyes had changed, too.

He removed the toothpick. His voice dropped to a guttural slur, and he bared his fangs. "Yes. And we're only slaves to the moon once a month, Senior Special Agent. But to answer the question on your mind, yes, we killed Ambrose. We don't consider ourselves vigilantes, though. We just have a strong sense of the natural order of things. We—" he waved his hand around to indicate everyone "—keep our territory clean. And I think deep down you know what we did was right."

Angela swallowed a large lump. She'd pushed the werewolf angle to the back of her mind in her effort to remain out of prison because the mind can play tricks when adrenaline if flooding its containing body. But seeing the chief's eyes drove it home; Evan had been a werewolf. And everyone around her was, too.

"Maybe, but did you have to, you know, eat him?"

"We only chewed. We didn't swallow."

"Thin difference, Chief."

She took her time as she reached into her purse, well within his line of sight, and pulled out a twenty-dollar bill. He didn't make any threatening moves; indeed, he continued to sit with his legs crossed, never flinching, nor tensing.

"You aren't upset? About me killing Evan?"

"Of course, we are! But he made a mistake. He should've turned you. Made you an ally, so to speak."

She hung her purse on her shoulder, moved to get up, but changed her mind. "Why didn't Ambrose disappear like everyone else?"

"Evan said you would've turned this town upside down looking for him. And we couldn't make you disappear—"

"—because the FBI would have scraped Redstick off the map looking for me."

"Probably." He put the toothpick back in. "You don't seem that scared, you know, considering."

She took a deep breath and blew it out slowly. "I've got a junkie for a brother, Chief. I used to chase child kidnappers, child killers, and child rapists. I've seen quite a bit of evil in the world. You may be scary, but I don't think you're evil. Hope I don't find out otherwise."

"Fair enough."

"You played me. And Officer McIver did his part. He had

me convinced he was competent, getting those pictures like he did."

"He is competent. Don't let that Barney Fife exterior fool you." The chief's fangs had receded. "And he didn't know anything about how Ambrose died until after the fact." He shook his head. "Senior Special Agent. *Angela*. Please don't fear us. We're on the same side. We have our own community, and we would like to keep it that way."

Angela took another sip of her tea.

Chief Wilcox continued. "There's no place else for us. We owe you. You could have dragged us into the investigation, but you didn't. Thank you."

Angela nodded thoughtfully at the idea of being owed a favor from a town of werewolves. She placed the $20 bill on the table and walked out to her car. As she started it, everyone on Main Street stepped out of their doorways. And as she drove out of town, every set of eyes she made contact with had turned pale blue.

Tom Bont

Episode 2: Task Force W

"**S**he put a curse on him, a hex," the young woman cried.

"Who did, Mrs. Hernandez?" Angela asked. Curses. Hexes. Not the usual fare for an FBI agent. But Task Force W didn't investigate the typical FBI cases. She glanced at Clint, her new partner, to gauge his reaction. Tall, dark, and mission-oriented, he'd been in Task Force W three years. He appeared to be taking the statement at face value.

"Lilith Blank," Mrs. Hernandez answered. "She's a witch, I tell you. Lives up in Denton."

Angela looked back at her. "What makes you think she cursed him?"

"Because Walter loved me!" She had surprise on her face as if the question didn't require answering. "Three years. That's how long he waited for my father to give his blessing. A man won't wait that long unless he loves a woman." She perched on the edge of her chair with her hands on her knees, twisting a tear-dampened handkerchief.

Angela took that moment to scrutinize Mrs. Hernandez's living room. It wasn't fancy. It was lived in. Comfortable. Wedding pictures on the walls showed Christi and Walter to still be newlyweds. A few others showed a cute, happy couple. Not the kind where the police catch the husband dead in another woman's bed.

Clint put his pencil to his notebook. Old school. "How long were you two married?"

"Six months." Christi dabbed her eyes. "We were already talking about children."

"That soon?" Angela asked. "Which of you talked more about it?"

"He did. He has a large family. Had." Tear dabbing again.

"How did you feel about it?" Clint pressed.

"I wanted a family, too, but I wanted to wait a bit," she confessed.

"And how did he feel about that?"

"He understood. He was willing to wait." Clint scribbled a few notes in his little book.

"But he met Lilith, right?"

"Yes."

Angela crossed her hands and rested them on her knees. "How did they meet?"

"Walter stopped to help her change a tire. He was like that. Always helping people."

"When was that?"

"Two weeks ago."

Angela knew she'd let her surprise show but quickly buried it by shifting around in her seat.

The man moved fast. Or Lilith did.

"How long after that did they start seeing each other?"

"I think that night." Christi sniffed and wiped her nose. "He came home, and I could tell there was something different. Said he had a good day. Helped some woman change a flat tire, but when he talked about her, his eyes lit up." She blew her nose and cast an apologetic look at them. "During dinner, he didn't talk much. Stared off into space. Daydreaming. As soon as we finished the dishes, he called her to check to see if she made it home okay. I was surprised he had her phone number! Then he left, saying, 'She's worried about the tire. Seemed to shake on the drive home. I'm going to check on it.'"

Angela jerked her head back in shock. "He drove all the way from Arlington to Denton to check on a tire?"

Clint shut her down with a stern look.

Just the facts, Hollingsworth!

Again, she'd acted unprofessionally and let emotions out during the interview. The FBI tolerated it when chasing child-killers, but she didn't chase those any longer.

"Yes! He didn't come home that night either. He swore to me that he slept on her couch, but he didn't. A woman knows. Don't we Agent Hollingsworth?"

Sometimes. Had the shirt. "What makes you think she put a curse on him?"

"He became obsessed with her. Every night for the next week, he was up there. He would come in the next morning, take a shower, and go to work. He wouldn't even wash her filth off before he came home. Then one night before he left, he said he wanted a divorce. The police came the next morning and *sniff* and *sniff* and told me that he'd died." Fat tears rolled down her cheeks as she bawled in heavy sobs. Angela slid over and put her arms around the distraught woman.

Clint's next question died in his throat when Angela tossed *him* a dirty look.

After a few moments and a final sniff, Mrs. Hernandez whispered, "A man waits three years for a woman, marries her, wants to start having kids, and within a week of meeting someone else, says he wants a divorce. Agent Hollingsworth, how do you describe that other than a hex?"

Two weeks ago, Angela would have laughed the first time someone asked her to take hexes seriously. However, since her run-in with a town full of werewolves and subsequent assignment to Task Force W, she figured a Magic

8-Ball would be more accurate.

Angela stared out the windshield at the pouring rain, trying to ensure none of the crazies on the road opted to take her and Clint with them should Darwin's Theory of Natural Selection pluck them from the tree of life. "Do curses or hexes or whatever really exist?"

"Absolutely," Clint forcefully stated. "I've only seen one though."

A large, passing truck splashed a thick wall of spray, forcing her to slow down and shift over to the right side of her lane.

"Excited?" he asked.

"About what, this being a W case?" A sly grin danced across her lips. She hadn't given it much thought. But now? Nostalgic, like skulking up her childhood home's hallway with her twin brother on Christmas morning. Their parents wouldn't let them into the living room until hot chocolate filled their cups and Elvis Presley crooned carols from the stereo. "Maybe a little. Do you think Lilith really put one on Walter?"

He glanced over at her and pursed his lips. "They're rare from what I understand."

Angela couldn't help but let her excitement show.

"Don't worry," he assured her with a chuckle. "You've earned your chops. A werewolf? That's the big kahuna. Everyone hopes for one like that. Relax."

Werewolf? Singular? Oh, crap, that's right! He doesn't know it's the whole damned town!

She kept her eyes on the road and took a deep breath. "I look back to Redstick and, well, it just seems too much on the surface. Then I run through the facts in my head, and I

32

begin to believe again."

"That's Task Force Weird for you."

"Weird?"

Clint chuckled. "What did you think the W stood for?"

"Wickersham," she answered. "The man who headed the first federal investigation team. At first, I thought it was for Werewolf." Contrary to popular mythology, Ichabod Crane didn't finish off the headless horseman. Wickersham did.

"Correct. But we find Weird better describes it." Clint twisted sideways in the seat. "Did you know there were actually two other men who worked with him. Eric Robinson and Christian Dietz."

She bounced a confused look at him.

He dropped another hint. "W. R. D. Last names?"

Realization struck her like a lightning bolt. *WRD. WeiRD!* "No, way!"

"Anyway, they don't assign anyone here unless they've encountered something, um, weird. Finding a werewolf in Redstick surely fits the bill."

"What did you run across?"

"I found a serial killer's skeleton."

"That doesn't sound too weird."

In a voice as dry as West Texas, he said, "Inside a dinosaur skeleton ribcage fossil."

"Oh."

Angela pulled up in front of Lilith Blank's house. It didn't flash *witchy*. Of course, Angela wasn't sure what kind of house a witch would live in. If Lilith even was a witch. She made a mental note to research witches as soon as she cleared her caseload. And curses.

The rain had stopped as they drove into Denton, so the

St. Augustine creepers covering the sides of the sidewalk dampened their shoes by the time they stepped onto the stoop. Clint stood four paces behind Angela and to her right as she rang the doorbell. After a few moments, a woman answered the door. Blonde hair, blue eyes, mid-30s. Thigh-hugging yoga pants told Angela this woman worked out and worked out hard.

"Can I help you?" the lady asked.

"Yes, ma'am. I'm FBI Senior Special Agent Angela Hollingsworth, and this is Senior Special Agent Clint Lane." They both showed their badges. "Are you Lilith Blank?"

"Yes, I am. What's this about?" Lilith straightened her back and blinked rapidly. Nervous. Expected though. The FBI doesn't knock on your door selling girl scout cookies.

"We'd like to ask you a few questions. May we come in?" Agents always suggested talking inside a suspect's house. People feel more comfortable in their own home. Comfort leads to overconfidence. Overconfidence leads to lying.

The more lies, the more opportunity Angela could trip her up. *Angela's Interrogation Tome, Page 4.*

Angela sensed hesitation from her, but when she peeked at Clint over Angela's shoulder, she gushed, "Absolutely!" and stepped to the side.

Angela's senses surged to high alert as soon as she passed the threshold. She'd spent numerous hours in scenarios where a simple invite into a witness's house switched to a close-quarters combat scenario. With Clint four paces behind her, he kept an eye on Lilith while Angela surveyed their immediate surroundings. The FBI drilled this behavior into all its agents until it became instinctual.

The front door led into a short foyer where a 1980s-style paneled living room unfolded into a breakfast nook at the end. An antiqued side table sat against the right-hand wall. To the left, a petite opening leading into the kitchen. As Angela noted available exits, Lilith turned on a giggle behind her.

"Hi! I'm Lilith! It's nice to meet you, Clint. What's this about?"

"It's about Walter Hernandez. And it's nice to meet you too, Lilith," he said.

He did not *just use her first name!*

Angela spun around. They were shaking hands, and his attention centered on Lilith alone. Angela leaned against the wall as if making room for Lilith to walk past her and scrutinized the living room. "Ahem. Ms. Blank, are you here alone?"

"Yes," she responded, her gaze never leaving Clint. "Other than your handsome partner here." She tore her eyes from him and stared at Angela as if it was the first time she'd laid eyes on her. "And you."

Lilith had usurped control of the interview and turned Angela into a third wheel. Clint's expression told her in no uncertain terms, *"Ask your questions so we can get to the good stuff."* She knew what constituted the "good stuff."

The three of them moved into the living room. Clint headed towards the end of the sofa where Lilith had sat. Angela beat him to it, though, plopping down in his intended spot and forcing him to pick the recliner across the room.

He lowered himself into the seat, and his eyes devoured Lilith as she parted her lips and her knees at him.

Angela knew she had to get a handle on this meeting soon, or they wouldn't get anything useful out of Lilith. "Clint," she said, patting her pockets, "I've left my phone in the car. Would you mind going out there with me while I get it?" Clint didn't need to go with her, but you never left a male agent alone in the same room with a female interviewee, and vice versa.

Clint's face closed up in frustration, but he nonetheless followed her towards the front door. "We'll be back in a few moments, Lilith."

As Angela opened the car door, she tipped her head to the side and gaped at Clint. "What the hell is going on in there? That's the most unprofessional display I've ever seen. You want me to sit out here while you do her in the living room?"

Clint caressed the back of his neck. "What are you talking about?" He gazed back at the house. "I'm being friendly. Trying to put her at ease."

"Yeah, well, you were trying to put something to her." She slipped her hand into her pocket and pulled out her phone. "Ah! I had it with me the whole time. Listen, Clint. Why don't I conduct the interview? You stay by the front door."

"I don't think that's necessary."

"I do," she insisted. "You're compromised." Agents never slung 'compromised' at each other unless they witnessed something untoward…like sexual attraction between suspects and partners.

Clint's head snapped up, and he glared at her. "Fine."

He didn't stand by the front door, but he did remain outside the living room, and out of sight of Lilith. He maintained the required line-of-sight to Angela, so she knew his big head had assumed control.

"How long have you lived here, Ms. Blank?" Angela asked.

"Call me Lilith." She glanced towards the foyer. "Where's

Clint?"

"He's watching the door," Angela answered. "Common procedure in certain situations. Now, how long have you lived here?"

"About four months. I have a six-month lease."

"How did you meet Walter Hernandez?"

"I've already answered these questions with the local police. Is this necessary?"

"I'm afraid so."

"Well, I had a flat tire, and he stopped and fixed it for me."

Angela went through the standard interrogation procedure, posing questions she already knew the answers to. She wasn't digging for new information. She was trying to spot inconsistencies. People have a harder time remembering lies than they do the truth. *Angela's Interrogation Tome, Page 4, Addendum.*

"He died while you two were having sexual intercourse. Is that correct?"

"Yes. He must have had a bad heart."

Lilith's answers matched the police report.

Dr. Fred Sherman, Tarrant County Chief Medical Examiner, leered over the rim of his glasses at Clint. "All men should die this way." He handed the report across his desk.

Clint chuckled. "Yeah, I suppose so, but if it's all the same to you, I'd prefer not to go at all."

He reached for the report, but Angela stepped in front of him and took it first. "Testosterone humor aside, we need to know what caused his death." While the two men slipped into a chastised silence, she slid her finger down the report until she got to the summation. "Says here that he died from an acute myocardial infarction brought on by severe cardiorespiratory exertion. He exercised himself to death? This is what Doctor Monroe said Ambrose died from in Redstick. You plagiarizing, Doc?"

"Nope. This time it's true. Poor Walter screwed himself to death. The man even went with a smile on his face." Fred showed a picture of an old man to Angela and Clint. Sure enough, the man had a broad grin frozen in time.

"That's not Walter," she exclaimed.

"Actually, it is," he asserted.

"Can't be. I saw his picture at his house. Late twenties. This man—" she pointed at the picture "—is at least 80 years old."

"Walter suffered from Late-Onset Hutchinson-Gilford Progeria."

"Late-Onset what?"

"Late-Onset Hutchinson-Gilford Progeria. It's rare. Typically only affects the internal organs, and then over several years. In this case, it spread like wildfire in a short time."

"English, Doc." Angela crammed a stick of gum into her mouth. "I just hunt bad guys."

"He had a rare disease that caused him to age up to five times faster than normal. But what happened here is the disease decided to ravage his system over a short time. Vigorous interactions with a younger woman? It's no surprise his 100-year-old heart gave out."

Clint speculated, "So, it wasn't murder after all?"

"Nope," Fred said. "Afraid not. DNA test confirms it."

"Case closed then." Clint headed for the door with a new-found hunger in his eyes. "I'm taking a few days of vacation while my desk is empty."

Angela licked a large dollop of mustard from her lip as a forward body-checked the center. The hockey puck scattered to the left and a Blues wing shot it back towards the Stars' goal. With a mouthful of hot dog, she yelled, "Defense, Big-D, defense!"

Heather yelled, "Yah, Blues!" Though from a traveling, military family, she claimed St. Louis as home.

The players passed and intercepted the puck a dozen times before the clock ran out. The Stars won the match, two goals to one.

Heather taunted everyone within earshot as she sent off a text. "Pure luck! No Skill!"

Angela pointed to Heather's phone. "Do I need to drop you off at the hospital?"

"No," she answered, sliding it into her back pocket. "The new resident's a little shy when it comes to narcotics. Likes to check with me on everything." They didn't get much chance to talk to one another as they jostled for position amongst the rest of the audience on their way to the parking lot, but once there, Heather asked, "When's the last time you visited Chris?"

"Last weekend."

Heather paused for a few heartbeats. "How's he doing?"

"Better from what the shrink's saying. Mostly still giving me the silent treatment though. And doesn't call Mom as often as he should."

"He'll come around."

"Maybe." She pulled onto 35E and headed north. "Mom and Dad? I don't think they ever will."

Her mom's words echoed in her head. *"You're supposed to*

be the responsible one! How could you let this happen?"

"Sorry."

"Thanks." She smiled warmly at her friend.

"At least he's still going to group," Heather offered.

Angela snorted. "No choice. He's a captive audience. No pun intended." She honked her horn at a moron shifting four lanes at once. A loud rumble roared past her, a jacked-up four-wheel-drive pickup truck. "Rednecks," she muttered.

A smirk lit up Heather's face. "Speaking of rednecks," she teased, "heard from Karl lately?"

"No, and I don't care to." She grew up in Hicksville, USA. She may have loved the slow lifestyle, the friendly neighbors, and the wildlife, but Karl epitomized everything bad about it—no ambition, no imagination, no future. And that's why she hated it, too.

Heather picked at her fingernail. "He still texts me to see how you're doing."

"What do you tell him? Never mind. I don't want to know."

"I told him exactly what you told me to. 'Never seen her happier!'"

"Maybe he should text that high school cheerleader I caught him in bed with." She wasn't really in high school, not by two months anyway. "I've given up trying to figure out what a 35-year-old man wants with an 18-year-old girl."

"If you don't know the answer to that," Heather taunted, "it's time for your physical. I need to make sure that certain parts of your anatomy haven't dried up and blown away." She keyed in another text and stared back at her friend. "Sister, you need to put yourself out there!"

"I've tried. All the men I run into are either four-wheel-drive rednecks who party at the lake every night or Lexusdriving salesmen who lay around my apartment on the weekends watching golf." She knew deep down that was just an excuse, though. She didn't have the time to devote to a relationship. They were over long before she caught him in bed with the cheerleader. Maybe the breakup wouldn't have been so bitter if the girl hadn't been a teenager. Nah. She also knew deep down that was something she told herself to calm her mind before bed.

Heather snorted. "I'll take either one of those compared to the god-complex-doctors I work with."

"You're a doctor. Are you saying you're the only one without a god-complex?"

"It's not a complex. I'm convinced. Besides, I'm tired of dating myself. Or my hands are anyway."

Angela dropped her forehead onto the steering wheel and gawked over at her friend. "Oh, my God! I can't believe you just told me that!"

"Damn, girl, it wasn't that funny! New job must be boring to get that kind of reaction."

"No, work's fine. In fact, I closed my first case today."

"Can you talk about it?"

"Yeah. Case of Progeria."

Heather's happy face switched to serious mode. "Progeria? Hutchinson-Gilford Progeria?"

"Yeah, the late-onset kind. Guy was cheating on his wife. Disease came on quick, and he died in his lover's bed. Wife's tore up."

"Progeria's rare, but late-onset is practically unheard of."

"That's what the coroner said."

"Did he say that's the second case in the metroplex this year?"

41

The first thing the next morning, Angela drove across town to the FBI's main office to visit Archives. Either Task Force W didn't warrant an office there, or someone decided it should be apart from the normal investigation teams. On the one hand, it made sense. On the other, it was a pain in the ass because all the records were elsewhere. A contractor was close to getting the data connection tied in, but the timetable changed each day.

She strolled into the main entrance and passed her ID card over the reader as she always did. The guard, Tony Santos, gasped and stared at her with surprise. "You've been promoted, Agent Hollingsworth. Congratulations!"

Angela studied the screen. She not only had been promoted, she now had W1 clearance. She had access to any case the FBI was investigating.

W1, Task Force W.

Only the Agent in Charge of the case could deny her access. Besides the AIC, someone of higher rank could technically deny her, but only by special request. This kind of access was not lost on her. It was big. Mind zinging like a pinball machine, she resolved to look into her missing papers concerning Redstick. "Thank you, Tony." She connected her ID to her lanyard and let it drop against her shirt.

Stepping off the elevator at Archives, she stood at the end of the hall staring at the main doors. The last time she'd stepped through them, she'd had to pull her weapon and shoot someone. Her boss. A friend. Or at least someone she believed to be a friend until he transformed into a werewolf and tried to eat her.

I wonder if they got all the blood cleaned up. Of course, they have. It's been nearly two months.

She straightened her badge and leaned into a forward

march towards the doors. She wasn't sure what she expected as they swallowed her and spit her out the other side, but things were quieter than usual.

Bill Olson, the Head Archivist, lazed behind the front desk reading a book. He was a young man, younger than she was, but his stooped posture and thin, messy hair made him look older. He perked up when Angela came through the doors, peering at her over the top of his glasses. "Senior Special Agent Hollingsworth. What brings you to my little cubby hole? And during the day when I'm around?"

"Hi, Bill. Need to do a search." She glanced around at the empty room. "Where is everyone?"

"System's down. Contractors cut a line while they were hooking up some satellite office."

"How long before they get it back up?"

"Don't know. What are you looking for?"

"I need a list of all reported cases of—" she pulled out the autopsy report for Walter Hernandez and slid it across the counter "—Late-Onset Hutchinson-Gilford Progeria or any deaths with related symptoms."

Bill took the report and flipped through the pages with a practiced hand. "I'll have to tap into the Centers for Disease Control archives to scan their reports. Don't have the data here. And I can't do that until they get my data link back up."

Angela shoved her hand into her jacket pocket and pulled out a piece of gum. "When?"

"How far back you wanna go?"

"Not sure." If this case fell under Task Force W jurisdiction, she'd require more than a few years to connect all the dots. "Let's start with the last ten. If we see anything suspicious, clustering maybe, take it back as far as you can."

Bill straightened his neck and whistled lowly. "Monday

maybe. Maybe longer. I have to learn what the symptoms are before I can search for them in the older style reports."

She crammed her stick of gum into her mouth. "Thanks. Call as soon as you have something."

"Will do."

The steel cage door clanked and a loud buzzer drilled into her ears as she waited for the guard to let her through. It was a familiar sight, the yellow and red lines, the gray chipped paint on the walls and bars, the Lexan windows at all the guard stations.

"Happy Saturday, Agent Hollingsworth!" the last guard in the gauntlet shouted.

"Happy Saturday to you too, Morris. Turn any screws this week?"

"Nope!" He took her Glock and two spare magazines from under the window and handed her back a receipt. "They keep promising me I'll get to soon, though."

This had become their usual banter over the last three months.

One of these days, I'm going to change the question and see how he reacts.

"Let me know how it goes!"

"Opening Five!" he yelled out.

Another loud clank and buzzer signaled her entry into a private visitation room where her twin brother sat, secured to the table.

"Hello, Chris," she said as she leaned over to give him a hug.

He sat there, stiff as a mannequin. "Hey," he finally answered back, refusing to move his lips.

That was more than she usually got from him. Her first

few visits, he refused to see her at all. She finally bribed him with a care package of cigarettes. He showed up with bruises decorating his face, some new, some old. Cops not only had a rough time in prison, but the immediate family of FBI agents did too it turned out. She'd called in a few favors and had him transferred to a block for "at risk" prisoners. He still had a rough time, but it was better than solitary.

She looked at the track marks on his arms. Mostly healed, they were more scar tissue than skin. "How are things going?"

"Okay."

"Wanna talk about it?"

"Not really."

And that's how they jump-started her visits. Today though, she had some different news. "I got a new job."

He perked up. "You not a pig anymore?"

Take ten deep breaths…One. Two. Aw, fuck the breathing exercises.

She pulled a stick of gum from her pocket. "I'll let you go on that one because I know life in here is rough. But you call me that again—" she put the gum in her mouth "—I'll kick your ass while you're still handcuffed to that fuckin' table."

"Sorry I let you down!" he spit at her. It was not an apology. She spent the rest of her time staring at the walls while he gave her the Look.

Way to go, Angela. One. I want one conversation with him that doesn't end in an argument.

When her time came to an end, she met their parents in the waiting room. "You could have come in," she told them. "We weren't talking much."

"Well, I suspect not," her mother snapped, "since you're the one who put him there. You're supposed to be the responsible one! How could you let this happen?"

"Anne," her father warned, "let it be."

They bestowed *their* Look as they rushed past to spend their half-hour with him.

Angela wiped tears from her face as she strode across the parking lot. She spent the rest of the day in bed and under the covers. And the next day. Other than eating a bowl of ice cream for breakfast. And lunch. And supper, though she put nuts on it.

Angela spent Monday morning at her desk sorting through email blathering on about the typical agency gripes; inaccurate reports; how appropriations were pinching budgets; people should refrain from using more than one piece of paper towel to dry their hands after washing them in the restroom. One piqued her interest. It entailed a reminder to those folks in the "weird" department to unload all silver rounds before shooting range practice. She made a mental note to check with Clint on whether that was a joke or not.

Her daily quota of deletions out of the way, she polished the Hernandez report.

Clint, face pale, collapsed down in his chair before she hit *Send*.

"Damn, partner," Angela blurted. "You look like warmed-over death. Too much vacation?"

"I think I picked up a cold or something."

One of the other agents on the task force, Brad Johnson, a grizzly bear of a man with a face always in need of a shave, yelled out across the room. "A cold? Guess that new girlfriend gave you more than you gave her!" Everyone in the office laughed except for Angela. "What's the matter, Hollingsworth?" he teased. "Don't like humor?"

"Like it just fine. When I hear some, I'll let you know."

"Ouch," Bill razzed. "Don't quit your day job, Johnson."

At least I think Bill's his name.

Angela circled back to Clint. "New girlfriend, huh?"

"Yeah."

"And here I thought you didn't know how to have fun." She leaned back in her chair. "Anyone I know?"

"Nope."

"When are you gonna bring her around?"

"Never."

"Do you give answers with more than one word?"

"Sometimes." A smile crept across his face and disappeared. "Morning, Kent."

Angela peeked over her shoulder as Kent Gladen, her new boss, walked into the gang room. He stopped at her desk, smoothing his slim black tie, the only tie she could recall him wearing, against his shirt. "Report on the Hernandez case?" he asked, his tone low and gritty.

"Should be in your inbox, right—" she pressed the *Send* button "—now."

"I need both of you in my office. Something weird in Wichita Falls."

Something weird. A joke?

Kent's only three decorating indulgences were an Ohio State Buckeyes Brutus bobblehead on the front of his desk, his Buckeyes coffee cup, and a picture hanging on his wall of a younger, military version of him along with some other soldiers. Burning poppy fields blazed in the background. The bobblehead, she'd been itching to poke since the first time she'd walked into the office. The picture, she'd stare at with intense curiosity until she realized he wasn't going to offer any information past what was depicted.

47

Taciturn, he also wasn't into small talk. "I talked with the Wichita County Sheriff, Elroy Ackerman, while I was driving in this morning. He has three murders I'm interested in. Someone skinned them. Need you to go consult and lend assistance if possible."

Angela asked, "Werewolves?" To date, Evan accounted for her only supernatural encounter.

"I doubt it. Not their typical M.O. Take some silver bullets with you anyway. Works on most things."

Angela shot Kent a look. "I didn't need silver when I killed Evan."

"Werewolf brains are just as sensitive as a human's," he drolled. "Destroy it, the werewolf dies."

Wichita County Sheriff Elroy Ackerman placed a picture up on his whiteboard of a body with the surface texture of a skinned, bloody grape. His sweaty underarms showed a man who'd been spending long nights and even longer days on a case. Aside from a shower, a razor might have done him some good, too. "Three nights ago, the body of John Aster, a bulldozer operator, was found in a culvert eight miles from town." He got back mixed gawks of horror and curiosity on Angela's and Clint's faces. "Well, we're assuming it's Aster. We found his truck nearby." He ran his hand across his black, stubbly head, and crow lines radiated from his brown eyes as he squinted at the picture.

"Two nights ago, Greg Spain, a local, self-proclaimed cattle baron, was found four miles from town in a creek bottom." He put another picture next to the first one. Skinned too.

"And last night—" another picture, same wounds "—the county judge, Wilford Craven. This time, in the parking lot of a local watering hole."

"Have the, um, skins been found?" Angela asked.

"For Spain and Craven. Not Aster."

"Whatever's doing this is getting braver," Clint muttered. "It's moving closer to town."

"I agree." Elroy continued studying the whiteboard. With a start, he glanced back at Clint. "It? I don't know anything other than a man who could do this. What makes you think it isn't a man?"

"The suspect might be human, but he's—or she's—a monster too." Clint pursed his lips. "It," he declared with finality in the tone of his voice.

Angela flipped through the coroner report. "Says here there weren't any knife wounds or claw marks. How did the suspect remove the skin?"

"Yeah, I wondered that too. That's when I called the Texas Rangers. If there's some cult overdosing on crazy around here, I was hoping someone might've heard about it. They said someone would call me back. About ten minutes later, I was talking with your boss. Supposedly, y'all handle stuff like this."

"We never get the standard murder," Clint confirmed. "We always get the weirdos."

Elroy squinted back to the pictures. "Well, this sure does peg out my weirdo scale."

Angela continued reading. "Aster and Spain both died from exsanguination. Blood loss? No stab wounds. No defensive wounds. Good God, they…they were skinned alive! Why would a grown man sit there while someone skinned him?"

"Drugs maybe? Toxicology reports haven't come back yet," Elroy confessed. "That's a preliminary you're reading.

I'm really hoping they were drugged, 'cause if they weren't, then we really do have some crazy cult on our hands."

Angela stepped up to the pictures and examined them in detail. "What can you tell us about these three? Any connections between them?"

"None that I know of. Judge Craven and Spain belonged to the same hunting club, but the dozer driver, Aster, didn't quite run in their circles."

Clint rubbed his jaw. "Sheriff, you have a deputy you can send out to the club? I'm curious if Spain and Craven had any dealings."

"Yeah."

"Thanks. In the meantime, can you take us around to the sites?"

They began at Craven's murder scene and failed to uncover anything other than what was in the report. A blood trail led east, but it faded after a hundred yards or so.

Elroy pointed to a mesquite tree. "That's where the investigators found his skin. Right here on the ground up against the trunk."

Spain's location had about the same amount of information, but its blood trail dribbled to the southeast for about half a mile. It had ended at a skin as well, this time hanging on a *No Passing* sign next to a pockmarked road.

When they got to Aster's, Angela volunteered to canvas the ditch. Like the other scenes, police tape stretched around the area. The sheriff's department had left a single patrol car parked nearby, but the tall grass and side of the trench shielded it from her. "Who found him way down here?"

"Johnny Hanson. Works for the public utilities. He was driving to work and noticed the ditch overflowing. We'd had a rain the night before. Aster's body had plugged up the culvert."

"So, the body could have been dumped here," she mumbled.

"Possibly."

"There's only one way to find out." She kneeled down, and her knees rustled the soft grass. Whatever water had collected in the ditch had succumbed to the dry Texas air and receded. Bone dry. The beam of her flashlight disappeared down the length of the culvert, but a glint reflected back at her from within.

"I'd be careful down there," Elroy warned. "You might find a—"

"—snake!" Angela screamed as she scrambled back along the ditch.

"Hang on," Elroy insisted. He showed back up a few moments later with a pair of long-handled tongs. "We keep a pair in the trunk. Never know when they'll come in handy." He stepped down into the ditch and seized the snake. "Rattler."

Angela wasn't particularly scared of snakes, growing up out in the sticks as she did, but she sure knew to grant them their space. Didn't stop the adrenaline from doing its job, though. Her hands were still shaking. "Little shit didn't rattle until I was right on it!"

"Yeah, they do that sometimes if they think a predator will keep going," Elroy admitted. He pressed the head of the snake to the dirt road and mashed his heel on it, killing it. "What'd you see?" he asked as he lobbed the snake's body into the tree line.

"Not sure. Something flickered up in there."

Did I really just say, "up in there?" Damn, I hate the country!

She pointed at Elroy's tongs. "Can I borrow those?" So armed, she crept back down into the ditch. Once certain no snakes hid in the mouth of the culvert, she stretched out with the tongs and snagged the sparkling glint. It was a high school class ring...on a piece of skin as well preserved as a glove.

Elroy produced a large plastic bag and held it open for her so she could drop the evidence into it. "That's Aster's high school class ring. All-State wide receiver three years ago. That's the award stamped there on the left."

"No scholarship?" Clint asked.

"No. Ripped his shoulder up pretty bad his senior year. Colleges walked away after that."

Angela considered the area around the ditch. "He was probably killed here. Or at least a bit further upstream. Too heavy to travel too far."

Elroy regarded the culvert. "I think you may be right. I'll call the coroner's office and get them to sweep the pipe for anything else that doesn't belong there."

They all silently scanned the area, when Elroy choked back a sob. "I've known Aster his whole life. Used to mow my lawn after my boy left for college. That bum shoulder didn't slow him down none. Played touch football every Saturday he wasn't working. Jogged. Lifted weights." He shook his head. "How does someone get the drop on a kid in that kind of physical shape?"

Clint shrugged. "I don't know, Sheriff, but we're gonna find out."

They spent the next hour scouring the area around the site under the assumption the coroner's report was correct; Aster's death occurred after the rain.

"Found something!" Angela yelled. She pointed to a

footprint.

Elroy dropped to one knee and inspected the ground with an educated eye. "Looks like a slipper. No treads to speak of. Disappears east into the brush though."

Clint stared at the sky. "Getting dark, too. Let's pick it back up in the morning when we can see something."

Angela unbolted her hotel room door to a pimply, redheaded boy. His nametag read, *Billy*.

"One medium pepperoni and jalapeno? That'll be $16.18, ma'am," he informed her.

Angela took the Rizza Pizza box from him and handed over a twenty-dollar bill. "Keep the change."

"Thanks! Have a good evening!"

Angela locked the door and dropped the steaming cardboard box onto the table. The newscaster on the television was talking about the murders, repeating what she already knew about the case. While a large slice cooled on the flipped-back lid, she plucked the crispy pepperoni slices that had fallen under the blade of the cutter and chewed them with determination.

Four hours on the treadmill, sprawled out right here.

She continued her pepperoni raid along the edges. She liked things orderly.

Nice and symmetrical. Like little trails leading to the treasure.

She halted her pepperoni genocide to concentrate on the center of the pizza where all the lines converged. She bounced up and rushed over to the map she'd taped to the wall. Digital maps were nice, but she liked to look at large ones. It bestowed a keener sense of dimension.

She grabbed her marker from the desktop and systematically drew a line in roughly the same direction each of the trails all headed. Taken to their guesstimated ending, they all converged in a large, undeveloped piece of property several miles outside of town.

Banging on the wall to the adjacent room, she yelled, "Let's go!" She folded the cooled pizza slice in half and ate it as she stepped into the hallway.

Clint wiped his hand across his sweaty forehead. "I must be losing my touch."

Angela turned the radio down. "Why's that?"

"I didn't think to put it all on a map like you did."

"I wouldn't worry about it," Angela argued. "It's been a long day."

He scoffed. "I don't make those kinds of mistakes."

"You can make it up to me, though," she razzed. "Seeing as I'm driving, call the sheriff and see if his deputy found out anything on Spain and Craven."

"We just talked to him two hours ago, he would've called if—" Clint's phone rang and he glanced at the caller ID. "Speak of the devil." He fumbled with the buttons a few moments and finally transferred the call on the car speaker. "Hey, Sheriff," he answered, "I've got Agent Hollingsworth with me. Go ahead."

"Got some information for you. Judge Craven refused to grant a restraining order against some kind of development on Spain's land. We're still trying to get the details, but there's a mound there that some believe the Wichita Indians used to bury their dead."

"Was it?" Angela asked.

"Unknown. The Wichita weren't known as mound builders. That's why Craven rejected the request. That's all I have. Where y'all headed?"

Clint glimpsed sideways at Angela. "Going out for something to eat."

"You won't find too much open this time of night."

"Thanks," Angela said. "Hey, before you hang up, you got some GPS coordinates from the court documents?"

"I'll see what I can find and send them to your phone."

About a half hour later, Angela and Clint pulled their car over a cattle guard leading onto Spain's property. Cow pies littered the road ahead. "Follow this dirt road another mile," Clint instructed. "Should lead right up to where the GPS says we need to go."

Angela leaned forward over the steering wheel. "Is it me, or is it getting darker?"

Clint squinted up at the sky. "It ain't you. The stars and moon are dimmed more than usual, too."

Angela focused on the road as a fog rolled in, shortening their headlight beams. Luckily, the GPS kept them on track.

"This is about as far as we can go on the road," Clint finally proclaimed.

They both eased out of the car and scanned the area. They couldn't see more than a dozen feet in any direction. The stench of rotten mud surrounded them. And it was a quiet as an undertaker's basement; no crickets, no wind, nothing.

"Which way did the GPS say we needed to go?" Angela asked.

"About fifty yards to our left."

Angela glanced over both of her shoulders. "What the hell was I thinking," she mumbled, "coming out here at night?"

"Same thing I was thinking." He swung his flashlight

slowly back and forth. "There's a bad guy that needs a catchin'." He pointed his flashlight at her pistol. "What loads you using?"

"The silver ones. Didn't get a chance to change out before we left."

"No, we want the silver. Most things supernatural don't like it. And if they aren't supernatural, it'll still leave a big hole." He checked his loads and stared into her eyes. "You ready?"

"Yes," she answered, pulling her Glock and flashlight before taking position two steps to his left and rear.

They stalked across a dampened field for about five minutes before Angela asked, "You okay?"

"Sure." He continued scanning the area with his flashlight. "Why you ask?"

"You keep dropping your hands. Your weapon too heavy?"

He bristled. "I'm fine."

Before she had a chance to respond, a loud screech froze them in their tracks. The earsplitting noise bore down on them from all directions at once before dying away. They spun their lights around in a circle, hunting for its source.

Clint whispered, "What the hell was th—"

He flew away into the fog, arms and legs splayed out.

A panicked scream disappeared into the dark. Angela gaped in shock, utterly alone.

"Clint!" she yelled, dashing after him.

Another shriek pierced the air, but this time she pinpointed its location—slightly to the left. First sound gives you distance. Second sound gives you direction. Works for matches at night, too. Her Uncle Bill had told her a soldier's superstition once about not lighting three cigarettes with the

56

same match. The third soldier usually got a bullet to the face once a sniper had range and windage.

She continued sprinting, not worrying about running into anything when she ran out into a clearing where the fog thinned enough to see.

Before her stood a twenty-foot high hillock. Off to her left, a parked bulldozer. The ground underneath, dew-damp, flattened grass. To her right, movement. She spun. Shined her light and pistol at it. Clint, face down and spread-eagle on the ground. Above him stood an old, Indian woman with long, sharpened, rake-like fingers, raised in the air, ready to strake Clint's back. When the light struck her, she glared at Angela and shrieked again, her mouth an unhinged maw larger than her head and full of needles. Angela squeezed the trigger again and again. The wraith shifted and dodged aside faster than she could follow.

Icy cold gripped Angela's neck. Before she could react, the ghostly old woman stood in front of her, clutching her by the throat with an overpowering clasp. Angela's feet dangled while she struggled for air. The specter swiped her pistol from her hand and into the tall grass. Its gaze burrowed deep into her eyes. A memory, one she had never experienced, rushed up: she lay on a slab of granite while a dark nebulous being with her brother's face took her without remorse or sorrow.

The witch muttered in a throaty tongue. Angela understood the meaning of the words even if she didn't recognize them. "You're the other half and not mine!"

It dropped her to the ground and glided back to Clint.

Aghast, Angela rolled over and glowered at the ghost. It raised its claw into the air, preparing to skin Clint like her previous three victims.

Too far away to stop it! No weapon!

She shoved herself off the ground, and a familiar object molded itself into her fist; Clint's pistol.

She fired three shots into the ghost's back.

With a shriek louder than the previous two, it dissipated into a rainbow fog, filling the air with the scent of a recently field-dressed carcass.

Angela rushed over to her partner and checked his pulse. Her shoulders slumped in relief to find him alive.

"How you feeling this morning," Angela asked as they sat down for breakfast.

"Like shit," Clint groaned. "I think I'm coming down with something." He set his cup of coffee down. "Maybe I was off my game last night. Didn't mean to snap at you."

"No worries. I...hello..." she muttered as she peered over Clint's shoulder.

An old Indian—older than anyone she'd ever set eyes on before—stared at them as he sauntered over to their table. He wore a copper-colored snakeskin blazer over a black, silk shirt buttoned up under a turquoise bolo, matching black slacks, and cowboy boots with shiny, gold tips on the toes. He slouched when he walked, but there was still strength in his legs. As he approached, his skin revealed itself weathered and as wrinkled as a wadded-up paper bag. He'd pulled his hair back so tightly into a ponytail, his head was as smooth as a bowling ball. And it didn't show the first sign of gray.

He stopped next to their table. "Are you the FBI agents?"

Angela was embarrassed to admit it, but she expected a Native American accent, "How" or something, not his flawless English. "Yes," she said as she and Clint stood up. "Can we help you?"

"Not really, no. But I can help you."

Clint waved his hand at a chair. "I'm Senior Special Agent Clint Lane. This is Senior Special Agent Angela Hollingsworth. Why don't you have a seat and tell us who you are."

"Thank you." The old man sat down and scooted his chair close to the table. It didn't look like he planned on leaving anytime soon. "My name is Lorne Tall Water. I'm a Wichita, and probably the closest thing my nation has to a shaman these days."

Mr. Tall Water reached across the table and took a piece of Angela's toast. She chuckled to herself and stopped. She had no concern about his lack of impropriety. In fact, she trusted the man as surely as she trusted her dad and had no clue why. She slid the rest of her food closer to him, and they dug in together.

"I had a dream last night," he confessed. "I saw you two in it. You almost died, Agent Lane. Agent Hollingsworth saved you."

After what she and Clint had experienced the night before, a Wichita Indian, dressed like a Hollywood movie producer, appearing at breakfast and disclosing he'd witnessed the entire skirmish in a dream didn't seem too outrageous.

Clint must have felt the same way. "You know who the old woman was?" He dropped a slice of his bacon on a small plate and set it in front of the shaman.

"The Wichita call her Skin Shifting Woman. She is what the white man calls a demon."

Now demons?! "What can you tell us about her?" Angela inquired around the huge bite of egg-smothered toast rolling around in her mouth.

"A long time ago, a great Wichita chief took a beautiful young woman as his wife. Her beauty was a legend among all the Wichita, and it was matched only by her generosity. One day, one of the tribe's old women came to her and asked for her help collecting herbs. The young bride stopped what she was doing and immediately followed the old woman into the woods. When the young bride leaned over to pick up the bundled herbs, the old crone wrapped a leather rope around the younger woman's neck and strangled her to death.

"Once the young girl was dead, the old woman skinned her and put the skin on. She could no longer tell the difference between the pretty bride and herself when she looked at her reflection in the lake. She went back into the village and relished in the newfound attention and respect. She enjoyed the love the chief lavished on her.

"In time, the skin rotted. The chief brought the tribe's medicine man to his house, and he discovered the ruse. The men in the tribe took the old crone from the chief's house and buried her alive, piling dirt on her grave every night for three full moons.

Angela covered her mouth. "Spain, Craven, and Aster disturbed her grave!"

"Yes," Mr. Tall Water agreed. "But she is not dead."

"Yes, she is," Clint claimed. "Angela shot her with silver."

"Silver only makes her disappear for a single sunrise. The cairn must be resealed."

Clint's phone rang. "Hold on a sec," he begged. "The sheriff."

While Clint roamed outside, Angela finished the last of her eggs. "You had a dream about us, huh? How does that work?"

"Don't know," he admitted. His eyes twinkled at her, and

a round smile lit his face. "If I did, I'd be dreaming lottery numbers."

Clint came back in and sat down. "Elroy found out that Spain and Craven were cousins. And Aster worked for the oil company looking to put a well on Spain's land."

Angela scowled at Clint. "How many people you think have been over that plot of land?"

Clint's own face flared with surprise. "More than those three."

"Mr. Tall Water, how do we reseal the mound?" Angela asked.

"I can do that, but you must ensure the cairn can never be disturbed again."

"I can assure you of that," Clint proclaimed. "Angela, call Kent and have him pass the word up the chain. Tell him we need a Form 1-63.A1 approved for the mound and the forty acres surrounding it."

Angela wrote it down in her field book. "What's a 1-63.A1?"

"It's a Task Force W form that requests an emergency ruling on declaring a location a federally protected landmark. Keeps the tourists off the hotspots."

"That's it?" Angela asked.

"That's it. Our job's done." He turned to their visitor. "Mr. Tall Water. Thanks for your help. You should be contacted today by the National Park Service. They're going to come in and fence the area off." He looked at his watch before pointing at Angela's plate. "I got a big date tonight. Eat up."

Angela had been filling out reports all Monday morning when Kent called her to his office. "Where's Clint?"

She stood before his desk and uncomfortably shifted her feet. Ratting on her partner wasn't her first choice for an answer, but if Kent didn't know where he was at, she was now more worried than not. "I'm not sure. I assumed he was taking another vacation day."

An icy glare froze his face for a moment. "He didn't say anything when you guys got back Friday night?"

"Other than he had a date, no sir."

"That'll be all," he said as he picked up his phone.

And with that, their meeting ended.

An email from Archives waited for her when she got back to her desk.

Angela,

Here's the information you requested on Late-Onset Hutchinson-Gilford Progeria. It wasn't hard to find once I knew which questions to ask. Most of the information was in the CDC reporting warehouse.

Numerous cases have been reported over the last 100 years. However, there are three clusters of particular interest. Each of the clusters consisted of four cases reported within a month of each other. And they all occurred within 50 miles of each other too. Each cluster was spaced 30 years apart from the next one. It was almost like clockwork.

Based on these data, I was able to determine that we're experiencing another cluster right now. Three cases have been reported in the Dallas-Fort Worth area. The patients' names were William Hardison, Tony Hall, and Walter Hernandez.

One final piece. All patients were men under the age of 40.

If the clusters follow their progression, we should see another case within the next week.

I hope this information helps.

Bill.

P.S. What are you chasing up there?

Angela transferred the email and all the research attachments to her tablet before sticking her head in Kent's office. "Need to meet asap."

He was putting on his inexpensive black wash-and-wear sports coat. "Make it quick."

She handed him the tablet. "Do succubae exist?" she asked. "I mean, I've read paranormal romance novels before. I know what they are. Mythologically speaking, anyway. But—"

"The short answer is yes. There is no long answer. Silver will kill them, though."

"I want permission to reopen the Hernandez case then."

"Granted." He handed the tablet back to her. "The first place we need to go is Lilith Blank's house."

Angela pulled up short. "We?"

"Clint's phone—" He stood and strapped his pistol onto his waist "—is at her address. Someone just used it to call Domino's Pizza."

Angela stood three men back from the SWAT team member with the battering ram. She didn't believe anyone inside would hear the noise; Led Zeppelin blasted through the walls. As soon as they received word over their ear comm they had a valid warrant, battering ram man dashed across the yard and swung his hunk of pipe steel at the doorknob. The door crashed open, and SWAT members poured into the house like water pours down a funnel. The team members cleared the house one room at a time.

All communications ceased.

"Master Bedroom, check?" Angela signaled. When no one responded, she rushed down the hallway. "Master Bedroom, respond!"

After surviving encounters with werewolves and an ancient Wichita demon, Angela considered herself an experienced supernatural investigator, but what was happening in the bedroom reminded her there were still things—weird things—her mind had yet to accept.

Every SWAT team member in the room stood staring at the peep show on the bed with glazed eyes and slack jaws. A young, well-shaped, blonde woman, younger than the Lilith she interviewed if the girl's muscle tone and skin were any indication, straddled an old man, giving him the ride of his soon-to-be short life. The air smelled of woman…and a touch of something else. Impending death. Like the reek of the old folks' home where her great-grandfather lived out the final months of his life.

She brushed past the men and raised her pistol. "Lilith Blank, stop what…what you're doing and get on the floor. You're under arrest!"

Lilith raised her head and shined a face on Angela 20 years younger than the one from a week ago. It belonged to a teenager on the cusp of womanhood. A loving smile glimmered on the succubus's face when it saw Angela's surprise. "This could be you," the demon revealed with a maturity in her voice out of place on a face so fresh. "You could stay young forever." She put one hand on Clint's chest and lunged out with the other, grazing the back of Angela's hand.

She wasn't sure why she didn't shoot, but by the time she realized she should have, electricity sparked. Her areolas constricted tightly as her nipples spasmed more violently than she had ever experienced before. The bolt of electricity scurried down her stomach, melded at her belly button and continued on its course of pleasure-pain until it crashed into her heart of femininity. Stars flashed in her eyes as the explosive orgasm ravaged her body and warred with her reluctant mind. She dropped to her knees along the edge of the bed as the ecstasy surged through her limbs and stirred her mind like pudding. It took every remaining bit of her mental faculties to maintain the grip on her pistol and not give in.

Before she had a chance to recover, another torturous flood of pleasure crashed over her. Stomach muscles ached from tension yet quivered with furor. Her body convulsed. Too much pleasure; she couldn't breathe. A primal blush exploded up and through her face. She fought the sensation, but lost control and stumbled into her second orgasm. Nothing existed as her body betrayed her through successive, cramping waves of pleasure. The animalistic grunts rolling from her mouth horrified her. As she settled down, her body forsook her one last time. She climaxed, and her hips scrubbed against air, seeking the source of her pleasure. Mortified and degraded, she slid down her teary whimpers to unwanted bliss.

"It can be like that all the time, Angela," Lilith cooed, her voice, a silk negligee, slipping over Angela. "Let me live, and I'll show you how to take it anytime you want."

A crackly noise slipped through the thunderous pounding in her ears. "Agent Hollingsworth!"

"Look at the men," the demon enticed. "See how easily they're controlled."

She examined each frozen SWAT team member. They pulled a pang of hunger from deep in her gut. The crackling in her ears strayed closer, a storm far away on the horizon moving towards shore. "Don't listen to her!" the voice urged.

"The Master can teach you how to take what's yours!" the

sultry voice promised.

"Agent Hollingsworth!" The turbulent voice moved closer still. "I order you to do your duty!"

"Duty," Angela murmured. She blinked and gazed down at Clint, at the love in his eyes for Lilith.

I want that!

Angela mashed her eyes shut in pain when a high whine of audio feedback whistled in her ear comm. When she opened them, her tall, dark, and mission-oriented partner no longer squirmed under Lilith. Instead, a feeble man, skinny and boney, lay dying there.

The spell ended like a wave on a rocky beach.

Compassion and pity replaced the aching lust. She snapped her gaze back to Lilith. Fear lived in her eyes where victory did moments before. Angela squeezed her trigger in rapid succession, and each bullet hole erupted in a kaleidoscope of dark colors while the ancient fiend's screech pierced Angela's mind with needles of icy terror. The body crumpled to the floor, aged centuries, and disintegrated into sand, while the demon's dying squeal left behind a potent migraine.

Clint cried out in anguish.

"How did you know?" Angela implored.

"Know what?" Kent posed back. He relaxed into his chair and sipped his coffee.

"Not to come into the bedroom?" Brutus the Bobblehead's smile taunted her. She so wanted to poke it.

"I had a hunch," he rasped.

She snorted. "Powerful hunch."

His tone was low and firm. "Not my first rodeo." He took another sip. "It was talking too much for something that should have been dead. It's the most powerful succubus I've heard about. Our other offices say the same thing."

Angela nodded. "Thanks, boss. You saved my ass."

He slid a typewritten sheet of paper across his desk. "I'm suggesting a change to our Standard Operating Procedure." It stated, going forward, all encounters with succubae would be handled with at least one heterosexual woman on the team armed with silver bullets.

"You did good. You saved Clint's life."

She frowned. "There wasn't much left to save."

"Not your fault."

She stared into her cup of coffee but could tell he was watching her. Her frown deepened. "How's he doing, anyway?"

"Fine, I guess, if you forget he's a ninety-year-old man who's lost his mind. They're giving him a full medical retirement."

"Will he ever get it back? His mind?" The agony in his bawling as they wheeled him from Lilith's bedroom gave her the night sweats.

"Doctors think so, but he's going through withdrawal." Another sip. "She did a number on his pleasure center. They're putting him in the same nursing home as his mother. They'll be next door to each other. He's actually physically older than her now."

Neither one of them talked for a few minutes as the ramifications of Clint's condition sank in. Finally, Kent broke the silence. "You've been touched."

"Touched?"

"By the supernatural. Those who've been touched usually end up with white hair. Yours is light brown. I guess you didn't hang on long enough."

She didn't tell him it had been light brown in college. It had darkened to black by the time she hit thirty-five. The succubus had shared with her whatever it had taken from Clint. Not much, just enough to gift her a taste. Even Heather and Chris had noticed the differences. She begged it off as the effects of being on vacation. Her gray hairs were gone. Her breasts stood out with a college-age pride. And her libido? Overdrive. She'd spent the four weeks she was on investigative leave prowling every bar in Fort Worth. And she'd slept with more men than she cared to admit. She didn't recall being that horny in college.

Maybe it was the flood of hormones all at once.

His voice brought her back. "Shooting was good. You're cleared. Don't have a partner for you, though. Hard to find one not in the funny farm after an encounter with the supernatural."

Angela grimaced. "I've been thinking about that." He stared hard at her, waiting for her to continue. "What all do you know about Redstick?"

"Everything that's in your report." He tilted his head to the side. "Why?"

"Danny? Why him?" Chief Jim Wilcox asked. He slouched across the Lucky Star Diner table from Angela as she finished her lunch salad.

She dabbed the corner of her mouth with a napkin. "He was sharp enough to get the cash machine pics at the 47 without being asked." A slight nod from him confirmed her evaluation of the officer's abilities. She put her fork aside and set her bowl at the edge of the table. "Plus, I need someone with supernatural experience, however light it is."

"The FBI's okay with a *lupus* on the payroll." He shook

his head in disbelief.

"Hell, no. That's why they won't know about it. And, truth be told, I'm not sure I like it either. But…I need a partner. That's why, besides me, only three other people would know about him." She nudged a stack of papers across the table. "We're going to hide it in an interagency cooperation form. All you have to do is sign."

He must have suspected she wasn't giving him the full story. He ignored the papers and pulled a toothpick from his shirt pocket and held it in his hand. He sat there and cocked his head, waiting for her to continue.

She caressed the front of her neck. "*You're the other half and not mine!*" echoed through her memories from the Wichita burial mound.

"Cockroach Chills for 500, Alex."

"And the answer is, 'Something eviller than Skin Shifting Woman and *a succubus.'"*

Who is the "Master" Lilith mentioned? Is it coming after me? Skin Shifting Woman seemed to think so.

She shook her head. "Jim, there's a Big Bad out there. I need more resources than the FBI can provide."

"What makes you think we can help?"

"I found some reports on *Lupus sapiens*. I got an inkling of what you're capable of."

He squinted at her for a moment, put the toothpick in the corner of his mouth, and signed his name. "I was hoping he'd replace me someday."

"It's not going to be forever. He'll be back, I'm sure." She took a deep drink of tea. "You think he'll do it?"

"Yep," he confessed as he relaxed into a chuckle. "Ever since he met you, the FBI is all he's talked about. He wanted to apply to the academy, but the problem we have with full moons put a damper on his enthusiasm."

"How did Evan handle it then?"

"He didn't take the venom until late in life, after he was already established. Then he took a leave of absence so he could learn to control it."

"Ah," she mumbled, faking an understanding nod. "So, will you talk to him for me?"

"Don't think I'll have to." He scanned the diner. "Small town. I'm sure the word has already spread. He's probably packed and sitting on his front porch waiting for you."

Episode 3: Twins

Angela stared out across the green pasture at the pulpy lumps of cattle carcasses.

I always wondered who investigated mutilations like this.

Redstick police officer Danny McIver stood at her side, fidgeting and restless. The air was electric. "You okay? This isn't that exciting—" The intense hunger on his face and his pale blue eyes cut her off.

Maybe teaming up with a werewolf wasn't that smart after all.

She took a step backwards and pulled the flap of her jacket to the side, freeing access to her pistol. She was glad she'd chosen to carry silver rounds after her last couple of cases. "Danny. Talk to me. You said you were a *Frenator*."

"I'm okay, Agent Hollingsworth." He twisted around and showed her a big, dumb smile. "I'm still in control."

"Just making sure." During his interview, he swore under oath he had total control over his *renovatio*, his transformation, with the single exception being on a night of a full moon. Members of the werewolf 'community' referred to those who couldn't control it as *Defrenatus*, who also, supposedly, were the root of all the horrific myths surrounding werewolves. In either case, he didn't strike her as a braggart, but anyone who pined to wallow in cattle guts didn't strike her as normal either.

He's a werewolf, Angela! He ain't normal!

She let her jacket slip back into place. "And stop calling me Agent Hollingsworth. Call me Angela."

"Yes, ma'am. Sorry, ma'am…I mean Angela."

"That's better." She let a smirk through. "We're going to

be working closely with each other. Formality is the first thing we have to toss out the window."

In an uncertain tone, he stated, "But you're my boss."

She put her hands in her pants pockets. "True, but we're also equal partners. It's like—" she scratched her nose "—we're married, but without the sex. And we don't live together. And we have to be brutally truthful with each other. Because if we can't trust each other, we're no good for each other."

His ears turned red at the mention of sex, but he nodded. "Is Angie okay?"

"Angie—Hell, no! There's only one person allowed to call me that, and you aren't him."

"Boyfriend?" he asked.

"No. Uncle Bill. He's a Houston detective. Used to regale me with stories of bad guys at Christmas time."

"I had an Uncle Bill, too!" he exclaimed. "He wasn't a cop, though. He worked in a sawmill. Lost two fingers on his left hand."

"See? We've already got something in common."

He stood a little straighter and stared hard at her, probing her with his eyes. "Brutally honest?"

"Yes."

"Why are you looking so young these days? You look ten years younger than you did when I first saw you."

Oh, crap!

She quickly spun around and scanned the field, scrutinizing the men in white isolation suits inspecting the various piles of hamburger meat. "And hitting on your partner is not acceptable behavior either."

"Aw, shucks, ma'am."

She couldn't tell if he was being sarcastic or not. She

glanced back into his hazel eyes from under her lowered eyelids. "If you must know, I hadn't had a bath or put on makeup that morning. You caught me on an off day." When he scratched his earlobe—typical body language for disbelief—she frowned. "And don't call me ma'am."

He took a few steps towards the nearest carcass. "I was just being polite. I call all women ma'am."

"I guess I should have known that. I *am* a Texas girl." She pointed towards the carcass. "I wouldn't get too close. Not until we've been given the all-clear."

"Oh, I wouldn't worry too much. There ain't too many bugs *lupis* can catch. None that I'm aware of anyway." He kneeled down and took long sniffs of the air.

"You got something?"

"Maybe." He took a few more sniffs and stood back up. "Smells kinda like *lupus*, but there's something else there." A small gust of wind picked up. He took off left. "This way."

She followed him for a few hundred yards before he stopped and surveyed the ground in the immediate area. "You would've been handy to have around during our…my last case." The image of Clint's aged and infirm body lying in Lilith's bed still plagued her.

"Why's that?" He dropped back to one knee and studied some sort of animal print.

"Three bodies with their skin missing, and the trails all went cold into the brush."

"Why didn't you bring in some hounds?"

"We probably would have had it taken longer to follow the blood trails."

"How'd you solve the case?"

"The Pizza Slice Intersection Method." She ignored his confused expression. "What did you find?"

He peered back at the print on the ground. "Not sure. Looks kinda like a dog, but these critters got an extra toe. See?"

"Can you track it?"

He stood and pointed towards the setting sun. "That way."

They followed the tracks for another hundred yards or so until they ended at a black top road below a small rise. Danny stuck his nose into the air before they scrambled down, and he eventually led them to a small copse of trees surrounding an old, abandoned church. "Mount Trinity, Est. 1932" read the carved sign out front. The peeling white paint on the sides and the boarded-up steeple told them this church hadn't been used in quite some time.

Danny's nostrils flared slightly. "The smell is strong here," he revealed. "Whatever got them cattle probably holes up here during the day."

Angela scanned the horizon. "Call in animal control?"

Danny dropped his hands to his side, cocked his head, and raised an eyebrow. "You really gonna stand there and tell a werewolf he needs animal control to come take care of a critter problem?"

Well, when he puts it like that. "Not what I was thinking. We aren't equipped to tranquilize them."

"Ah!" he exclaimed. "Forgot I wasn't back home."

Angela tried three times to get a cell signal but couldn't. "Never mind. I'll cover the back." She eased around the church, trying to peek through cracks in the boarded windows as she passed them. Near the back, tree line sat a five-gallon bucket, upside down but held off the ground with a couple of bricks. As she made for the door, it opened, and Danny stuck his head out.

"What the hell are you doing?" she asked incredulously. She grabbed him by the arm and pointed to the trees. He followed her.

"What's going on?" he asked, genuine confusion on his face.

"You don't fucking clear a structure without your partner!" She hated being the asshole senior agent, especially after their earlier conversation. "Don't move faster than me like that again. You copy?"

"Um, I, uh, don't understand." He scrunched his eyebrows together.

"We clear together. You may think you're Superman, but I've dropped one of you with a single shot to the head. You're not invulnerable. We back each other up. We work as a team, or I'm shipping your ass back to Redstick. This is your last and only warning."

He bristled, but he took her lead and tersely nodded.

She empathized with him. She'd been on the receiving end of one of these ass-chewings shortly into her first assignment, only hers was much worse. No one liked them.

But we all move on, or we move off.

"So what did you find in there," she inquired.

"The front and back doors were pushed shut. No doorknobs. Nothing inside that I could see, but the smell is definitely strong. They either just left or they're invisible."

"Or there's a basement." She kicked a bucket over. A pipe with a small cone rain guard on top of it stuck up from the ground. "Ventilation pipe."

The inside of the church resembled any other country church constructed in the late 1800s or early 1900s. The only three pews left were stacked against a wall. The pulpit was missing. The wall behind the stage was faded except for where the cross had hung in the distant past. Disintegrated doors led to back rooms.

They scouted for an entrance to the basement for a solid ten minutes before Danny discovered a hatch under the desk in one of the rooms. A trail led from it to the back door through the dust and dirt scattered everywhere. Angela crinkled her face. "I don't need your nose to detect that."

She pulled her pistol and followed Danny into the basement. The steps creaked and groaned as she crept further into the darkness. The stench of rotten meat flowed up and punched them square in the face.

Angela shined her flashlight around. "This looks like something out of an old Frankenstein movie." Beakers, bottles of various chemicals, Bunsen burners; everything a mad scientist desired was laid out along the shelves and workbenches. A bloody operating table sat in the middle of the floor, a centerpiece for the house of horrors.

"What the hell is this place?" Danny asked under his breath.

Angela stepped around two large, copper spirals mounted to wooden stands. "Are these Tesla coils?"

"I don't kn—shh…Did you hear that?" Danny swung around and pointed at a ratty sheet hanging on the wall.

Angela readied her weapon. A woman whimpering. She stepped back quickly and nodded at Danny. While he pulled the sheet to the side, she shined her flashlight and pistol into the opening. "FBI! Announce yourselves!"

A weak, female voice cried out from the darkness, "Help us, please!" Angela's light revealed the long, dank corridor before them. Steel cages with doors touching the low ceiling stretched along both sides for roughly thirty feet. Moist earth, human excrement, sickness, and death molested her like a sour dish rag. Something stirring restlessly echoed up to her.

"We're over here!" A dark, slender hand slipped through the bars about halfway down.

Angela crept along the passageway, heel to toe. "Ma'am, are you alone?" she demanded.

"No," the girl answered back. "My brother needs help."

Angela looked into each cage as she stalked by. "Jesus wept," she muttered. Dog, pig, and human bodies rested in weeks-old feces and moldy straw.

"Where are the people who put you here, ma'am?"

"I don't know." *cough* "We call him the Doctor."

"It's just one man?"

"That's all we've ever seen."

Angela got to the cage with the young girl. She was black, late-teens perhaps, and malnourished. She wore nothing more than the ragged remains of a dress. Angela took the girl's hand while Danny continued past her, finishing his visual assessment. "I'm Angela. What's your name?" She holstered her weapon and tried to unbolt the cage. Locked, she quickly scanned the immediate area for a key.

"Felicia, ma'am. Felicia Jefferson." She indicated a young boy laying on a bed of moldy straw in the cage beside her. "This is Ja'son. He's my brother. I think he's dead, but I don't know. He ain't talked today."

Angela grabbed his wrist and took his pulse. She let out a huge breath and nodded gently. "He's just sleeping." Without taking her eyes off Felicia, she urged, "Danny, I need the keys." She studied both of the kids. "You look alike. You twins?"

"Yes, ma'am."

Danny yelped, triggering a shot of adrenaline to tickle her

face. He sprang backwards, batting at something in front of him. Angela snapped her hand around to rest on her pistol. Whatever had spooked him though, had toppled to the floor. He stomped on it and glanced at her, a nervous frown on his face. "What? I hate spiders."

Angela's heartbeat slowed to thundering. "Dammit, Danny," she grumbled as she shook her head.

He pointed into the cage in front of him. "You've got to see this."

"I'll be right back, Felicia," Angela told her.

As Angela stood up, Felicia's hand shot out and gripped her arm. "Don't leave me!" she screamed.

Angela smiled, and every dead child she'd investigated crouched behind those bars. "I'm going right down there to look for some keys."

"No! He'll come back!" Felicia sobbed. "He does things to us!"

She gripped Angela's arm tight. She stooped back down. "Felicia, I'm a twin too."

"Really?"

"Yep. And you know what?"

"No, ma'am." The tears still flowed, but the panic had backed off a heartbeat.

"Well, Ja'son knows you're here." She took Felicia's finger and pressed it against Ja'son's neck. "You feel that bumping? That's his heartbeat. As long as you feel it, you'll know he's just sleeping."

Hope radiated from Felicia's face as her eyes dried up and her mouth formed a firm line.

"He needs you to be strong for him, Felicia. I won't leave you down here. I promise."

She crept back towards Danny. The cages along the way

78

contained either dead dogs, pigs, or humans. When she stopped next to him, she took a sharp breath as the strongest sensation of deja vu she'd ever encountered washed over her. "Woah! What was that?"

Danny's head snapped around to her. "You felt that too?"

"Yeah." In the cell in front of them, a live animal, what appeared to be a cross between a hairless German Shepard Dog and a pig, stared back at her. Without warning, it charged the cage door, snarling and growling. They both hopped back a step. Long, sharp teeth tried to bite through the steel bars. "What the hell is that?" she asked.

"Other than ugly, mean, and pissed off? No idea. This is what killed them cows though." He pointed to the cage behind them. A pile of dirt and a hole in the back headed towards the surface showed how—whatever it was—got out.

Angela realized she was in the zone when she lifted her empty coffee cup to her lips for the third time. And each time she'd stood up to go fill it, another gruesome piece of evidence held her attention hostage. She finally transferred all the pictures taken from the church to the conference room's media table, stretching them out and arranging them in the order she experienced them. On the wall in front of her were pictures of Felicia and Ja'son alongside images of 14 dead dogs, nine dead pigs, and eight dead people from the cages. None of the human bodies had identification on them. It would take months to determine who they were, if they could at all.

Danny paced back and forth in front of the pictures of the dead. His temples bulged in and out as he repeatedly clenched his jaw like he was chewing gum.

Speaking of which.

She slipped a stick into her mouth. Danny's frustration stood in contrast to her own attitude. She'd witnessed it in dozens of other agents in the past, including in the mirror after spending a long night staring at a murder scene. Helplessness. Anger. The only cure was taking down a bad guy. In his current state of mind though, she knew he'd likely strike out at any suspect with a facial twitch he didn't like.

"Angela," he burst out, "who would do something like that?"

His voice thunderstruck her calm. She rested her hands on the table as she pressed herself onto the stool. "Sit down, Officer," she ordered.

He stopped pacing and stared at her. When she refused to break eye contact, he flared his nostrils and took a seat.

Humph. Just like my Chris's hunting dogs. They all need to know who the big dog really is.

"Danny, I believe what we're dealing with here is the classic Visionary Murderer."

"What do you mean?" He shifted on his stool, hooked his cowboy boot heels onto the lower rung.

"The *Doctor* believes he's onto some scientific breakthrough. He's performing experiments at the behest of some internal demon…." She opened her eyes wide and closed her lips for a moment. "Hell, it might be a real demon for all we know," she muttered. "Anyway, we sometimes see these crackpots in cults. But no matter how smart he is, he's still a psycho. And like all psychos, he wants to get caught. He'll get careless because he wants to show the world what he's created."

Danny snorted. "He doesn't seem like the careless type to me."

"I know." She glowered back at the pictures of the

laboratory. "He's also showing traits for your typical Organized Serial Killer, too. Meticulous."

He licked his lips and blinked his eyes. For a brief moment, her brother's hunting dog's excitement appeared on his face. "So, what do we do? Wait for him to surface? How many more—"

"No," she argued, looking back at him, "We don't wait for him. You want to catch him? Help me read the evidence. He's left us a map. We just have to find it."

Danny regained control. He stood and pulled his jeans up a little higher. He licked his lips again and asked, "Okay, what's he trying to create?"

"Start with this." She slid the digital picture of the mysterious animal across the table to him. "The lab rats are sequencing the DNA, but it may be some time before we know with any certainty."

"You got it," he exclaimed with renewed direction.

Her pep talk had an amazing effect on him because a short time later, he interrupted her with a low whistle of disbelief. "You are not going to believe what this thing is."

Angela peered at the main screen. The FBI's facial recognition software was running on the picture, searching the internet. Right there on a conspiracy website called, *They Walk Among Us,* were several different images of the same type of creature. "Well, what is it?"

"We have us a real-life Chupacabra." A huge grin stretched across his face. "I didn't think these things were real!"

Angela peeked over her shoulder to make sure they were alone. "Danny, coming from a werewolf's mouth, that has got to be the most ironic thing I've ever heard."

They worked late into the night, sorting through the

evidence, and arrived early the next morning to start again.

Kent came into the lab as they sat down at the terminals. "That was good work out there, you two," he said, his voice low and abrasive.

"Thanks," they answered.

"Any progress other than what's in your report?"

"Nothing concrete," Angela grumbled. "Still waiting to hear about our tipster."

Kent slid a folder across the lab's main table. "The call came in from the 'Groupie.' That's what we call him anyway. He usually calls with realistic-sounding tips he's gleaned from redacted Open Records Act requests. It's mostly tabloid trash. Still got to follow up though."

"Better lucky than skilled," Danny sassed.

"Today anyway." Kent's icy glare flashed for a moment. "Time to let him know that we know who he is."

Angela nudged Danny's elbow as a short, skinny rat-man with little, beady, brown eyes eased through the front doorway and stood back against the wall next to the door. "Is that him?" He had thin, mussed hair of an indeterminate shade of greasy, toasted bread, and clothes two sizes too large for him.

"Could be. Doesn't exactly blend in with the rest of our friends here."

Fat Charlie's, the smoky, stale beer stinking biker bar they were huddled in, wasn't overly crowded, but it was crowded enough with the type of men and women who wouldn't have appreciated one FBI agent and one police officer lounging in their midst. They needed to blend in.

The Groupie had insisted on meeting here. "*It's a public place, and they don't like cops so don't try anything stupid like trying to arrest me.*" Of course, he only said that was after he got control of himself. Receiving a call from the FBI on his latest burner phone rattled him a bit.

Angela had to admit Danny could dress down when he needed to. He used his *lupus* virus to grow hair along his cheeks, jowls, chest, and the backs of his hands, the latter being a bit too weird for her. Mixed in with a little grease under his fingernails, he passed for an authentic scumbag. Couldn't maintain a normal eye color, though. They were that freaky shade of pale blue identical to all the other werewolves in Redstick.

He'd shrugged when she brought it up. "Part of my *Luna Amator* clan heritage. It's the first thing to change when I'm performing a *renovatio*."

She didn't possess the same abilities, but she did happen to be a woman. It didn't take much—tight jeans and t-shirt, hiking boots, and lots of cosmetics. No tattoos, but a light jacket hid their absence. Puppy noses proudly sticking out from her shirt—thanks to an overzealous air conditioner—finished off the façade. Danny turned out to be the consummate gentleman. He didn't stare unblinkingly like the large, sweaty potbellied bartender or even try to steal surreptitious glances at them.

Rat-Man took a few moments to scan the bar, and when he spotted Angela and Danny, scurried over along the wall, and straddled a barstool.

So much for our disguise.

The bartender set a cold, draft beer in front of him. It appeared Rat-Man was a regular.

"Marion Dinkleton?" Angela asked as he took a sip of his beer.

Rat-Man sputtered as he tried to inhale the brew with a

surprised gasp. After wiping the mess from his face, he gaped at Angela and pronounced, "Speed. My name is Speed."

"Okay, *Speed*. I'm Angela, and this is Danny. Why don't you tell us what you know?"

Speed shook his head. "Nope. Y'all promised a tip-reward for reporting the killing field if I met with you."

Danny pulled out an envelope and handed it over.

Speed looked shyly over both shoulders and huddled over his prize while he counted it. Convinced he hadn't been taken advantage of, he visibly relaxed. "Okay. What do I know…well, I know we're all in for a world of hurt."

"Who from?" Danny asked.

"The Forsaken Dweller. It's hungry, and Earth is its own personal pan pizza."

Angela resisted the temptation to search for a Candid Camera crew but forced a severe expression. "Forsaken Dweller?"

"It's from a parallel universe."

"A parallel universe?" Danny quipped. "Like on Star Trek when Kirk and them went to a different Enterprise?"

"Yeah, exactly!" Speed exclaimed.

Danny sat a little straighter and pulled his shoulders back. Angela wasn't sure if the prideful grin on his face was because he guessed the answer or because he'd managed to squelch a laugh. "Okay," he argued, "but I don't remember no big monster eating everything up."

"Joke all you want, Agent Danny-Boy, but it's coming. I'm talking H.P. Lovecraft here."

"Who?" Angela asked.

"H.P… Never mind. Think monster of biblical proportions."

"Well, it'd have to be if it's gonna eat a whole dang

planet." Danny leaned back in his chair, done with the conversation.

"Let's assume this Forsaken Dweller is coming," Angela allowed, picking up the questioning, "why would it do that? Aren't there enough planets in its own universe?"

Speed guzzled the last of his beer, snapped his fingers at the bartender, and pointed at his mug. "You saw what was in the church, right?" The bartender dropped a fresh mug in front of him. "Those weird-ass dogs? The human experiments in the basement? That's just the start."

Angela raised an elbow onto the bar. "The start of what?"

"I don't know!" he exclaimed, taking a deep swallow from his beer. A few burly bikers took a keen interest in Speed's excitement. "But someone from its universe is already here. And they're performing other experiments that are way worse than those. There should have been some kinda proof where the main lab is at."

"I tell you, Speed, I just don't know," Angela grunted. "Why don't you come on down to our office." She stood and reached into her pocket for her handcuffs. "Seeing as you know so much about the church, maybe you can help us figure out what these mysterious beings from the other universe are trying to do."

Speed glanced at the both of them in turn and smirked at Angela with his eyes. "Can I finish my beer at least?"

While Danny stood and monitored the bar, Angela pointed her head at the mug, "Sure, go ahead."

Speed finished the beer in a long series of gulps and flipped the mug over on the bar. When he removed his hand, five of the larger bikers huddled near them stood up, their chairs' wooden legs scraping across the gritty linoleum floor. They formed a semi-circle, blocking Angela's, Danny's, and

Speed's path to the door.

Their apparent leader had a shaved head along with blue flame tattoos running up his neck from under the top of his vest. He stepped to the front. "I'm afraid Speed's with us. See, he's our wrench. Keeps our bikes purring. I'm afraid I can't let you take him."

Angela shifted in front of Speed. "My name is Angela Hollingsworth. I'm an agent with the Federal Bureau of Investigation." She pointed her head to the side. "This is Officer Danny McIver."

"FBI? Fucking Bitches Incorporated?" Blue Flame Man wisecracked. Angela's nose whined about his lack of regular dental hygiene procedures. "You ain't no FBI agent…unless they're hiring high schoolers these days." He eyed her breasts. "You wanna play house? You can be my bitch."

Danny slipped out in front of Angela and Speed before anyone had a chance to stop him. One moment he was off to the side and the next he wasn't. "I don't think you boys underst—"

Blue Flame Man punched him in the mouth. "I wasn't talking to you, shithead."

Danny's head whipped to the side from the whack. His bottom lip showed the first signs of a split by oozing blood down the corner of his mouth. He slowly righted his head, looking Blue Flame Man right in the eyes. Most men would have gone down under such a blow.

Five against two weren't good odds, werewolf by her side or not. She slipped her hand under her jacket, and her fingertips had barely brushed the butt of her Glock when one of the other men rushed forward and pinned her to the counter. He seized her wrist and slammed it on the bar before she had a chance to skin her weapon.

"Uh-uh, Honey. You stay right there." Honey Man had utterly immobilized her.

She sincerely wished this had been a television show where upper body strength didn't matter in a brawl against huge, hairy bikers.

He pulled her pistol out. "Little girl here had a hog leg on her!" He put it in the back of his waistband and winked at her. "That's way too much gun for you, sugar."

Most of the bar's patrons were yelling and beating a hasty retreat to the door. Speed disappeared out of her periphery. Two of the men had pinned Danny's arms against the bar and had taken his weapon. He wasn't resisting though. Blue Flame Man gut punched him. When it connected, the officer grunted and fell to the floor, bloody spittle flying from his mouth.

He stayed on his knees but slowly lifted his head and stared into Blue Flame Man's eyes again.

The fifth man in the group was shorter than the rest, but still above six feet. He sidled up next to Blue Flame Man. "Look at his eyes, Angus. Ain't them some of the weirdest eyes you ever saw?"

The corners of Angus's eyes twitched at the pale blue *lupus* eyes glaring back into them. He whirled around on Shorty. "Cooch, you dumb shit! Stop using names!"

"You just used my name!" Cooch complained.

"It ain't your real name!"

Cooch gawked at Angela, a shiver of fear bouncing around on his face in the shape of half-formed words and jerky head movements.

"That's right, Cooch," she snapped. "We there at the FBI have lots of files on people. Some of those files even list nicknames. So far, I've got two. Yours and Angus's here."

She scanned the others. "What about y'all? You gonna make my job easier? My ID's in my pocket if you don't believe me."

Angus backhanded her across the face. "Now see what you made me do?"

The sharp, stinging crack across her cheek was one of experience. Angela's head snapped to the side like a ragdoll, and she squinted one eye, trying to get the tearing to stop. The second blow was perfectly executed to cause pain but not permanent damage—an experienced woman beater obviously. Shaking her head, trying to clear the gathering fog, Angela slid back and up against the bar. She attempted to wrench her arm free but only succeeded in pulling up face to face with Angus.

"Let me kiss that and make it feel better." He grabbed her by the hair and licked her from chin to forehead. Tasting her. When he pulled back, the look in his eyes was clear. He had passed the point of no return. This wasn't going to end well for her if the swelling and throbbing on the left side of her face was any indication.

Angus ordered, "Search her."

Honey Man rummaged around in her jacket and pulled out her badge. "Oh, man, we are so screwed," he whined as he handed it over.

Angus snatched her badge, scoffed, and focused on her with laughing eyes. "Fake." He glanced over her shoulder. "Where the hell did Speed go?" He looked around at the empty bar. "Cooch, go outside and watch our bikes." When he didn't move fast enough, Angus yelled, "Move it!"

He twisted back to Angela's breasts and pulled a switchblade knife. "Time to taste something else." He slowly gripped the bottom of her shirt with his free hand and sliced upwards in long, deliberate strokes. The fabric parted like silk threads under a scalpel.

So concentrated on the forthcoming rape, no one was paying attention to what was happening on the floor next to them until the werewolf reared up with a loud, rumbling roar and ripped its clothes off as if in pain.

Along with the bikers, Angela spun around and backed off, peeing a bit in surprise.

Danny-Monster pointed its blunt snout at the ceiling and howled. A near-replica of Evan-Monster. Long-legged. Over seven feet. Covered in bristly, short, brown fur. Huge, sharp teeth protruded from its snout. It stank of two-day-old road kill.

She still had the occasional nightmare where she relived Evan stalking her in Archives, but she'd fooled herself into believing werewolves weren't dangerous. The human mind was not equipped to understand something so predatory, so well designed to eat her. Humans had been at the top of the food chain for millennia, or so they thought. The monster standing before her, growling and roaring into the faces of Angus and his crew, distorted her worldview in an instant.

Angus and his men staggered back, Honey Man among them, and stared at the horror. Awestruck fear blotted their faces white. The howl overrode their fight or flight instinct and anchored them in place. If she had not known the creature standing before her was her partner, she would've been right there with them.

Danny-Monster took one, long step towards them and snarled. It snatched Angus by the throat with lightning speed, pulled him close, and raised him up into the air until his nose sat even with its snout. Growls rumbled from its chest. It sniffed and spent a moment considering him before it stuck its tongue out and licked him from chin to forehead, slowly and deliberately. Tasting him.

Thanks, partner.

A wet trail snaked its way down the leg of Angus's dirty jeans and splashed onto the bar floor beneath him. Danny-Monster's lips curled up in disgust, and it chucked the biker away, sidestepping the puddle.

Proving he had control of his curse, Danny pointed at the floor with a menacingly long talon.

The rest of the crew stumbled into seated positions.

Angela stepped forward, keeping one eye on Danny, and took her pistol from Honey Man's waist. She turned around and punched Angus square in the nose.

She held her bruised hand under her arm and mumbled, "Say hello to my little friend."

"I'm telling you, man, that fucker right over there is a werewolf!" Angus scowled at Danny as the deputy sheriff slammed the police cruiser door shut.

The deputy laughed and shook his head.

"I mean it, man!"

"Yeah," Honey Man insisted, "those aren't even his clothes. He stole 'em from my pack after he changed back."

Angela signed the arrest report for another deputy while the bikers continued their tirade. "Thanks for your help. We'll have the Marshall Service pick them up in a few days."

"No problem," the deputy replied.

"What are they yelling about anyway?"

"Something about your partner here being a werewolf?"

"A werewolf?"

Danny was leaning against the fender of one the cruisers sharing a cup of coffee and a laugh with another deputy.

"Him? I thought werewolves were supposed to be hairy? And only on a full moon?"

"They've probably been cranking," he guessed. "Explains why they would assault you two like that." He clicked his pen and put it in his shirt pocket. He studied her from under narrowed lids, his sunglasses shadowed under the brim of his hat. "How the hell did y'all manage to handcuff four bikers anyway? In a biker bar?"

"Danny over there?" She tilted her head at him. "Yeah, well, he's some kind of martial arts expert. Tai Chi, I think. I pulled my pistol on two. He wrestled the other two by himself. And two got away."

The deputy didn't seem too convinced, but he nodded anyway and handed her a copy of the arrest report. "Y'all have a safe drive back now." He took the brim of his hat in courtesy and walked off.

Angela whistled for Danny as she scanned the crowd for Speed. No sign of him or Cooch.

We'll get them.

Danny and Angela slid into their seats at the same time. She put the key into the ignition, stopped and twisted in the seat towards him. "We're going to have to work out some kind of signal. I don't want to have to change my panties every time you decide to go all wolfy on me."

"You're not going to get fired, are you?" Angela asked. She looked around at the hospital lab.

"Nah," Heather answered, waving her hand as if to brush off the question. "No one uses these labs this time of night. And the dayshift spills more materials than I'm going to use." She pulled a pair of rubber gloves on. "You know, I'm an ER doc these days, not a hematologist," she confessed. "Why don't you have your FBI lab look at it?"

"Because they're so backlogged right now," Angela complained. "It'd be months before I got the results back."

"You haven't changed a bit since college. Danny, is she this impatient when she's not around me?"

Danny's face turned a shade of red. "She's not that imp— p—patient with me," he stuttered. He tried to relax by leaning on the table and ended up flipping a hefty, stainless steel tray loaded with medical utensils off the edge. The clangs, clatters, and smashes grew louder as he tried to catch everything at once and succeeded only in flinging it all in every other direction.

Heather giggled. "Here, I got it," as she rushed over to help him. She peeked out from her hanging hair, and her eyes smiled brightly at him. Angela knew the look. That boy was in trouble.

Werewolf? Human? Can they even do it?

That was a visual she didn't need. They finally stood up with everything back on the tray. Heather cradled it with one arm while she placed her other hand on Danny's chest and slowly slid it over to his bicep. "Why don't you go sit down on the couch over there."

He twisted his head back and forth until he spied the couch and rushed over to it.

Angela flipped the top of the cooler back while Heather grilled her. "Where did you find him?"

"He's on loan from the Redstick Police."

"They sure grow 'em nice out there."

"There's a whole town full of them," Angela groaned. "Go help yourself." She pulled out a rack of chilled test tubes, each with a different blood sample from the church basement. "And don't say anything you don't want him to hear. He's got excellent hearing."

"817-555-1234," Heather murmured.

"What was that?"

"My phone number. You call me enough. You don't have it memorized?"

"Your phone number is 'Heather' in my phone."

They both twisted their heads as Danny ripped a section of magazine cover off, a phone number scrawled across it, and tucked it in his pocket.

"Heather!" Angela whispered harshly, "he's my partner! Leave him alone!"

"All that means, sister, is that he's available."

Danny's face turned red again. He stood. "I'm gonna go hunt down a soda. I'll be back."

As soon as the door slipped shut, Heather squealed under his breath, "Isn't he just darlin'?"

Angela rolled her eyes. "Are you gonna help tonight or scare off my new partner?"

"It's my night off. Give me a break, okay?"

While Heather worked in the lab, Angela and Danny watched a Magnum P.I. marathon in the hospital visitor's lounge. Halfway through a particularly cheesy gunfight, Heather texted, "Done." Angela shoved the bag of microwave popcorn into the trash, and she and Danny made their way upstairs.

"Are you sure these samples aren't contaminated?" Heather asked.

"The place we found them was pretty grimy," Angela admitted. "The whole place was contaminated. Why?"

"I've got samples here from three distinct species,"

Heather said. "Humans, pigs, and dogs. That's why it's taken me so long. I had to triple-check everything. This fourth sample? I'm not sure what it came from. Now don't try it at home, but I think it would serve as a viable transfusion for all three distinct species."

Danny scratched his nose. "Why those three?"

Heather leaned against the workbench and crossed her arms. "Well, pig and human? They're close already. We've even gene modified certain pig species to produce type O blood to prove we could use it in an emergency."

Danny scrunched his brow as he hugged his chest. In a quiet voice, he asked, "Why the dog?"

"I don't have a clue. It's possible they were working to combine the human and dog blood too. Pigs and humans are close. Human and dog? The coagulation profiles are way different. Maybe this tri-xeno profile was an accident." She handed a printout to Angela. In any case, the sample labeled 'P-9' is human—and dog—compatible too. Somebody's up for the Nobel Prize on this if I didn't screw up my testing."

Angela and Danny stared at each other for a few quiet moments.

Heather sighed. "I can't ask where you got this, can I?"

"Unfortunately, no," Angela muttered. "I can tell you that you've made life rougher for me." She smirked. "Does that make you happy?"

"Yep!"

Angela looked around at the mess. "Are you going to get into trouble? Using hospital resources?"

"Nah." Heather paused. "They give me quite a bit of leeway as I'm taking the night shift in the ER. They're hoping I'll change my mind and move back upstairs to their research labs." She slipped off her rubber gloves. "All right, kids, get out. I gotta clean up."

As Angela and Danny walked through the parking lot, he handed her his cell phone. He'd brought up some tabloid news site. The headline read, *FBI Werewolf Squad Targeting Outlaw Bikers!* Below was a picture of Angela and Danny outside the biker bar, only Danny's head had been replaced with Lon Chaney's 1940s wolfman picture.

The steel cage door clanked, and the loud buzzer set her teeth to rattling. The familiar sight of yellow and red lines, gray, chipped paint along the walls and bars, and the Lexan windows at all the guard stations greeted her as usual.

"Today's not your usual visiting day, Agent Hollingsworth," the last guard in the gauntlet stated.

Master of the Obvious!

"Official business this time, Morris."

He took her Glock and two spare magazines from under the window and handed her back a receipt. When he decided she wasn't going to engage in their usual, friendly banter, he pointed to her hands. "Is that a book? And a carton of smokes?"

"Yeah." She raised a notebook recovered from the church basement and thumbed the pages while she gripped the carton under her arm. "They've been inspected." She turned and faced the last gate and waited for it to open.

He paused long enough that she considered asking him to open the door.

Just as I thought. Anything out of the ordinary throws this guy off.

Finally. "Opening Five!" followed by another loud clank and buzzer. She stepped into the private visitation room. Her brother waited, secured to the table, only this time with a curious look on his face. A guard stood at the door.

"Hello, Chris." She didn't lean down to deliver the standard hug.

"Today's not Saturday," he said. "What gives?"

"Remove his cuffs, please." She delivered a pounding glare to her brother. "He'll behave himself."

Chris massaged his unshackled wrists and stared at his sister as the guard stepped back to his position by the door. She always insisted on keeping him chained to the table. She wasn't afraid of him assaulting her but wanted to hand out the tough love instead. Today though, he was part of her investigation, and he was going to snitch for her whether he realized it or not. She needed him off-balance first, though. He eyed the carton of cigarettes and the notebook as she sat down at the table.

While at the office earlier, she'd tried her hand at deciphering the writings in the notebook. Brad walked by scratching his three-day-old stubble. He looked over her shoulder, and instead of his usual inane attempts at humor, offered a professional evaluation. "That's Lithuanian."

She stared up at him. "Really?" She thumbed a few more pages. "How the heck do you know that?"

"My grandmother emigrated from there. I've seen some of her letters."

"Lithuanian," she muttered.

After seeing the church basement, I'd have figured Transylvanian instead.

She laid it out on her desk. "Can you read it?"

He examined it for a few moments. "Some basic words. Nothing useful. Give Southern Methodist University a call. They got a Baltic humanities group or something. Someone over there ought to be able to help."

"I know someone else a little closer to home." Picking up

the notebook, she drove immediately to the prison and arranged to have her brother waiting for her.

Chris wrung his hands and twisted his fingers as he continued to eye the cigarettes. Angela suspected he wanted to reach for them, but she knew he knew better. *Hands Behine the Yellow Line* was etched and painted on the table. Of course, *Behine* and *Line* rhymed, so maybe the misspelling was on purpose.

"You studied Lithuanian in college."

He wrinkled his nose at her and nodded slowly. "So?"

"Why Lithuanian?"

He shrugged. "Easy Credit." He stared back at the cigarettes.

"You're just being humble. That's a hard language to learn. You made all As." She knew exactly how to stroke his ego. Sadly, it worked both ways. *Twins. Sheesh!*

"Oh, it is. It's also one of the oldest languages in the world too."

"No!"

"Seriously!" He bobbed his head sharply and scooted forward in his seat. And before she knew it, sitting before her, was the brother she grew up with, not the crazed ex-junkie who beat the shit out of their dad. "Fifty-five hundred years with little to no drift in pronunciation or structure."

"College was a long time ago." She plucked at a cuticle with what she hoped was a mildly disinterested look on her face. "You've probably forgotten all about it." She stilled her hands and barely raised an eye to his, gauging if she could continue with this dance.

His laughter filled her heart with familiar and long-lost warmth. "It's hasn't been that long, Ang. Why you ask?"

"I ran across something at work. That's all." She nudged

the carton of cigarettes a little closer to the yellow line. "So, why would you take Lithuanian? Seems pretty esoteric to me."

He glared into her eyes, and the warmth cooled. "Thought it might be something interesting to do. Pretty girls with foreign accents. You know. Besides, I needed some electives. I didn't really like the class. I would have preferred PE fencing or karate. But I needed...why the interest?"

"So, you could read it if I brought something here?" She elbowed the carton. Just. A bit. Closer.

"For you, no fuckin' way. For a carton of smokes, you can bet your ass I would."

"Whew! I thought I was going to have to go see a stranger." She slid the notebook up against the yellow line and spun it around so he could read it.

He looked over at the guard. "Can I touch the notebook?"

"You know the rules, Chris," the guard said. "Nothing can go back and forth while you're unsecured."

Chris swung back to his sister. "You'll have to turn the pages."

As soon as she flipped open the cover, he leaned forward and read the first few lines. "Where did you find this?"

"Some crazy was doing experiments on a young girl and her twin brother. We think he was making notes in here about it."

"Twins?"

She recognized the flicker in his eyes. They were her eyes. Anytime something about twins popped up in the news, or they passed a pair on the street, their thoughts always skipped to each other. Their twin bond was something their parents could never understand.

Yet, I still sent him away.

"Are they okay?" he asked.

"The girl, miraculously, is still alive. And healthy. Her brother died, though. I want to find this asshole."

"Yeah, there's a reference here to blood matching. Felicia has the tri-xeno…" Without warning, his face paled, and he swallowed a lump. "He was giving them pig and dog blood?"

Angela narrowed her eyes. "Yeah, a real sicko, huh?"

He read a few more pages, and with each new one, he coiled his hands tighter and tighter into a ball.

Finally, he sat up straight in his chair and scooted away from the table. "Guard, I want to go back to my cell."

Panic racked his eyes. And worry. It reminded her of the time she'd climbed a tree and couldn't get down. He'd thrown their Frisbee up there on purpose, and she'd gone after it because he didn't like heights after the Rudolph incident. He'd run back and forth between her and the house, unable to decide whether to stay and help or get their parents. He was afraid for her, as she suspected he was afraid for her now. "What wrong, Chris?!"

"The guy who wrote this is whacked. He's collecting twins." The unspoken sentence lay on his lips, *We're twins!*

She knew what he was thinking because the same thoughts had gone through her head when she found out Ja'son had died. Her heart ached for Felicia. Even with the trouble Chris had caused their family, she wouldn't have wished anything so grievous on him.

Before she had a chance to say anything else, he stretched across the yellow line and grabbed her wrist, forcing her to look into his eyes. "Stay away from this one, Ang," he strangled out around a gasp. "This guy is whacked!" Chris's grip was desperate and painful as he got louder and louder.

"Whacked, Ang! Don't do it! Don't!" He had pulled her half over the table before chaos burst through the door. As the guard pulled him off her, another one rushed in to help restrain him. Soon, the only sound was the slamming of the metal door on her empty room.

Angela and Danny listened to Dr. Albert Martinkus, SMU's Baltic Studies chair, read to himself for three hours as he translated the notebook. He had insisted they leave it with him, or at least let him scan it in, but Angela refused both requests. Evidence, however "weird," was staying in her possession. Losing evidence would put her on the fast-track to the Fertilizer Tracking Office.

He flipped the last page and looked at them with a wide grin and a sparkle in his eyes. "Someone's got quite the imagination."

"Why would you say that, Doctor?" Danny asked.

"These are obviously draft notes for a science fiction novel. What's so amazing is the time the writer spent recording it in Lithuanian."

"Care to explain?" Angela implored.

"Well, for instance—" he flipped a couple of pages back on his yellow pad "—this reference to blood 'majic.' The word the writer used is not the real word for magic. Its more literal meaning is, um, 'science,' as in something made by hand instead of naturally occurring. And the references to animal sacrifice and electricity—" he blew a short raspberry "—I'm not a scientist, but I recognize quackery when I see it. This is definitely a work of fiction."

Angela let out a long sigh. "I don't suppose the author signed his name, did he?"

"No," Albert said. "In fact, now that you mention it, I

can't tell *what* the sex of the writer is. It's usually a man because women were illiterate back when this dialect was used. But you could tell it was a man writing. Here—" he pointed at the notebook "—the pronouns are all gender neutral. Could be a modern slant, but I can't say with any certainty."

Danny shifted uncomfortably in his seat. "What do you think the story's about then?"

"If I had to guess…a werewolf."

A flush rushed up Angela's arms, across her shoulders, and down her spine. "A werewolf?" She stared at Danny.

Danny's eyelids fluttered, and he swallowed a lump. A bead of sweat formed on his upper lip.

"It's what it looks like to me." Albert smirked and handed the notebook across the desk. "Science fiction. For instance, there is a reference here to a barn—" he referred to his notes again "—in the Village of the Hall. That's where the narrator's going to conduct his final experiments before implementing the 'plan.' A mad scientist's lab in the Village of the Hall? I don't know of a town with that name."

"Thanks, Doc," Danny said, standing up. To Angela, he seemed in a rush to get out of there. "And, um, we're going to need your yellow pad, too. Sorry." He shrugged in the shy country-boy way she recognized from Redstick.

Angela pulled onto Highway 183, and traffic trapped her in the right lane for over a mile. "This is what I love about Texas," she griped. "People think speed limits are suggestions and blinkers mean to speed up and cut me off." She cranked the temperature down a couple of degrees and relaxed back in her seat for the ride to Fort Worth. "So, what was that all about back there?" she asked Danny.

He stared down at his phone. "Village of the Hall" he muttered. He held his up phone and showed her a map. "Hallsville, maybe? Out on I-20, east of Dallas. Barn country anyway."

"Maybe. But that's not what I'm talking about." She poked him in the arm, and he shifted his gaze to the side of the road. "You know something. Spill it."

He took a deep breath and chewed the inside of his cheek for a moment. "I think someone's trying to create *lupus*." He nervously tapped the cap on his water bottle. "This is the definition of bad."

Angela shrugged. "What's so bad about it? You're *lupus.*"

"Right. And—" he took another deep breath "—I'm a *Frenator.*"

"And?"

"Right. It takes years, sometimes decades, to learn how to do that unless you've got the mental discipline to do it faster. The Nazis liked the idea of a werewolf super-soldier, but they weren't willing to wait that long."

"Nazis?" she snapped. Neither of them said anything for a few moments, but she blinked her eyes and nodded in long, slow arcs. "They tried to create their own artificial version of a werewolf."

"Right. And Dr. Josef Mengele was ass deep in it. He experimented on death camp prisoners. Worked on a strain of the virus to make *Frenatus* off the bat." A dark shadow crossed his face as he paused to stare out the windshield. He radiated a deep uneasiness that wrapped around her like a cold cloak. He took a long drink of water. "He experimented heavily on twins, Angela. One theory he had was that all twins had some kind of supernatural link. Had the crazy idea the link was the key to creating *Frenatus*. He tried to put the secret to that link in a bottle." He held his water bottle up to make his point.

"Was he successful?"

"Yes. Sort of. The victims all ended up as psychotic monstrosities. *Intelligent* psychotic monstrosities. Insane *Frenatus.*"

"So, we're not looking for a Dr. Frankenstein. We're looking for a Dr. Mengele wannabe."

"Right."

"Is there an antidote to Mengele's serum?"

"Not that I know of. The real *lupus* infection might inoculate you. It fights off everything else."

Angela frowned. "But wouldn't that make the person a werewolf?"

"Yes," he admitted. He took a deep breath and slowly let it out. "The alternative though, is being a monster. A true monster."

Angela wasn't sure of the difference, but she didn't argue the point aloud. However, she had to admit, if it made a werewolf shiver, she didn't want to run into it.

We're gonna need a bigger boat, ahem, silver bullet.

"Why would the Forsaken Dweller want to create a pseudo-*lupus*?"

He tightened his lips and shook his head. "No idea." He snapped his fingers. "You know, some supernatural rituals use *lupus* blood. Summoning demons and the like. Maybe that's what's going on here. Creating their own *lupus* blood bank, kinda like humans using pigs for the Type-Os." He took another drink.

"Seems like a lot of work. Why not just get some blood from a real werewolf?"

Danny snorted water out through his nose and stared at

her in disbelief. "You volunteering to hold one down long enough to stick a needle in its arm?"

Angela read the sign as they whooshed past it. Hallsville, Texas. Population 3,775.

Just call it what it is. Hicksville, Texas. Why can't the bad guys hang out in a city?

Propped up on the car door's window frame, she rested her chin on her palm. A deep sigh fluttered past her lips. "I'm completely untrained for this type of work."

"Pardon?" Danny asked.

She glowered at him. "Do you realize they don't teach one, not one class on the supernatural at the FBI Academy?"

He scoffed. "Why would they?"

She sighed again. "Because this baptism by fire shit is starting to get next to me."

He turned the radio down. She didn't like country music, but they'd agreed on a truce; the driver picked the station. "Don't sell yourself short, Angela. You're more equipped for this than you think you are. You don't know all the lore behind the scary stuff, but you've astounded me with your investigation skills. In the couple weeks I've worked with you, I've learned more than I did in the ten years I was a cop in Redstick."

She shook off the compliment. "What good is my tradecraft if I don't know what the hell a mad scientist's lab looks like from the outside?"

"It was good enough to tell you we needed some thermal imaging of the area."

She shrugged. "It wasn't good enough for a search warrant, though."

"So? It's good enough to go snoop around. Maybe we'll

see something wrong."

"True!" They shared a conspiratorial smile. "And there's always that nose of yours. I suppose you could smell something you shouldn't."

"Exactly!"

They'd left Fort Worth early to investigate a barn aerial surveillance showed to have a massive thermal signature. If they'd been with the Drug Enforcement Agency, they would have taken a particular interest in it but for entirely different reasons. Pot growing operations used lots of solar lamps. Technically, Task Force W didn't care what the owners were doing in their own barns as long as they weren't creating new versions of werewolves, hiding a renegade succubus, or disturbing ancient Amerindian burial grounds. Oh, and summoning Cthulhu monsters.

Yes, summoning Cthulhu monsters was right out.

Especially ones with a name like The Forsaken Dweller. She surprised herself by knowing what a Cthulhu monster was, but ever since Speed had mentioned Lovecraft, she'd been reading his stories. She'd even found a small bookstore in Arlington that carried those types of books.

"Besides," Danny said with a crooked grin, "You can't feel sorry for yourself. I look up to you too much."

"Just shut up and drive, smart ass."

"Someone went to a lot of expense to make that barn look old and rundown," Danny murmured. "Artificial siding. Corrugated metal roof. Definitely retro." He ran his binoculars over the large pasture surrounding it. Tall pine trees shrouded three sides. A 200-yard gravel trail ran from the barn's massive doors in a locked metal gate next to the main road. "Jump the fence?"

"Nooo," Angela pronounced, drawing it out as if it was the only answer. They both knew the lawsuit the owner would slap them with if they trespassed.

"What do you suggest th—" He lowered his binoculars and blinked rapidly at her. "Did you hear that?"

"What?"

"A woman screamed." He tilted his left ear towards the barn.

"I'm not pulling a fake probable cause out of my ass, Danny."

"No, seriously," he exclaimed as he stood.

She knew he wasn't making something up. He *did* hear something, something her human ears couldn't. She rushed back to the car with him.

A light chain and combination lock secured the gate. As she requested backup, Danny drove through the gate, ripping apart the chain, and raced up the driveway, a long trail of caliche dust spiraling behind them. He slammed on the brakes and skidded to a stop as they closed in on the barn, kicking up even more dust. They both leaped out, pistols drawn and racing for the side door.

Screaming, whether it was a woman's or not, came from the barn. She'd heard girls cry out in their sleep after a kidnapping rescue, but what pried its way out through the cracks in the walls and around the doorframe made her palms sweat and knees tremble.

Danny opened his eyes wide. "What the hell was that?"

"Together!" she hissed while *Bad Girls, Bad Girls, Whatcha Gonna Do?* sang in her head.

He pointed his head at the doorknob, raised his eyebrows, and Angela gave him the go-ahead. He twisted the knob, and the door swung in with a quiet squeak. Angela followed it, taking up position on and scanning the inside right. "Clear," she whispered loud enough for only Danny to hear her.

Her little talk from the church about working together as a team must have stuck because he stayed with her the whole time. He shadowed her, taking up position on and scanning the inside left. "Clear," he echoed back to her. "I feel like I need a lead vest," he added under his breath.

They both stared at a scene from Mary Shelley's worst nightmare. Flashing arcs of lightning shot across the inside of the barn, and they undoubtedly did more to ruin their night vision than the brightness of the East Texas afternoon sun they'd escaped from on the other side of the door.

Tall Tesla coils with jagged spikes failing to obey the standard laws of geometry poked out along their length, appearing and disappearing from sight. The longer she stared at them, the harder she clenched her teeth from frustration until pain shot through her jaw. She had to look away. Dark crystal chains with glittering loops connected the coils to pulsing blobs of pasty, blue-veined flesh. Another set of chains attached the fleshy bulbs to the feet of three metal stretchers forming a three-pointed star in the middle of the floor. The heads tilted up at the center, forming its heart, where a tall, thin, and naked man stood. He faced away from them, but his skin was as pasty white and translucent as the fleshy pods around him. His organs convulsed each time a bolt of lightning flashed, and she imagined a sickening squelch along with them. A bank of switches, knobs, and analog dials reminiscent of the worst monster flicks Hollywood had to offer formed a semicircle around Angela and Danny.

Angela took the lead and crept to the right across the

dusty, wooden floor. Danny stalked left. They stayed hidden behind the control consoles should the alien, or monster, or whatever Task Force W called these things, chose to swivel around. As she got to her side of the console, she chanced a peek around the corner. One stretcher contained a woman, the second one, a man. The third one held one of those chupacabras…chupacabri…

What the hell is plural for chupacabra?

All three were restrained. Danny crouched below the other end of the console, one eye on her and the other on the alien. She nodded once and stood up.

"Freeze! FBI!" she yelled, "Cease all…cross-universe experiments and put your hands behind your head." Considering the FBI refused to train her on how to arrest cross-dimensional beings, she was quite pleased with herself and her ad-lib adjustments.

The monster spun around and stared at her. Its face comprised a mixture of insectoid eyes, beavertail nose, and a tri-jawed mandible for a mouth lined with long rows of needle-sharp teeth. It looked like the drawings produced from Felicia's description.

Angela wasn't sure how she knew it, but the look was a glare. The mad alien scientist did not appear to be happy with her interruption. The lightning didn't cease, but it did dim as the Doctor took two steps towards her. Its shoulders flinched as Danny put a three-shot set into it, center mass. The lightning show increased again and struck the creature multiple times.

The bullets spawned no damage whatsoever.

Oh, fuck! Not Dr. Mengele!

It spun around and tilted its head in Danny's direction, folded its jaws shut, and lowered its nose flap. Three stalks with large bulbs on their ends flowed out from the crease and pointed in his direction. The bulbs pulsated and glittered for a moment before slipping back out of sight. Its mouth unfolded again, and it chittered. It sounded happy. Too happy. Angela guessed a ready supply of *Lupus sapiens* blood showing up unannounced was more than it could have hoped for.

She squeezed her trigger in rapid sets, knowing her shots were scoring, until the slide on her pistol locked back, telling her it was time for a new magazine. Each shot made the monster twitch, but it didn't drop. Lightning bolts continued to fly. She stepped out from behind the safety of the control console and dropped her magazine from her pistol.

The creature ignored her as it spewed a long stream of rotten mushroom-colored webbing at Danny. He screamed when it hit him. It was hard to tell if it was in agony or abject terror considering his aversion to spiders. Smoke roiled from where the strands landed on him. By the time she'd inserted her second magazine and cocked her pistol, the monster had entirely cocooned Danny in its smoldering webs. He toppled over.

The creature whirled back on her and unfolded its mouth.

"I don't think so, scooter!" she yelled as she dived behind the bank of consoles, belly crawling while she peeked under them. The monster was walking towards her end of the machinery. She sprung to her feet, dashed over to Danny, and stood over his still body. "I'll burn in hell before I let you near his carcass," she screamed.

The creature paused and regarded her. It rested one arm on the top of the console and wagged a finger in annoyance at her.

Her situational awareness training kicked in. Two

magazines. Target armed with a…web-shooting…mouth-thingy. Immune to kinetic energy. And silver.

The last few moments flashed through her mind. Every shot she and Danny had made resulted in a lightning bolt striking the creature.

Time for my own experiment.

She pointed her pistol at it and squeezed off a round.

A lightning bolt crackled from the three Tesla coils, merged in mid-air, and struck the alien. The bullet hole sealed shut as if it had never been there.

Lightning heals it!

She whipped around and shot three rounds into one of the jaggedly spiked coils. The bullets disappeared as the area around the otherworldly twines warped as if she'd dropped three pebbles into a still pond.

Deja vu struck hard, harder than in the church basement.

The creature squeaked and hurried towards her with long strides. Its mouth stretched open and quivered. Webs shot from it like cotton candy from a spinner run by a deranged Dr. Seuss.

She darted towards the back of the laboratory, away from the creature, to give herself time to figure out how to stop the lightning. She stepped closer to one of the pulsating blobs of flesh. Glittering sparkles of static electricity traveled up the crystal chains to the coils. She filled the blob with silver rounds. It burst in a loud schlorp of gooey, greyish pus.

She held her hands to her ears as the creature's shrill and fearsome screech pierced them like a hot needle.

She poked her head around a large crate in the back shadows to investigate if her efforts did more than merely piss it off. It continued loping towards her.

Still invulnerable.

She slammed her last magazine home and aimed at the second blob. It took nine bullets to burst it.

The creature screeched again, but this time it heaved crates to the side as it stormed after her. She continued her circuit around the laboratory.

Options were limited. Shooting the remaining blob might burst it, but she'd be out of ammo. And defenseless. If she shot the creature, the lightning would heal it.

Math is math. I need more bullets.

Angry growls echoed across the barn.

He's alive!

A howl stabbed the air.

"It's about damned time, you redneck!" she yelled. Danny-werewolf made her decision for her. She fired her remaining shots into the final blob. Damaged, it still didn't rupture.

Shit!

She glanced at Danny, at the werewolf. Every instinct in her monkey brain screamed evil incarnate. Every instinct except her first one; her first instinct was to hide.

Will I ever get used to seeing him like that?

The webbing had burned zebra stripes into his fur. He dropped to all fours and rushed towards the alien, snout snarling, and slaver dripping freely.

The alien quit chasing her and turned its attention to Danny.

Her curiosity nearly overruled her discipline. She wrenched her attention away from the battle royale evolving before her and raced around the outside of the control consoles to where Danny had dropped. She still managed to catch most of the scrap out of the corner of her eye.

Danny sprinted on all fours and launched himself at the

alien.

It had the same idea because it dropped to all fours too.

They clashed in midair as a writhing tangle of fur, claws, and webbing, tumbling to the ground. Digging talons tore splinters the size of pencils from the floor as they both maneuvered for an advantage. Danny growled and bit while the alien screeched and shot burning strands of arachnid horror. Their claws tore mercilessly at each other. A lightning bolt from the remaining flesh pod healed the monster's latest wounds. It struck Danny, too, but didn't have the same effect; he scrambled back, shaking his head in pain.

Angela bent over, retrieved his pistol, and aimed at the remaining pod.

He blocked her view as he jockeyed for an upper hand against the alien. She sprinted off for a better position and glimpsed over her shoulder when he screeched in pain.

Another grey spray of webbing that would have made an abandoned farmhouse full of spiders proud webbed Danny's left arm to his chest. The fur on his back and neck snapped out straight, like a pissed off porcupine. Wounded and one-armed, he leaped back in, clawing a swath through the alien's midsection that would have gutted a horse.

Lightning lit up the barn.

Angela found herself standing before the last pod.

She took aim at the gelatinous, pulsing sac of goop and put half her magazine in it before it burst.

She turned, made eye contact with the alien, and let a slow grin spread across her face.

It unrolled its mouth towards her as she triple-squeezed the trigger in rapid succession. White, nauseating, goo exploded from the alien's chest while Danny's last act of vengeance separated its head from its body. Lightning exploded from its neck stump, catching her partner square in the face and sparking small fires in the lofts, the wooden crates in the back, the walls, everything. As she reflexively ducked, the bolt threw Danny back into the console, hard.

The lightning trickled down to nothing after a few moments, but the fires spread. She scooted over towards Danny but slowed when her survival instinct told her he might be playing possum and snorted. "Werewolves don't need to play possum." The smell of bad hamburger meat pummeled her nose. Burned hair and flesh covered it up enough for her to get close to him, though. She considered slapping his snout to wake him up, but that annoying survival instinct got the better of her again.

She gently placed a hand on his chest. "Danny?" A heartbeat. Strong and sure. She pulled back an eyelid. His eyeball rolled back into his skull.

This is one hurt puppy.

She snorted at her own stupid joke as she took a leg and tried to pull him towards the exit. G.I. Jane, she was not. Seven feet of werewolf was heavy.

The man and the woman behind her in the stretchers screamed for help.

Angela walked over to the gurney when Danny sat up and removed his oxygen mask. "Welcome back, stranger."

While the female paramedic checked his vitals, he blinked and scanned the scene around him in confusion. It no longer looked the same as when they'd stormed the barn earlier. Angela understood his confusion. A dozen police cars, all with their lights blinking, sat in various spots throughout the field. Men and women with a whole alphabet soup of big white letters on their backs hurried around. The fire department was busy watering a garden of charred ground where the barn once stood.

He twisted his neck one way and the other, releasing two long strings of cracks. "What happened?"

"You got struck by lightning," Angela answered. "To the head. I've never seen anything like it." She looked at the paramedic. "Burned all your clothes off but left you untouched. Even your hair." They both knew he didn't have clothes on.

"Lightning?" Danny asked.

"Yeah," Angela replied with a slow shake of her head.

"And I lived?"

"Yeah."

He sat a little straighter and grinned that shy, country boy grin of his. "Heck, I must be a total badass."

The paramedic tossed a pair of scrubs onto his lap. "I guess we can start calling you Danny Danger, huh?"

"Oh, hell, no," Angela argued. "Don't even go there."

Convinced Danny wasn't going to die on her watch, the paramedic went to check on the other two survivors.

"I remember taking its head off," he muttered. "Then nothing. Say, how'd you get me out of there?"

"Arnold Cooper. The man who was on the stretcher inside." Angela pointed her head across the way.

"How'd you convince him to drag a werewolf to safety?"

Angela handed him his pistol and badge.

His voice rose in pitch. "You threatened a civilian at gunpoint?"

"No. I deputized a civilian with extreme prejudice."

Danny pursed his lips and nodded to Arnold, who returned it with a nervous smile.

"You think he's gonna say anything?" Danny asked.

"Don't think so. Once we got his sister out—his twin sister, by the way—and you'd changed back, he calmed down. I guess after being forced into some mad experiment by—whatever the hell it was—seeing a werewolf was probably mundane."

Danny grimaced at the remains of the barn. "Any evidence left at all?"

Angela shook her head.

"So, we don't know if there are any other labs around."

"Nope. Not at all."

He leaned back on his elbows and tilted his head to the side. "Angela Hollingsworth and her trusty sidekick, Danny Danger." He stared off into the distance with a wide smile. "I think there's a comic book deal here."

Tom Bont

Episode 4: Doorman

Two One Eight Elmwood Drive. Spelled out.

Must be hard on the mailman.

A dozen rose bushes along the front of the single-story, red brick house were headed towards hibernation for the winter. A mowing constituted the limits of its weekly maintenance for the rest of the yard. "A little fixing up, it'd be pretty," Angela told Danny. "Not that I'm interested in moving to the outskirts of Marshall, Texas. Too Hicksville for my tastes, I don't care how big it thinks it is."

"If you say so," he murmured. He'd drawn his mouth into a straight line, chewing on his lip.

"What's wrong?" she asked.

He paused before he whispered, "Death."

"That's why we're here," she sassed. "Dead body. Remember?"

"Yeah, but…the death is wrong."

"Well, I don't know too many that are right." When he didn't answer, she crossed her arms and studied him. Beads of sweat coated his forehead. "What makes you think that?" she demanded. "We haven't even seen it yet." When he still refused to answer, she grabbed his arm and pulled him towards the street. More privacy. "What's got you so spooked, Danny?"

"There something wrong about this whole house." He painted the entire structure with twitching eyes as if he expected something to jump out at him.

She scanned it too and cocked her head to the side. "No spiders that I can see."

He jerked a quick glimpse at her and let loose a staccato chuckle. "Yeah, right?"

"Here comes our escort." A man in his late thirties with curly blonde hair, brown eyes, and an FBI windbreaker swaggered towards them. "If you want to stay out here, let me know now," she told Danny.

He glanced at the FBI agent. "No. I'm okay." He rolled his eyes to the side to gaze back at the house. "It's just giving me the willies. That's all."

The local FBI agent shook hands with them. "You must be Angela Hollingsworth," he drawled. "I'm Justin Bates." He squinted at her as if trying to recall where he'd seen her before.

"Yes, I am, and it's nice to meet you. This is Officer Danny McIver."

"Police Officer?" Justin asked. "Where you from?"

"Redstick. Up north a ways."

Angela interjected. "He's a subject matter expert we tap from time to time."

Justin appraised Danny for another moment before he nodded. "Well, we've got a good one for y'all today. Locked room mystery."

"Why is the FBI interested in a man found dead in his own house?" Danny asked. "This seems like a local matter to me."

"He was caught up in a sweep and interviewed about the disappearance of two teenagers a few months back. You may have heard of them. Felicia and Ja'son Jefferson? Their names came up in one of your case files."

Angela snapped her head up. "The animal who kidnapped those kids is dead in that house?"

"We don't know." Justin allowed with a long shrug. "But

I'm beginning to have doubts about his alibi."

"Who found him?" Danny inquired.

"Local police. Welfare check. Didn't show up at work last night. Hadn't missed a day in like eight years or something."

Angela put a stick of gum in her mouth. "And the house was locked down tight?"

"Yeah. All windows are either locked or painted shut. Doors chained or dead bolted."

"So, who's the stiff?"

"Conrad Sabine. Caucasian male. Age 42. Divorced. Lives here alone. Found nailed to his easy chair with a single arrow through the heart. The trajectory of the arrow shows it came from the fireplace. The problem is there's not enough room to stand there and shoot a shotgun, much less a bow and arrow. That's why we called you guys. Is this a Task Force W case?"

"Won't know until we look it over." She did a double take. "You know what Task Force W is?"

"Just that you're called in on the cases that typically defy logic." He scratched the back of his neck. "I've heard your investigation methods are unconventional."

"You could say that," she drolled in a voice as dry as the Texas grasslands in August.

"How do you get assigned?" he asked. "Were you a quota assignment?"

Angela stared hard at him for a moment and wrestled with the temptation to ask if that would be the Mythical Woman Quota because their Redneck Asshole Quota seemed to be all filled. Fighting the urge to snarl a snide comment, she leveled her gaze instead. "I shot my old boss."

He laughed, but when neither she nor Danny joined him, he nervously smacked his dry lips, blinked a couple of times, and pulled his head back. "Sorry. I didn't mean…I meant—"

She spun towards the house. "Walk us through the scene, please," she ground out through a clenched jaw.

Justin took a couple of jogging steps to catch up and held the door for her and Danny after they put their booties, hairnets, and gloves on. The open concept living room sat off the carport. The first thing she spotted was a leather recliner with an arrow sticking out the back of it. Dried blood had tinted the arrowhead dark brown, and a blackish dripline streaked from the hole to the floor. She crept around the other side. Conrad, obviously, lounged there as if he'd fallen asleep—other than the arrow buried in his chest. The shaft lacked one of its fletching flights. A book lay on the floor next to him. There was no television. Only a stereo with classical music CDs piled on it. A comfortable-looking couch and another recliner, both full of books. From the spines, Conrad preferred crime and mystery procedurals, mostly conspiracy-based. The sofa and recliner must have doubled as an overflow because even more books entirely filled the wall-mounted bookshelves. There were three other ways into the room: a hallway, a back door, and the dining room. And down the chimney, if you were Santa Claus.

Angela leaned over and focused up the length of the arrow shaft, judging its trajectory back towards the fireplace. "Has the backyard been canvassed?"

"Yes. Results negative."

"I assume the doorknob here—" she pointed to the back door "—has been cleared?"

"Yes, ma'am."

She stepped out onto the back patio and surveyed the overgrown yard before examining the bricks on the back of the fireplace, about where she figured the arrow would have come from. "Danny, what do you see there?"

Danny leaned in and inspected the section of the bricks she was pointing at. "Looks like a feather in the mortar."

"Agent Bates," Angela called out, "I'd like this section of the brickwork removed and sent to the lab. I want the feather in the mortar here compared to the feathers on the arrow."

He glanced back and forth between the feather and Angela. "You think they're the same?"

"I don't know. Let's let the evidence tell us."

Justin raised his eyebrows and tilted his head towards Danny.

"If she thinks it's important, I'd bet a silver buffalo nickel she's right," Danny told him.

Justin laughed and shook his head. "Waste of time if you ask me, but I'll get your bricks for you."

Danny watched him walk off. "I guess he failed the task force's entrance exam."

"Yeah, but not because he's a chauvinist. I deal with that shit every day. He failed because he made an assumption before all the evidence was in."

"Agent Hollingsworth?" A young, female police officer in uniform stepped through the doorway. "We got the background on Mr. Sabine. He's clean as a whistle. No priors. Solid citizen by all accounts."

Justin grabbed Angela's attention over the young cop's shoulder. "Agent Hollingsworth, could you come in here, please?"

Angela followed Justin into the house to find half a dozen other agents with crossed arms observing her.

"Agent Hollingsworth—" Justin indicated an older agent standing to the side "—this is Field Supervisor Harvey

Anderson."

Harvey indicated the body but kept his gaze on her. "Agent, have you ever seen Mr. Sabine before today?"

"Not that I recall, no. Why?" She glanced around at everyone and immediately knew what it would be like to tiptoe through Redstick in the middle of the night during a full moon. These men had hungry eyes.

What the hell's going on?

Danny edged up next to her and straightened his back. "Angela, don't say anything." The cop she first met in Redstick materialized next to her. He took a single step forward, placing himself in front of her, and faced down an entire room of armed men. "Is she a suspect?"

"This doesn't concern you, Officer," Agent Anderson growled.

"The hell it doesn't! You asked for us personally." He flared his nostrils and took a deep sniff. "But I understand your hesitation. You don't want to outright accuse her of anything, so you're hoping she'll ass up and say the wrong thing. Does she need her attorney?"

Three of the men uncrossed their arms and exchanged dour expressions with each other.

Agent Anderson shifted uncomfortably from one foot to the other. "We aren't accusing her of anything."

"Yeah?" Danny growled. "Well, I'm calling bullshit."

Angela stepped around and rested the back of her hand on Danny's chest, gently forcing him back. "What do you want to know, gentlemen?"

Anderson blinked and pointed a lazy finger at Justin. He handed her an evidence bag with a picture sealed up inside. "We found this in that book next to the chair. He'd been using it as a bookmark. Maybe."

Angela took the bag and scrutinized the picture. "We didn't know who that was until you showed up. This is you, right?" He pointed to the picture.

It was her—and Heather—eating lunch a few weeks ago. A masculine hand had written on the back, *The Forsaken Dweller has prepared her with a gift.*

"Yes, it's me."

"Who's the other woman?"

"My friend, Dr. Heather Wiley."

"What's the gift it's referring to?"

She paused for a moment. "I'm not sure." She continued to stare at the picture.

"Do you know who this Forsaken Dweller is?" Anderson inquired.

"Psycho," Danny answered. "Leads some cult we've been tracking." When no one challenged him, he stated clearly, "Any other questions, contact our boss, Kent Gladen."

As they left the house, Anderson called, "Agent—" He tilted his head at the evidence bag still in her hand.

Angela pulled out her phone and took pictures of the picture.

Danny usually had a comment for every crack in the road and every worn-out piece of architecture they passed while they drove from one scene to the next. But during the drive back to Fort Worth, he didn't utter a word.

"Okay, Danny, what gives?"

He rested his arm across the top of the steering wheel. "Tell me about the *gift*."

She stared out her window. "What gift?"

"Angela, I may look and sound like a dumb country boy, but I'm not a dumb country boy. I pulled the report on Lilith and Clint."

"What?" Angela swallowed a lump not too dissimilar than an ice-cold ball bearing. It slid down her throat and pulled her stomach to her feet.

"A succubus that leaves its victims looking older. A succubus that's lived at least 100 years. That we know of. The reports from the SWAT team members all agreed Lilith was a teenage-aged girl. A teenager is not someone I would expect an FBI agent with Clint's record to pursue romantically."

"Fuck," she mouthed.

"I found your entrance photo ID to the Academy. There's not much difference there. That's why people probably haven't picked up on it. But, Angela, I'm *lupus*. Age smells. And you smell younger than when I met you in Redstick."

"Fuck," she mouthed again. She wanted to be angry. She hungered for it.

How dare he!

She'd worked hard to control her emotions through life, but ever since Lilith, she'd been a malfunctioning hormone factory. The littlest thing triggered the wrong reaction. She pulled out a stick of gum and stuck it in her mouth.

Yes, he would dare. He's a fuckin' awesome cop.

"I need to know what happened in that room, or I'm carrying my hairy ass back to Redstick, and you can fight this Forsaken Dweller yourself because you told me if we can't trust each other we're no good for each other, and the bastard's gonna win anyway." He took a deep breath.

Tears welled up in her eyes—damned teenage hormones—and once she started talking and sobbing, she couldn't stop. She hadn't realized how much she'd been holding back. She told him the whole story. "…and you know what hurts the most, Danny? Clint is lying in some bed, waiting to die, while I'm living on his dime. I haven't visited him once because I can't face him. I know it's not my fault, but that doesn't make it any easier."

They drove in silence for a few moments. He gently bit his lower lip. "Would you give it back if you could?"

She didn't expect that question. In fact, she had never once asked herself that question since it had happened. She wasn't sure if she avoided it on purpose, or if it had never crossed her mind. She surprised herself when she whispered, "I don't know." She sniffled. "I'm sorry I lied to you, Danny. I haven't told anyone. Not even Heather. How could I?"

"I understand," he consoled her quietly. "And I accept your apology. But don't lie to me again, please. I don't think I could stand it." He was quiet for a few more moments before pointing to a field along the side of the road. "Hey, would you look at that! I haven't seen a tractor that old since they closed down the mill and Uncle Bill took to farming."

"Hairy ass?" she half-choked around a phlegmy laugh.

"Part of the werewolf package."

"Thanks," she said, and added with emphasis, "Partner."

Heather stared intently down the long shaft of stainless steel. She peered slightly to her left, deliberately pulled her arms to the right, and pulled them back to the left a little faster. The putter tapped the golf ball and sent it rolling across the green. It bounced against the wooden corner, flew over the ramp, and disappeared under the windmill wing. A few moments later, the *plunk* *plunk* *plunk* of the ball dropping into the metal cup told Angela her friend was now eight strokes ahead. As if the happy dance she was doing on the Astroturf didn't.

Angela shook her head and laughed loud enough to attract the kids' attention at the next hole. "When do you find the time to practice?"

"Only when I'm out with you," Heather bragged with a big smile. "Doctor reflexes, I guess."

Angela cut her laugh off as a man with a cell phone took pictures of the area. One of them included Heather and her. She was about to go over there when a kid bumped her arm. She spun around. Two more kids, all standing on a stone wall, posed for a picture.

"That's all," the man yelled. "Let's go!" He cast a wary face at Angela and protectively put his arms around the kids as he ushered them out.

"What was that about," Heather asked.

"What?"

"I thought you were fixin' to draw down on Family Man over there."

"I don't like people taking pictures of me without my permission."

Heather pursed her lips and put one fist on her hips. "Since when have we ever been shy, sister?"

Angela pulled her friend to the side and let the next group play through. "Since I found this on a dead, child-kidnapping suspect 200 miles from here." She pulled out her phone and brought up the picture of them eating.

Heather stared at it. "What? Who?" Her face turned pale. "What the hell?"

"Yeah, that was pretty much my reaction. Like I said, the guy's dead, but I don't know if he had an accomplice or not."

Heather watched Family Man leave through the gate with his kids and wife. "What was his name?"

"Conrad Sabine. You ever heard of him?"

"No." Heather stared back at the picture for a few moments and handed it back.

"You still have your pistol?"

"Yeah, but I haven't carried it in months."

"Time to dust it off," Angela advised.

"You think someone's coming after me?"

"No, I don't. I don't want to take any chances, though."

Heather stepped up to the next t-off position and put her ball down. "Hey, you think I could get that cute partner of yours to take me to the range?"

"Is that the only place you want him to take you?"

"Sister, it's been a year since I've had a man in my bed. Been too busy. But a man with handcuffs? Hmm, hmm!"

"Hey!" Angela stepped up to her ball. "We swore off cowboys!"

"You did. I swore no such thing."

"True," Angela admitted as she swung her putter. "But you don't want to know where a cop's cuffs have been. Trust me on that one."

"Well, he's got big, strong hands. I might just have to take a couple days of vacation for that."

Angela shook her head with a subtle chuckle. "Hussy."

Danny dropped a folder on Angela's desk as she sat down. "The report on the arrow. Took forensics long enough. Four weeks? Hell, I could have held a séance and got quicker information."

"You're here early," she grumbled, ignoring his too-damned-cheerful early morning banter.

"Went for a run before I came to work," he explained as he dropped into his chair and put his hands behind his head.

"God, I hate you," she complained.

"Why's that?"

"I hate morning people."

"I'm not people." He sported a huge grin. "I'm your partner."

"Everyone's a morning person until noon or a cup of coffee. Whichever comes first. Speaking of which, it's your day."

He hopped from his chair. "Sonny Jim," he burst out. "I forgot." He pulled a cup of coffee from behind his computer screen. "Here."

"Sonny Jim? Wait. What's going on here…? Oh, crap, Danny. You didn't go out with Heather, did you?"

His ears turned red. "No. Well, yeah. Well, not really. It wasn't a date or anything. I cleaned her pistol and taught her how to shoot."

Angela crossed her arms. "Danny, her dad's a United States Marine Corps general. She's more qualified to shoot that weapon than you are."

"Oh." He scrunched his eyebrows and gently sat back down in his chair. "So, it was a date?" A hint of a smile crept across his face.

"Men." She picked up the proffered cup and held her finger in the air, signally he should hush up. She closed her eyes and took her first sip of coffee for the day.

Black, just the way I like it. The boy's coming along just fine.

She flipped open the cover on the folder. "Give me the highlights."

"Sabine's DNA matched up to an unsolved rape and murder from six months ago. Lisa Reilly. Unsolved until today, that is." Kent came up and listened to Danny's report. "And the arrow is an authentic museum piece. The fletching you found in the mortar? As you suspected, it was a perfect match for what was left on the arrow. As if there was ever a doubt, regardless of what Justin had to say. Looks like we got us a real-life, supernatural hunter on our hands."

"Justin was an ass," Angela said. "Worse, he was a moron." She flipped a few more pages in the folder. "I'm tired of thinking every dead, bad guy we find is the result of a vigilante. This looks too coincidental, though."

"What's your next move?" Kent asked, reminding her he was standing there behind her.

"Well, we need more information on the arrow," she said. "We need to find someone who can tell us where it came from, who made it, everything."

"Keep me updated," he said, his voice no more than a gravelly whisper.

Angela closed the folder. "Yes, sir."

As Kent strode purposefully away, Danny stood and put his jacket on. "Let's roll. I'll tell you all about my date."

"Agent Hollingsworth," the receptionist said. She was a young woman with light brown hair and a pug nose. Sandy, by the nametag on her desk. "Ms. Mastier will see you now."

She led them from the lobby, with its squeaky vinyl couches, and through a pair of sandblasted glass doors. They followed a long hallway until they entered a corner office. The understated plaque on the door read Diana Mastier, Comptroller, ACME Protection Underwriters, but the inside was anything but understated. Granite topped tables, polished oak bookshelves and a magnificent view of downtown Grand Rapids, Michigan from two solid walls of floor to ceiling windows. Angela slowed her pace in awe as she walked in. She wondered what the nighttime cityscape must look like from there.

As soon as they stepped into the office, a beautiful, statuesque woman in her late 30s rose from behind a large, mahogany desk. She stood a smidge below six feet and had the type of chest Angela wished for—proud, but not so large as to cause backaches. Black hair, curly and long, and when she stepped out from behind her desk, athletic thighs and stomach brought to mind Angela's unused gym membership.

If I were into women, this is the woman I'd be into.

"Hello, Agent Hollingsworth. It's nice to meet you." She smiled, and her sharp, brown eyes twinkled with warmth. "I'm Diana Mastier."

"Hello, Ms. Mastier. It's nice to meet you too. This is my consulting partner, Officer Danny McIver."

Danny stepped forward to shake her hand. Shock rattled Angela; his eyes were pale blue, signaling the start of his *renovatio*. Angela hoped Diana would accept it as his natural color. His forehead had a sheen to it. He tightened his lips, quickly released her hand, and stepped back. The only other time he'd acted so uncomfortable around a woman was when he met Heather. But he was clumsy then, not on the verge of changing.

He stuttered, "I...I j-just remembered something I forgot to do," he stammered, heading for the door. "I'll be back in a few minutes."

I'm not the only one attracted to her, it seems.

Diana's smile dropped to a smirk as Danny disappeared out the doorway. She looked back at Angela. "Can I get you something to drink? Water? Coffee? A soda?"

"No, thank you. I'm fine."

"Great!" Followed Angela's gaze to the skyline, she turned and looked over her shoulder. "Pretty isn't it?"

"Yes, it is."

"I'm a Grand Rapids native and have yet to get tired of it."

"I bet."

"So, Agent Hollingsworth, what can I help the FBI with?"

Angela handed her a warrant. "I believe this will explain everything."

Diana took a moment to read the document. "A Request for Help?"

"It's not a Search Warrant. It's not legally binding. It's a request from the government that you voluntarily help us with a case. We're not asking for open access to your systems, but ever since 9/11, we've found it necessary to work more closely with the private sector than ever before. This request shows you we are on official business and not looking for dirt on your company."

Diana leaned back against her desk and crossed her ankles. "Our client confidentiality prevents us from sharing this information without an actual search warrant."

"We aren't here to seize information. We're simply asking your help to clear some things up. The line between confidentiality and something we could glean from data mining government records is fine but distinct. You, not we, will make the call when we go over that line."

Diana's smile returned. "And if I refuse, 200 FBI computer experts will take over my data center, shutting me down for weeks while you dig for what I could give you in a few moments."

Angela grimaced. "Yeah. I would really hate to do that. It would get the job done, but the stack of paperwork I'd have to fill out would destroy my Thanksgiving. Plus—" she crossed her arms and rubbed them "—it's too damned cold here. I'm a southern girl. I like beaches and drinks with little umbrellas in them."

Not that spending it in silence with Mom and Dad is something I'm looking forward to anyway.

Diana laughed. "Well, we wouldn't want that, now would we. Consider me at your disposal. What information, in particular, are you looking for?"

Two days ago, Angela had sat down at her desk and connected to Archives through her own workstation.

Welcome to the 21st century!

She was quite pleased she didn't have to drive across town to Archives any longer. She and Danny had spent a few hours with the coroner generating a list of search terms. They were working under the assumption someone was going after unsolved murder-rapes. If there were any unsolved murders under unusual circumstances—such as locked room mysteries—they wanted to compare those victims' DNA with any unsolved sexual assaults.

Her connection to Archives might not have been the fastest leaf in the stream, but as soon as she pressed the *Enter* key, two results popped up. Three more. Seven more. "Search Complete," the screen read after about half an hour.

A baker's dozen—if you count Marshall—with nearly identical MOs.

After a few moments, it dawned on her why no one had made a connection before. The cases spanned twenty years and over the entire country. Every perpetrator was a man with no priors, his DNA connecting him to a crime at least six months old. The interesting part was their method of death; they were categorized under the FBI's *Other* column.

These were typically things like arrows, knives, or swords. Three of the men had broken necks from what three separate coroners swore were bola attacks. Those three deaths had been assumed linked a couple of times, but without additional evidence, there was no way to pin it on any one person. Angela, however, had one final piece of evidence to connect them.

Their victims.

She sent the results to Danny and Kent, and they spent the next few months scouring through records, conducting interviews, assigning other agents around the country to conduct interviews, and reviewing past interviews.

"…so, after all that work," Angela revealed with a pointed look, "we found one, and only one, link connecting them. Each of the women had a life insurance policy underwritten and paid out by ACME Protection Underwriters."

Diana's eyes and mouth opened in surprise. "We underwrite a large number of insurance policies, but this is just too fantastic to believe." She gazed out her window for a moment and slowly turned her gaze back. "You think someone at my company is responsible?" She held the information request up. "That's what this is for."

"Yes. We think someone who has, or had, access to these accounts when they paid out might lead in a more positive direction. Who would have access to these women's accounts?"

"This office. Claims, too."

"So, you would have access to the records?"

"Technically, yes, but I don't get into the system."

"How long have you worked here?"

"Eight years." Diana threw a piercing look at Angela.

"You can check with Human Resources."

"We will, thanks. How many in Claims? Over the last twenty years?"

"All of them? None. Not unless one of them hacked in," Diana confirmed. Her face was a mask of distraction as she looked off to the side, blinking and mouthing words only she could hear. Finally, she spoke up. "I'll look into it and get back to you."

"We need to look now."

Diana glanced back at the request. "Yes. Of course. Follow me."

Danny caught up with them in personnel. Simple searches showed over the last twenty years, there had been four different people heading Claims. One was retired. One used a wheelchair. One died eight and a half years ago.

The current one, Wallace Ingraham, had taken an early lunch.

Danny checked his watch. "It's only 9:30. A little early unless he's on Nova Scotia time."

Diana immediately picked up the phone and punched in a number. "Security? This is Diana Mastier. I need you to locate Wallace Ingraham and hold him until I get there."

While Diana talked with her security department, Danny kept his distance from her. To the untrained eye, it appeared normal; he was fiddling with his phone. Checking his mail. Observing the area. But to Angela, she knew the difference. Diana spooked him...like the house in Marshall. He was more relaxed than he was upstairs, but his eyes were still pale blue.

"...already left?" Diana repeated into the phone as she glanced over at Angela. "How long ago? Thanks. Contact me the moment he returns." She hung up the phone. "He left the building about half an hour ago."

Danny called their office. "Kent, we need a Wants or Warrants Check on Wallace Ingraham. Records can contact Diana Mastier here to get the particulars…Yes, sir…That's fine. Just have them send the report to our phones. And put out an APB on him. He's a Person of Interest. Requires a Level One Interview. Thanks." He hung up his phone. His hands shook.

Angela nodded to him and Diana. "That's all we can do for now."

Diana had taken up a place behind the personnel agent and stared at the computer screen. "I can't believe Wallace is suspected of murder. I don't know him that well, but I like to think I'm a good judge of character."

This kind of shock was typical. *He was such a quiet boy. Got along with everyone. Used to mow my yard. My son would never do that!*

"It's always the quiet ones, Ms. Mastier." She turned to Danny. "I think we're done here. You?"

Danny nodded in short, jerky movements.

The elevator doors shut, and Angela spun on Danny. "What the hell was your problem? A pretty face and you go all wolfy?"

"No!" he rubbed the back of his neck. "I don't know what the hell was happening. It took every ounce of willpower I had to hold my *renovatio* down. It was like I was sitting under a full moon. That's never happened before!" He held his hands up and to the sides. "I swear it, Angela."

She studied him. He looked calm now, eyes their normal hazel, if not a bit nervous. "What do you think caused it?" She scoured her brain for clues; she had no idea what would cause a werewolf to werewolf. "Did her perfume smell like raw meat to you or something?"

He scoffed and grimaced at her. "No. A smell sometimes makes us antsy, but that wasn't it. Besides, I have complete control *except at night under a full moon*."

The elevator doors slid open, and they followed the signs to the parking garage.

"Can you lose your *Frenatus* thingy?"

"There've been cases of *lupus* reverting to wildlings, but only under extreme psychological or physiological circumstances. Torture's a sure-fire way to cause it."

"Am I working you too hard?"

He scoffed again. "No. I do need a vacation, though."

"Where you going? Home?"

"No. Orlando. *Viam Lupus* Monastery."

She knew that was where *lupus* learned how to be a *Frenator*. She looked sideways at him as she opened the car door. "Granted. I'll make sure Kent approves it."

He relaxed into a sigh. "Thanks."

"Two weeks, Danny," she said. "If you can't figure this out in two weeks, you're back to being a beat cop in Dumbfuck, Texas."

The man strutting up to Angela and Danny didn't look like a college professor at all. He looked like a rodeo cowboy with his boots and shiny belt buckle. "I'm Dr. Mark Canard. Can I help you?" he asked in a thick drawl. His eyes gleamed with a squint borne of spending quite a bit of time in the sun.

"I'm Agent Angela Hollingsworth. This is Officer Danny McIver. Thanks for meeting with us. We've come to check on our arrow."

"Nice to meet you both," Mark responded. "I apologize

for taking so long to get back to you. To be honest, I blew it off as a well-made reproduction when I first saw it. How wrong I was! Follow me, please? I'll show you why I'm so excited."

Dr. Canard led them down a few corridors until they arrived in a room with an excessive assortment of ancient weaponry. It all hung on the walls, mounted in racks, or stored in drawers—half of which were open, showing their contents. A large table in the center of the room had an assortment of arrows spread out across it. "These are the same type of arrows as yours."

Angela frowned. "These don't look anything like ours. These are old and partially disintegrated."

Mark's face lit with joy and amazement. "That's what's so spectacular. Your arrow is one of these—" he pointed to the table "—except it looks like it was made yesterday. The same paints, wooden shaft, goose feather, everything. Either the ancient Greeks made your arrow or someone who knows more about the craft than I do made it. Where did you find it?"

Angela spoke in low, even tones. "Someone shot it through a rapist's chest."

"Wow!" Mark cocked his head to the side, and a sly grin twisted his lips. "Artemis lives!"

"Who?"

"Artemis," Mark stated. "Daughter of Zeus and Leto? Twin sister to Apollo?" At the mention of a twin, she and Danny shared a grimace with each other. "Greek Goddess of the Moon and Protector of Young Girls? The Stainless Maiden?" When she and Danny stared at him with blank looks, he shifted into full professor mode. "The Romans called her Diana, though. Neolithic man called her Callisto.

To the Minoans, she was Britomartis. Her favorite weapon was the bow and arrow. Your arrow is Greek. She's Greek. And she had a soft spot for abused women."

Angela glanced at Danny. "What the hell have we gotten ourselves into this time? A Greek Goddess? Roaming around, killing off rapists?"

"No, of course not," Mark sniggered. "It was the first thing to come to mind. That's all."

"Can you tell us where it was manufactured?" Danny asked. "Any serial numbers on it?"

Mark let out a short, sarcastic chuckle. "You don't understand. This arrow, from everything I can tell, was made 2,700 years ago." He pulled out a sheet of paper with a bunch of graphs on it. "I ran it through the spectrometer. The materials in your arrow, they perfectly match the materials in these—" he pointed to the arrows on the table again. "As I said, it's either a perfect forgery or an authentic specimen from that time period."

"Who has the kind of skill to produce something like that?"

"Me, maybe a dozen other people around the world," Mark guessed. "But even we would have a hard time. The tree to make the shafts went extinct over 500 years ago."

Angela pulled out a custody transfer form. "Thanks for your help. I'll need the arrow back." She had a mental flash from *Raiders of the Lost Ark* and a large warehouse full of Greek arrows. "And that list of names. You can use this email address here." She handed him her business card.

"No problem," he agreed with a large smile. "It's in the spectroscopy lab." He held the door open for them to follow him.

They headed down the hallway to another room. Mark

unlocked the door, and Angela stared around at what could have been a scene from a 1960s science fiction show. Computer screens populated half a dozen desks. Cables ran from behind them, up along the walls, and converged in the middle of the ceiling where they dropped down to a large, off-white metal box. "This is the mass spectrometer." Numerous smaller contraptions hung off the larger box where colored lights blinked off and on. He pushed a few buttons on the side and the large door on the main box opened.

It was empty.

Mark stared at the barren interior before stepping back and scanning the laboratory. "I don't understand. It was here this morning," he said, concern blanching his face.

Angela and Danny wandered around the lab and lifted sheets of paper here and there and looked for the arrow while Mark opened up cabinets. "I personally saw the arrow this morning. Other than me, a couple of graduate students have a key, but they're not scheduled to work today. Well, security has one too, but they never come down here."

"You have a security camera?"

He snapped his fingers "Yes, I do! Lots of expensive machinery. Insurance demanded it." He pulled up a screen on one of the computers, and they spent the next two hours scanning through the various camera feeds.

Four hours earlier, the screen flashed white as if a bright flare lit up the room. When the image cleared, a woman dressed in hunting attire reminiscent of the *Ben Hur* movie stood there. Flowing hair rippled down and around her breasts in a non-existent breeze. She elegantly brushed the length of it back over her shoulder as she strode across the room, her face a bright smudge.

Squinting at the image, Danny asked, "Can't you clean that up a bit so we can see her face?"

Fiddling with the controls, Mark made confused and frustrated noises as nothing he did cleared the screen. The woman took the arrow from the large stainless-steel chamber, and in another blinding flash of light, she was gone. The entire picture was clear, except the smudges in the video obscuring her face.

Mark slid back into his chair, crossed his arms, and tugged at his earlobe. "You know, we were joking a few minutes ago about Artemis being alive. But seeing that woman?" He pointed at the screen; complete awe etched his face. "That is exactly how I would expect her to be dressed."

Later that evening, sitting at her desk, Angela reviewed a report from Michigan. The Michigan field office had captured Wallace Ingraham and brought him in for questioning. He fessed up to selling drugs out of his office—explaining why he rabbited when the word spread the FBI was there—but not to murder. They were convinced of his innocence due to his airtight alibi. His uncle had passed away, and forty mourners all vouched for his presence at the funeral on the same day Lisa Reilly had been killed. After the events at the museum, she was convinced they were hunting for a woman anyway.

She badgered the tech department to get some decent facial shots from the video, but they claimed there wasn't enough to work with. The techs insisted the light where her face should have been was real. She sighed and sent an APB and a BOLO to all field offices in the continental U.S. She resisted calling the woman Artemis, but that was their working name until they had an actual suspect.

Suspect. We're dealing with someone who's probably a Greek goddess, for Christ's sake, and we're calling her a suspect.

Angela knew what everyone would say when they saw the pictures of the woman in her costume even if the face was smudged out—the same thing she would have said before being assigned to Task Force W. *To-ga! To-ga!*

Let the ribbing commence.

Angela was careful not to let the glass and wood frame door slam shut behind her. The Arlington winds were blustery, and she didn't want the rickety door to shatter on impact. A cardboard sign on the back of the door read, "Thanks for visiting The Dusty Spine bookstore." The fragrances of mildew, old glue, paper, and spilled coffee greeted her as she pushed it shut.

A young man with black hair, brown eyes, and more ink on him than a tattoo parlor wall sat behind a worn-out wooden counter flipping covers on a stack of books and making notes in a notepad. At the sound of the door closing, he looked up. "Can I help you?"

"Maybe," Angela said. "I'm looking for some information on Greek gods." She held up the book in her hand. "And more books by Mr. Lovecraft here?"

"*Mister* Lovecraft." A welcoming smile lit his face as his gaze drifted to the book. "I see you're a recent convert." His smile was genuine, and his voice wavered to the tenor.

"How can you tell?"

"That book looks brand new." He stepped around the corner to greet her. He wore sandals and shorts, and tattoos decorated his legs too. "And nobody," he teased, "would refer to Lovecraft with such an honorific. The man was nuts. A genius of horror, but nuts." He held his hand out politely

141

and raised his forehead as he tilted his head at the book. "May I?"

Angela handed the book over, and he flipped through it. "No brown thumb marks on the pages, no coffee stains. Tsk, tsk, tsk. You read it so fast, it didn't have time to cure properly."

Angela couldn't help but smile. "I've always been a fast reader."

"A fast reader." He flipped to the front cover. "And a repeat customer. Thanks! I predict a lucrative relationship here." He winked at her.

"I bought it a couple of weeks ago."

"Let's see if my salesman skills are as good as I think they are. Follow me." He took off down an aisle of tall bookshelves at a brisk pace. "I'm Randy, by the way. Randy Tracer."

"I'm Angela." She struggled to keep up with him. He wasn't that much taller than her, but his long strides ate up the floor in a methodical, practiced way.

"Did you like it? The book?" he asked over his shoulder.

She hadn't considered whether she liked it or not. She liked to read, and her tastes did tend towards the paranormal, but reading it was less about the potential for enjoyment than it was for research from her last case. She thought about it— "Yes, I did. Thanks."

"No problemo." He stopped when he got to a shelf with an entire collection of Lovecraft books. "I'll let Tiffany know she picked out a good one for you."

Tiffany was the young girl who'd sold her the book on her first visit. "Is she your sister? Y'all look alike."

"Sister?" His eyes twinkled, and his mouth split open into a wide grin. "No, she's my daughter. But thanks for the

142

compliment."

"Daughter?" she exclaimed. "Well, you're holding onto it!"

"Must be the tattoos." He grinned.

"You own the store then?"

"Yes. It used to be my wife, Lucy, and me. She died a few years back. It's just Tif and me now with the occasional high school or college help."

"Sorry."

"Thanks, but it's okay." He ran his finger along the spines of a series of Lovecraft books. "Let's see. Most of his books are collections of short stories. Need to find one without a bunch of duplicates from the one you just read." He stopped when he came to one named *Dream Cycle* and pulled it off the shelf. "This one's got some good stories in it. You should like it."

Angela took the book, scanned the front and back. "I don't suppose he's ever written about something called the Forsaken Dweller, has he?"

Before he had the chance to answer, a young woman squealed in surprise and a loud crash from an aisle over startled them. "Tif!?" he yelled, concern in his tensed-up shoulders. With a start, he bellowed, "Watch out!" as the bookshelf fell towards them. Angela crouched and prepared to jump to the side, when he hooked his arm around her waist and pulled her to the floor, landing on top of her and shielding her from the avalanche of books. Luckily, the heavy wooden shelf leaned against the wall and stayed there.

When the last of the books finished toppling around them, he slowly lifted himself off her. "You okay?" They kept eye contact the whole time as they sat up.

He hadn't been on her long, but his scent still lingered

and left her with a brief flash of him giving her a backrub. She shook the thoughts away and did a quick check of arms and legs. Other than a few minor bumps, "Yeah, I'm fine. Thanks. You, though—" Blood ran down his forehead. She grabbed his hand and pressed it against the wound. "Hold it here. Where's your first aid kit?"

"Tif, you okay?" He scanned around looking for his daughter. "Should be some bandages behind the counter." He crawled for the end. "Tif!?"

"I'm okay, Dad," she answered. "Sorry!"

"What the hell were you doing…?"

When Angela got back with the box of bandages and some sanitized wipes, Tiffany was standing in front of her dad with a chastised look on her face. "Well?" he demanded from his daughter.

"I'm sorry, ma'am," she whispered. "I was on a ladder. I heard you two talking. I eavesdropped. Leaned too close to the shelf."

"Why were you eavesdropping?"

Angela let them sort it out. She took out a couple of the wipes, blotted his forehead, and put a butterfly bandage on it.

"Maybe I should leave," she offered.

"No, don't do that," he begged. "Are you gonna sue?"

"No." She shook her head. "I'm okay. Accidents happen, right?" She questioned Tiffany with a stare.

The young woman sighed. "My dad hasn't laughed like that since mom died. I got nosy."

Both Angela's and Randy's faces flushed.

"Oh," Angela uttered. "Sorry."

Randy softly ran his fingers over his bandage and looked at the shelf. "This is going to take all day to sort out. Get started, young lady. Your bowling party is canceled."

"Dad!"

"We're not leaving tonight until we've righted everything, Tif." He turned back to Angela. "You were asking something when my personal hurricane interrupted."

Angela thought back. "Oh, yeah! Forsaken Dweller. Has Lovecraft ever written about it?"

Randy puckered his lips to the side and frowned. "Not that I'm aware of. Sounds like something from his mythos though. Leave some contact information, and I'll check for you."

"Okay, thanks." She cradled her new book close to her chest.

"No problemo," he replied. "In fact, if you want, I'll trade you this one—" he held up the other book she'd brought in "—for that one."

Angela tilted her head to the side. "How do you stay in business making deals like that?"

The twinkle in his eyes returned. "Least I can do for dropping my store on you."

Angela laughed. He did have a sweet smile. "Okay. Sure."

"Good." He slipped the book under his arm. "Anything else I can help you…oh, that's right. Greek gods. Anyone in particular?"

"Artemis?"

"She's my favorite. Early supporter of women's suffrage. D'you know that?"

"I know she didn't put up with uppity menfolk," Angela teased.

"Ha! That's one way to put it. But you have to appreciate how immature the Greek gods were compared to the Romans'." Angela's confusion must have shown. "I take it you've never raised a teenager." He glanced over at his daughter as she piled books against the outer walls. "No? A friend of mine, Scott, explained the difference one day over a bottle of Fighting Cock. The Greeks and Romans shared gods and goddesses. Different names, but the same jokers were always sticking their noses in man's business. Scott theorized the only difference between the two versions was the Roman ones had gone through puberty; they weren't as childish as they'd been three centuries earlier. He thinks that explains why the Roman Empire was so much larger. The gods were tougher. I don't buy the theory, though I do agree with him on their maturity levels. In either case, I've got a whole shelf on Greek mythology." He spun around and took off at a quick walk, stepping over spilled piles of books. "If it's still standing. Tally Ho!"

Angela put the book to her nose and inhaled the scent of book paper as she tried to keep up with him.

Angela placed a pile of reports on Kent's desk. "Here're the follow-ups from those chupacabra sightings."

He grimaced at the stack. "Got a shorter version?"

Angela pointed at the stack. "That *is* the short version. DNA report also came back. Part dog. Part pig. Someone's gene-splicing."

Kent took a sip of coffee from his Ohio State Buckeyes mug and leaned back in his chair. "I saw Danny came back from Orlando a few days ago. Haven't seen him around the office though. Where's he been?"

"Down in the tech department." She sat down. "He's been giving the guys hell for calling it quits on the museum video restoration so fast. He's a closet nerd, by the sounds of it."

A soft ping from Kent's computer interrupted her.

He set his cup down and clicked his mouse a few times. He turned the monitor around for her.

A flush zipped up her neck as she stared at the face on the screen. Her phone beeped. "Hollingsworth." She put it on speakerphone.

Danny's voice echoed back. "Have you opened the picture yet?"

"Yeah. Kent and I are in his office looking at it now."

"Who is it?" Kent wanted to know, frowning at the picture.

"You're probably going to fire us," Angela groaned, "but that is Diana Mastier, ACME Insurance Underwriter's Comptroller."

Kent resized the picture, so it filled his entire screen.

"I can't believe we stood two feet from her, Danny," Angela ground out.

"Me either," he grumbled.

"That's Artemis." Kent blinked and pursed his lips. "Danny, anything in your history about the moon goddess affecting your *lupus* infection?"

"Hmm. Like what happened in Michigan when I was around her? No, sir. Voodoo witches have been known to cast spells that can interfere with it, though."

"Voodoo's real?" Angela asked.

"It's all real, Agent," Kent said, as if the distraction was an annoyance, "until we find out it isn't."

"So, we're gonna accept this, too?" she demanded, standing straight. "She's the moon goddess until we find out otherwise?"

"Correct." Kent ordered, "I'll issue an arrest warrant." He picked his cup of coffee back up. "Danny, thank your new friends down there."

"Oh, they're most happy with the result. Or should I say, they're happy I'm leaving."

A few minutes later, Danny hopped into the gang room with a soda in his hand.

Angela stared at the can as he set it on his desk. "Soda," she muttered.

"What was that?" Danny asked.

"Soda," she repeated. "Diana didn't say pop. When you left us in her office. She said soda. People from Michigan say pop, not soda. I didn't catch it at the time. She's not a Grand Rapids native."

Angela and Kent forwarded the restored pictures to Michigan. What they got back didn't make them happy. Diana quit the same afternoon she'd met with them, packed a suitcase, and drove off. She left her cell phone on her kitchen table. They located her car at the airport. No cameras showed her anywhere near the terminal though.

"Dig into her past," Kent ordered. "Find out everything you can."

ACME Protection Underwriters sent over their files on her. Diana Mastier, or at least the woman everyone knew as Diana Mastier, didn't exist before eight years ago, one week before ACME had hired her. All of her references were bogus and no longer traceable. Angela refused to believe she'd only been working at ACME for eight years, not with all the connections between the victims.

With dead ends stacking up like cordwood, Angela pulled out her remaining bullet. She instructed the onsite ERT techs to scan for any information on any other women working at ACME who quit or retired shortly before Diana hired on there. Two folders appeared in her inbox within the hour.

The first one was Sabrina Garcia. Her Hispanic features ruled her out. The other one, Diana Imarets, didn't look like her either. She'd worked there for 25 years before retirement.

Same first name, but Diana is not uncommon.

Angela didn't like coincidences, but the two women didn't look anything alike to the naked eye. She set them off to the side, typed their names into her report, and stopped, her finger wavering above her mouse before she saved the file. She stared at her screen and muttered, "No way!" She grabbed the book on Greek mythology she'd bought at the Dusty Spine and opened it to a page near the center.

"Danny, listen to this: 'Sometimes, when the gods wished to walk among men, they would change their names to a riddle, for instance, rearranging the letters. If a mortal ever figured out the deception, they were usually granted a boon.'" She slid the pictures over to him.

He picked them up and read the names. First one, then the other, and back to the first one. "Mastier. Imarets." He laughed aloud. "Artemis. Didn't Canard say Diana was the Roman version of her?"

"Yeah."

He took the two pictures back down to the tech department, much to their chagrin, and ran a facial recognition batch. There was a greater than 93% probability it was the same woman. The bone structure was near identical.

"Didn't even bother to change her first name," Angela muttered, reading Danny's report.

He ran his fingers through his hair. "Diana, Artemis, whatever her name is, she's been around awhile."

"No, shit." Angela crammed a stick of gum between her lips. "I'm not sure I'm equipped for this. How the hell do we

149

track a Greek goddess who appears to be immortal and can wink in and out of secured areas?"

Danny leaned back in his chair. He stuck his tongue into the side of his cheek and stared out the window at the evening sun. Unexpectedly, he spun around and faced her. "Sonny Jim, Angela!" He stood and flapped his hands at her. "You walked into a town full of werewolves and stared down the chief of police while you ate a Caesar salad. There is no one *more* equipped for this than you."

She quit her smacking and glared at him.

"Think about it," he argued, "I'm no different than any other redneck except I grow fur and howl at the moon...Okay, scratch the moon part. Rednecks will do that given enough beer."

Angela snorted.

"The point I'm making is that the supernatural is still natural. It's just super different. She ain't no goddess. All she is, partner, is another bad guy doing bad things."

"*She ain't no goddess?*" Angela mocked. "Yeah, you're a redneck." She turned back at her computer screen. "Okay. Enough pep talk. Let's use some old-fashioned police work." She tapped a few keys. "We need a list of all ACME payouts from the last six months for murder-rapes. Compare that list against any unsolved cases in our records. She's been avenging women for millennia. She's not going to stop because two mere mortals found her out." She spun around in her chair, took careful aim, and in a most unladylike fashion, spit her gum into Danny's trashcan, a good five feet away, with a resounding "Pwuh!"

Danny peeked over the edge of his desk to make sure it landed in the can and shook his head when it hit bottom. "Artemis is only going after the unsolved cases where the suspect has no priors. Pure luck if we find any connection."

"I agree, but I want to exhaust all avenues first before we start rolling dice."

Hours later, the only thing left was to review the images of the evidence in Diana's work desk. As Danny set a bag of Chinese food on his desk, Angela stood up in excitement. "Found it!" she exclaimed, a new burst of adrenaline waking her up. "Valerie Smythe, she's on the Unsolved List, was raped and killed while out jogging. Here's her payout voucher."

"Oh, hell," Angela moaned as she read the report. "She was a month pregnant." *Child-killer and probably didn't even know it.* "Hey…bingo!" She turned her monitor to the side so Danny could see a picture of the sticky-note they found inside the file. Diana had written an address and a name on it. "Run a check on Greg Pastorin."

"Okay, Agent Hollingsworth," Kent grunted. "You wanted this guy—" he indicated the man they were all staring at through the two-way mirror— "get a confession."

"You got it, boss."

Kent stayed behind to observe and oversee the recording operations while Danny followed her into the room. He took a position standing in a corner behind the suspect. Angela gently closed the door and sat at the table, facing both of them. "Greg Pastorin," she intoned, opening a folder.

"That's me." His gaze darted between her and the folder. "What's this about?"

She ignored the question. "I see you've been read your rights and that you've waived your right to remain silent and to have your lawyer present."

"Yes. Should I have my lawyer?"

"I can't advise you one way or the other in that regard." She dropped her hands in her lap. "But if you've done anything illegal, I'd ask for one."

"No," he shook his head. "No, I've nothing to hide."

"Good!" she pronounced. "We've just got a few questions to clear up." She inwardly gave herself a high-five.

No lawyers today!

She read from his background check. "No criminal record. One speeding ticket 20 years ago in Lincoln, Nebraska."

Greg stared at Danny's reflection for a moment and addressed her. "Yeah? So what?"

"Blood type, AB negative." She placed her hands on the folder and scrutinized him, cocking her head to the side a bit. "That's the rarest blood type in the world. Accounts for less than 1% of all Caucasian men. Did you know that?"

"Yeah," he answered with a quick nod. "How did you know I have AB negative?"

"Oh!" she moved her hands off the folder. "We got your army records."

He folded his eyelids down under a harsh squint. "Why would you—"

"Do you know a Diana Mastier?"

"No. Should I?"

"Well, she knows you." Angela pulled the yellow sticky-note from the file and placed it on the table. "She knew who you were and where you lived? Why would she be interested in you?"

He read the note. "I have no clue." He looked at Danny's reflection as he shifted from one foot to the other and crossed his arms. "Like I said, I don't know her."

"We found this sticky-note in one of her case files. She

152

works—worked—for an insurance company."

"Who is she?"

Angela took her time putting the sticky note back into the folder. When she was sure it was aligned correctly with the edge of the folder, she rested her hands on it again. "The case file was for one of Diana Mastier's customers."

"Who?"

"It's not relevant right now," she declared dismissively. "What is important is that we didn't want to bother you with this, you know, in case it turned out to be nothing." She paused while she moved his folder to the side, revealing a second folder underneath. "But it still bothered us. Why would she be so interested in you? So, we dug around some more.

"The lady's folder we found that sticky note in? She'd been raped and murdered a while back. And she was pregnant. I have a special hard-on for people who kill kids, unborn or not. So, you can imagine the gusto I put into finding their killers."

He slowly sat back in his chair.

Denial. *Angela's Interrogation Tome, page 2*.

"We had DNA evidence, but a name and address aren't enough to get a search warrant. But it was enough to request your files from the government. You know, because we're all one big, happy tyranny and like to share all our stuff, like records."

Two little beads of sweat bloomed on his forehead.

"And the darnedest thing came to light."

He crossed his arms.

"You have the same blood type as the person who raped and killed Diana's customer. And even though it is the rarest of the rare, it still wasn't enough. But combined with your name in the folder? Well, the judge signed the warrant so fast, I thought he would melt the tip off his pen."

"The woman's name," Greg asked. "The one who was raped and murdered. Was it Valerie Smythe?"

Angela snapped her eyes open in surprise. "What?" She put a piece of gum in her mouth. "How do you know Valerie Smythe, Greg?"

He closed his mouth, and his face relaxed as he slowly nodded his head. "I raped her and killed her."

Angela's heartbeat throbbed in her ears. Danny stood straight and dropped his arms to his sides. She needed to make sure she got this again. "Would you repeat that, please?"

"Are you recording this?" he asked.

"Yes," she said with a slight nod, swallowing a lump that had materialized in her throat.

"Good. I, Greg Pastorin, raped and murdered Valerie Smythe. I caught her while she was jogging, dragged her behind some bushes. I shoved an old pair of my underwear in her mouth so she couldn't scream. I slapped her a few times to let her know I wasn't fooling around. Not yet, anyway." A twisted grin darkened his face. "I ripped her clothes off. There should be a scratch mark on her left breast where I got carried away." He examined his left hand's fingernails. "She knew it was coming. I didn't want to, but orders are orders. When I finished, I squeezed her neck until the cartilage and bones cracked under my thumbs."

Angela had interrogated rapists before, but she'd never parked her ass across from one who'd related the crime with such calm. The scratches on Valerie's breast were never released to the press. This guy did it all right. "You said, 'orders were orders.' Who gave the order?"

He met her gaze, heartbeat for heartbeat, as if the question was obvious. "The Forsaken Dweller. Who else?"

Angela stood so fast, her chair slammed back against the wall. "What did you say?"

"It's okay," he confided to her in a soothing tone, admiring something off in the distance only he could see. "He passes along his regards, Agent Hollingsworth, and says to enjoy his gift while you can." He smiled brightly, closed his eyes, and slumped forward onto the table.

Danny rushed over and pressed his fingers against Greg's neck. "No pulse! Kent! Get an ambulance!"

He and Angela performed CPR until the paramedics arrived, but they were unable to revive him.

Angela sipped her coffee and eyed Greg Pastorin's house from down the street. Stakeouts never changed it seemed, even when stalking the supernatural. "It's starting to drizzle. Danny, can we roll up the windows now?" The weather had flopped to the chilly end of the thermometer the last few weeks, and she didn't like cold weather.

"I need them open," he informed her. "I need the breeze." To make his point, he turned his head to the side and took a whiff.

Angela set her cup in the holder and grabbed her jacket from the backseat. "You know what bothers me about Sabine?"

Danny looked at her with raised eyebrows and a slight headshake as she fumbled her arms into the jacket's sleeves.

"Why she didn't retrieve the arrow from the house."

He shrugged and took another slight sniff from his open window. "Well, if she shows up, we can ask her."

She sipped her coffee. "Yeah. I still think it's a long shot.

Her showing up."

"Best shot we have though." He chuckled at her. "Besides, it was your idea!"

"So? I didn't say it was a good idea." She sighed and shook her head. "She's got to know we would've searched her desk."

"Maybe. Maybe not. She doesn't know how much we know. Explains why she went to the trouble of leaving a trail to the airport and not popping out to wherever she pops to."

The last vestiges of the sun had sunk below the treetops when Danny snapped his head to the side and took a deep whiff. "She's here."

Angela leaned forward in her seat and peered through the windshield. "Where?"

"Down towards the house."

Angela keyed her walkie-talkie. "Hotel Lobby, this is Bellhop. Our VIP has arrived."

"Roger, Bellhop," the radio repeated. "Standing by."

"We're bringing the luggage now," Angela relayed. "Out."

Angela and Danny left their car and made their way along the sidewalk towards the rear of Pastorin's house. The FBI had cleared all civilians—and dogs—five houses deep in all directions. If you didn't have FBI stenciled on the back of your jacket, you weren't supposed to be in the area. They cut left down a side street and let themselves into an alley bordering Pastorin's backyard. Along the privacy fence, stood tall bushes that hid them from anyone who might look in their direction. They climbed the two ladders SWAT had placed there for them and peered over the top.

Diana Mastier—Artemis—stalked along the back of the house. Angela expected to find her dressed in a forest green Roman toga with leather sandals laced to the knees, not modern rip-cloth tactical pants, a Beatles t-shirt, and leather boots. She had pinned her long hair back with a gold barrette, though.

Angela ordered, "Now!" into her throat-microphone and lights flooded the backyard as she and Danny shoved the false fence panel to the ground. They dashed across the yard in classic 4 o'clock and 8 o'clock positions. "Artemis, daughter of Zeus and Leto, Goddess of the Moon, lay down your bow and arrows and put your hands behind your head!" Only in Task Force W could an agent get away with saying something that crazy. "*Stop! You're under arrest,*" was so retro.

Artemis froze and slowly raised her hands to the side. She turned around and narrowed her eyes. "You know who I am?"

"Drop the weapon now!" Angela yelled at her.

"Drop it! Drop it!" Danny bellowed with a guttural growl as he covered her flank. His eyes were pale blue.

Their shock and awe arrest technique didn't faze her; she carefully leaned the bow against the back wall of the house and leisurely put the three arrows into her quiver. She snapped her head to the left when three FBI SWAT team members scrambled through another false fence panel. Then to the right when three more came from another.

Angela ordered, "Hold!" The SWAT team members spread out and red targeting lasers peppered Artemis's center mass. Angela crept up; Danny kept his distance. "Turn around and put your hands behind your head," she ordered.

Artemis complied.

Angela holstered her weapon. As soon as she clutched Artemis's wrist, déjà vu snagged her with such fury, the world twisted sideways. A loud pop slapped both of her ears, and when the world straightened back out, she stood next to an old water well fashioned from white stones. Forest surrounded her, the trees fat with age, and the limbs gnarly and knotted. Honeysuckle floated on the breeze. Moonlight filtered through the leaves from a clear night sky. Birds chirped all around.

Artemis stood at the edge of the tree line with a loving smile on her face as she witnessed Danny's *renovatio*.

He growled and drooled, snapping at thin air as his bones rearranged themselves and his skin stretched taut over his elongated limbs. His eyes raged more than she recalled from the two times she'd stared into them before. Crazy lived there now.

Angela drew and pointed her weapon at him. "Get back," she yelled to Artemis. If he was losing control, they were both in danger.

"There's no need to fear," Artemis informed her with a loud whisper. "There's a reason I'm known as the moon goddess." She stepped closer, and her face glowed a pale white. It all shined on him. When he finished, he rushed her, but she coolly raised her hand, halting him in his tracks.

Danny the werewolf crawled around in a circle, reminding Angela of a lost puppy she found as a child, but growling like a *lupus* ready to chew an arm off. Artemis snapped her fingers, and he scooted over and pressed up against her leg in a heel position. Angela was halfway between scared and pissed off. The fearful part was glad Artemis had control of him. The pissed off part, Danny's partner, didn't like him being so easily mastered, at least until the raving wildling stared into her eyes. This was not a *Frenator*.

She knew the difference now.

"That's a good boy," Artemis purred, gently stroking her hand on his head. After a few moments, Danny's eyelids drooped. "Angela, please put your weapon away. I may be long-lived, but I'm not invulnerable."

Angela wasn't sure what to do. Her pistol wavered someplace between Artemis and Danny. She finally made the decision to trust she wasn't going to die and holstered it.

Artemis smiled at her and gazed back down at Danny. She snapped her fingers again and pointed to the woods. Danny took off like a shot, growling and yipping. He soon disappeared amongst the trees, a happy howl echoing from all around them.

Angela scanned the trees around her. "Where are we?"

Artemis laughed and pointed towards the sky over Angela's shoulder.

Angela blinked and slowly turned around. The Earth hung low over the horizon.

Where are the damned moon rocks?!

The world again turned sideways, but this time, it also went dark.

Angela awoke alone and stretched out on a couch straight from the Roman era. It had but one arm on one end, raised in a curved fashion. The entire thing was upholstered with supple leather over padding. The room around her was fashioned in ancient Hellenic grandeur. Urns and amphorae, marbled in silver, white, red, green, and turquoise, sat on small shelves and tables. Murals of huntsmen, soldiers, and bards with lyres decorated the walls, framed in zigzag and spiral motifs. The more prominent mosaic depicted a man and woman in Roman hunting garb stalking ferocious beasts in a forest. The woman could have been Artemis, though the stitch work had blunted any facial features. Could the man be her twin brother, Apollo? Angela could only guess. Gauzy white drapes billowed across a terrace entrance, wildlife song floating on the breeze. Breathtaking, yes, but she had to shake off the awe and get back on the job.

Her pistol and badge sat on a small bureau near her feet. She reached for them but considered the fact if Artemis had wanted her dead, she already would be. Good sense and even better training won out, and as she strapped the pistol to her hip, she muttered, "I'll be damned if I walk around this place with who knows how many werewolves on the loose, not to mention a perp with finger-snapping control of them."

Investigating the terrace showed the house to be a villa, also of Hellenic design with columns and peaked roofs, perched atop a large hill overlooking a forest stretching to the horizon. Again, a waning Earth hung low in the sky.

"Welcome to my home, Delos." Artemis implored from behind her. "How are you feeling?"

"Fine." Angela twisted her head around on stiff shoulders. "Where's Danny?"

"I turned him loose. He's running around, doing what *Lupus sapiens* like to do." She gazed out into the forest as if she could see him. "When I created them, I didn't anticipate their savagery would be so profound. I let them play when I can. Keeps them balanced."

"When you created them." *A Greek Goddess created werewolves. That's something for the Task Force Weird archives.* "He's okay though, right?"

Artemis giggled. "Yes. He's fine." She stared deeply into Angela's eyes. "You'll have to excuse me, but you've piqued my interest. How did you figure out who I was?"

"You left your arrow at Conrad Sabine's house. And we caught you on camera taking it from the museum. Google's awesome when you need answers."

"Conrad Sabine." Artemis nodded with understanding. "He suspected I was after him. He placed wards around his nest."

"Wards?" Angela clapped her hands once. "You couldn't get into the house! That's why you left your arrow behind."

"Correct." Artemis lifted one eyebrow in confusion. "If you know who I am, why do you chase me?"

"Because you're a murderer." As soon as the words left Angela's mouth, she knew she didn't believe them. The cop in her still wanted to blame someone, though. She pivoted back to admire the wooded vista.

"Quite the view, isn't it?" Artemis asked.

"Yes." Angela did a little hop. "Gravity seems normal."

"Parlor trick," Artemis told her.

"Doesn't look like the moon either."

"How do you know? You ever been here?"

Angela scoffed. "Well, when you put it that way, no. Are you telling me the government's been lying this whole time?"

"You have not been lied to. The moon from your continuum looks exactly as you would expect it to."

"Continuum? A different dimension? Wait! Have you ever heard of the Forsaken Dweller? Is this where he's from?"

Artemis's mouth dropped open, and her voice pitched up an octave. "You know about that?"

Angela licked her lips and tilted her head to the side. "All I know is that he, it, whatever, has popped up in my caseload lately." She feasted her eyes to the side. "Do you mind?" she pointed at two glasses sitting next to a glass amphora of water with lemon slices floating in it.

"Please," Artemis answered, "let me." She poured them each a glass. "And allow me to show you what these *murders* truly are." She waved her hand through the air, and it was as if a completely different world was overlaid on the one where they stood, life-sized, fully colored, translucent. It showed a man strapped down to a metal gurney. Lightning bolts arced and shot through the air in the background. An alien, identical to the one she and Danny had encountered in Hallsville, lumbered into view.

Nervous energy flooded through Angela, and she glanced back and forth between the image and Artemis. "Danny and I killed one of those!"

Artemis paused the playback. "That's a doorman," she told her. "Actually, their names can't be pronounced with human vocal cords, but doorman describes their function. They're there to open a portal for the Forsaken Dweller." She waved her hand and resumed the playback.

The doorman placed a rotten mushroom-colored worm onto the man's cheek. He bucked against his restraints as the worm crawled up into his nose. He sat still for a moment while his face crinkled up as if he had to sneeze, but he took a deep breath instead and screamed in unadulterated fear and pain. He passed out a few moments later. Artemis turned the video off.

"The worm eats sections of the host's brain, replacing it with its own cerebral structure." Artemis took a long drink from her glass. "I doubt your science could find a difference between it and human tissue. Anyway, it takes about six weeks for the incubation period to complete. It's no longer human at that point. It's a drone in constant contact with the Forsaken Dweller. It's got free will only so long as it carries out the dweller's plans."

"This explains why Sabine knew about me," Angela muttered. Then a bit louder, "He had a picture of me. I may have been next on his list."

Artemis stood a little higher. "For you to have grabbed the dweller's attention, even for a moment—" a feral grin darkened her face— "is impressive."

"Do you think he'll send another one after me?"

"Maybe." Artemis shrugged. "It's not used to being interfered with. It may have simply given the order and forgotten about you." She stared hard at Angela. "Hope that's what happened, anyway."

Angela acknowledged the advice with a nod. "Why are they killing women?" she asked.

Artemis grimaced with a light shake of her head. "It's not just women. They also target men. But to answer your question, I'm not certain. It's speculated the victims are, or will be, a threat to the dweller's plans. I've never been able to stop one ahead of time to find out."

Angela sat down. "And the rapes?"

"Also unknown, though I suspect it's simply a power thing on the drone's part. Being under control for so long, maybe it's a release valve or something."

Angela understood. Rape wasn't about sex. It was about power.

Artemis sat on the bench next to her. "We're on the same side, Angela. I'm one of Earth's protectors. The drone known as Greg Pastorin has to die. It's not human. It's not murder."

"Thin line." Angela shook her head. "Besides, he's already dead. Some kind of mental suicide. Right there in the interrogation room."

Artemis pursed her lips and softly bobbed her head. "Yes, that happens every time I've tried to question one, too. The dweller kills it before it has a chance to reveal anything." She let loose a deep sigh. "It's all I can do to stay ahead of them."

"Is there any way to detect them? The drones?"

"*Lupus sapiens* can," Artemis confessed.

Angela stared at Artemis. "Yeah, you said that you'd created them. Why?"

Artemis laughed. To Angela's ears, it was musical. "It seemed like a good idea at the time. Afraid to try again, though. They were to be my bloodhounds. Unfortunately, only the wildlings have the ability. And they would rather eat than track. Plus, as you've seen, they lose their ability to *Frenis* when around me. *Frenatus* can usually detect them when they're dead. That's useless, though. I need them when they're alive."

"That explains Danny's heebie-jeebies when we were around Sabine, but not Pastorin."

They sat there listening to the wind through the trees and the wild forest noises. Jasmine wafted up over the railing.

"I'm not sure there's a court that could try you," Angela finally confessed. "Not to mention, there's no prison that could hold you."

"True, but I would prefer that you knew I was a good guy."

Angela clenched her jaw but nodded her head in reluctant agreement. She hated to let a case go, but there was nothing she could do. If there was ever an extra-jurisdictional dispute, Artemis positively filled the criteria. Angela scratched her ear. "Kent's probably called out the National Guard looking for Danny and me."

"Don't worry about that," Artemis told her. "I can get you back within a couple of seconds of the time we left. Take as long as you wish. Consider it a vacation if you want." She stood up. "Clothes more fitting to our environment are next to the changing screen behind your couch. I have to check on dinner. My brother will be here soon."

"Your brother?" Angela asked. "Apollo?"

"Yeah." She dragged the word out. "I'm not sure how happy he's going to be when he sees I've brought home a stray *lupus*." She tilted her head and stared at Angela. "And a human."

"You're not…human?"

"No." Artemis rubbed her arm.

"And…Apollo…doesn't like humans?"

"Not really, no. Thinks you're useless."

"Why's he helping Earth then?"

"Spite. The Dweller took our world from us. We were children when that happened. Killing it is his only goal now."

Angela's thoughts roamed to the pistol on her hip. "Maybe you should take me home."

"Uh, huh," she said as she smiled and shook her head. "My house. You're my guest. I like you. He can go eat at Micky Ds if he doesn't like the company."

Angela lounged at her desk and reread her report, for the fifth time, on the events surrounding Diana Mastier's disappearance. The report read like a pulp science fiction novel.

Artemis had shown an intense curiosity about Angela's combat and police procedural abilities. Artemis might have been a well-seasoned vigilante, but she conceded Angela's skills exceeded hers where it counted. So, while Danny spent two weeks pelting helter-skelter through the forest around Delos, Artemis's villa, Artemis's *moon* villa, she and Angela spent two weeks getting to know each other, way more time than either of them initially planned on.

Apollo had spent more time around the villa than Angela would have preferred. He was everything a Greek god should have been. Tall and muscular with a full head of red hair tied into a long ponytail. Clean shaven. Angela didn't mind the occasional bristly face, but his smooth cheeks and chiseled jaw accented his sparkling emerald eyes. When he recited her name in his baritone voice, it was so low, she could almost count the vibratos in it. When he smiled, which was rare, she lost all sense of time. When she gazed into his green eyes, she almost forgot the reason she was even on that moon. And if he hadn't been such an ass, she would have found all his other assets quite attractive.

She had tried to squeeze Artemis for information on the Forsaken Dweller, but there wasn't much to glean. It was eating planets, one after the other, and no one understood why. She and her brother were of a race who called themselves the Diutinus, which interestingly enough was Latin for Long-Lived. They were refugees from their own continuum and had taken on the responsibility of protecting Earth. The twins had been working here for over 4,000 years, hunting and killing doormen and drones.

None of Artemis's compatriots believed Earth would be able to help on a cosmic scale, so they refused support. Artemis was the sole exception, being captured by Angela in Greg Pastorin's backyard.

When she and Danny reappeared back amongst the SWAT team ten seconds after they'd vanished, with weapons holstered and hands raised, all hell broke loose. Kent broke it up, screamed something about the whole scene being an official cluster fuck, and ordered everyone to stand down. It was the first time she recalled him ever raising his voice above a loud whisper.

Artemis did not come back with them. Angela understood her reasoning. SWAT team members with itchy trigger fingers would have probably shot her full of holes once she'd blinked back in.

Angela shook her head, and with a slight grimace, hit the Send button on the report. She held up the arrow in her left hand, a gift from Artemis.

"Your boon," she'd said with a full-lipped smile. "Break this when you need me."

In hindsight, Angela wished she had asked for something more portable instead. Like a phone number, maybe.

Tom Bont

Episode 5: Reunion

Anne's dyed brown hair whipped around in the late fall wind. She pulled the flaps of her coat tighter and hunched her shoulders as another icy gust rushed across the empty parking lot, worming its way up her sleeves and down her neck. "How much longer you reckon?" she pleaded through chattering teeth. Her husband, Ben, flipped her coat's collar up for her.

"Pretty soon, Mom," Angela answered back for the fourth time in the last 15 minutes.

"Miss Anne, you still quilting?" Heather leaped in, running interference.

"I sure am. In fact, your mom and I been working on a new pattern. We hope to have it done in time for next year's Houston convention." Anne frowned at her. "She ain't showed it to you yet."

"I haven't been over there in a while," Heather admitted. "Work."

"Tsk." Anne shook her head. "You need to go see your mom. With your dad overseas, she's all alone in that big house."

Heather winced and dipped her head a bit. "Yes, ma'am, Miss Anne. I'll do that."

Angela debated reminding her mother of the fact Heather's parents hadn't lived together in over ten years. Ben gave her a quick, subtle headshake, so she took a deep breath of wintry air and held her tongue.

Instead, she glared back at Heather, watching her lean into Danny, seeking warmth. Danny's ears deepened to red at Angela's surrendering leer while Heather mouthed a quick, "What?"

The county jail's heavy metal door swung back with a loud screech and clank, nicking off Angela's sarcastic comeback. Chris stepped out into the sunlight and raised his arm, shielding his eyes. He wore the same cheap suit he had on the day the jury convicted him.

The day I took him from Mom and Dad. I think his time in jail has been harder on them than on him. They look older. No, they look old.

Her mom rushed to him first and hugged him fiercely. He tried politely breaking it, so he could see everyone else, but she wouldn't let go until she'd gotten her fill.

She mumbled into his shoulder, too low for anyone to understand. She finally stood back, both hands on the sides of his face, and kissed him on the cheek.

Chris squeezed his mother's hands before he faced his father. "Hey, Dad."

"Hey, Son. It's good to see you."

Then they embraced, too. Angela believed she caught Chris whisper, "I'm sorry, Dad." Admitting fault had been a requirement as part of his treatment while inside but overhearing him utter the words now without the threat of further incarceration hanging over his head hefted the heavy weight from her shoulders she'd carried ever since she'd stepped down from the witness stand.

Lastly, "Hey, Ang."

"Hey, Kis," she muttered.

They gave each other a stiff hug. He smelled clean, but his clothes, in storage for over a year, held the ever-present odors of old paint, stale urine, hot electronics, greasy jail cell hinges. And desperation. They pulled back from each other, and he mumbled, "I'll never forget what you did for me." Resentment, though, clouded the new wrinkles around his eyes. She knew he meant, "to me." The pit of her stomach turned as cold as the set of his chin.

Don't make me break their hearts again, Chris.

She didn't dwell on it long, though, as their parents grappled them into a group hug.

"Let's hit the road," her dad urged. "Christmas Turkey's getting cold."

Dallas Police Department Detective Billy Torres stared at the man in the interrogation room a moment longer before handing the case folder to Angela. "Phillip Duke. He's the fourth one this month."

"I still don't understand why you called us." Danny rolled his eyes, bored out of his skull. He had become accustomed to cases a little more exciting than smash and grab robberies. "Liquor store robberies ain't exactly our area."

"Under normal circumstances, I'd agree." Torres stroked his large, black mustache. "But these aren't your typical liquor store armed robbery suspects." He rubbed his hand across the back of his neck. "Look. We're not asking you to take over. As you said, it's not your jurisdiction. Consultation only. Your task force supposedly handles the off-beat cases?"

"Yeah." Angela's answer was vague and automatic as her attention was elsewhere. She studied Mr. Duke with a practiced eye. The suspect needed a good night's sleep to start with. Professional. Manicured. Suit. Missing his tie though; they take those weapons before they chucked them into the tank. She skimmed his folder. "He's a lawyer?"

Torres bobbed his head as he produced three other files. "And two computer programmers and an engineer. None of them remember anything about the robberies."

Danny scratched his chin. "That's convenient," he drolled.

"Yeah, tell me about it. Caught them all at home, too. Nice homes." Torres brought up a file on his phone and read from it. "One was cooking. One was watching TV. Two were taking naps. Naps! Only hardened criminals can sleep after a stick-up."

"Okay," Angela admitted, "I agree with you. Not your typical stick-up men." She reviewed the pictures from three of the robberies, the ones with working cameras. The images weren't top quality, but they were good enough for facial recognition. She eyed the pistol in the first suspect's hand. Brushed stainless finish. Semi-Automatic. She flipped to the second picture. To the third picture. "Did you recover any weapons?" She flipped a few more pages. "Any of the cash?"

"Nothing."

"How many robberies involve a Beretta P-92? Or a Taurus PT-99?"

"It's a popular weapon," Torres smoothed out his mustache. "Why?"

"Popular enough to be used in three crimes where the suspects all claimed loss of memory?" She flipped the pictures around and showed them to the two men. "I'm curious about the other one." She flipped open the fourth folder and read the statement from the store clerk. "*He shoved a big silver pistol in my face.* Make that four robberies."

Danny and Torres gazed at Angela, mouths agape.

Danny cranked his head towards the detective and winked. "She's my hero. You know that, right?"

Torres shook his head and scrutinized at the pictures again "I can't believe I didn't catch that." He ran his hands over his suddenly-red cheeks. "I guess the wife's right. Time for a vacation."

"Come on, you guys," Angela mocked. "What are you? Straight out of the academy? We find this weapon, and we find who's responsible for these robberies."

Angela squinted at the suspect again, and her phone alarm beeped. *"Dinner with Mom, Dad, and Chris"* flashed at her. *If I'm fast.* "Detective, you mind if I ask him a few questions?"

Torres raised his hand towards the door in friendly invitation.

She wielded every page from *Angela's Interrogation Tome.* Either he was a damned fine liar, or he honestly didn't remember.

As they left the police station, Angela's phone rang. "Hey, mom."

"Angela?" her mother bawled. "Have you seen Chris?"

Angela pulled into Thirsty Liquor Store's parking lot. She and Danny had been hitting all of Chris's old haunts. "Thanks again, Danny."

"No problem, partner." He stepped out of the car and scanned the area. "Busy place for this time of day." Head on a swivel, his nostrils flared, and he exhaled sharply with a pinched expression. "I don't see his ride anywhere."

"Me neither." She understood Danny's distaste. Urine-soaked bricks and the rat-infested dumpsters offended her nose. His must have tolerated it as easily as a sucker punch. She took in the assortment of old, beat-up cars. Part of her hoped Chris's car was here, but another part hoped it wasn't; the big sister in her truly yearned for him to be working a job somewhere. The cop in her knew he wasn't. You don't miss meetings with your parole officer. She tightened her coat against the wind. "He used to hang out here on the corner, buying and selling his drugs."

They rushed inside out of the cold and stood at the counter until Jesus the Clerk finished with the customer in front of them.

"Can I help you?" he monotoned.

Angela showed her badge along with a picture, a large mugshot of Chris. "Have you seen him around here lately, Jesus?"

He took the picture and glared at it. He didn't appear nervous around her at all.

Probably used to cops coming in all the time looking for someone.

"Si, I've seen him."

Angela snapped, "When?"

"A couple of days ago." He handed the picture back. "Bought a beer or something."

Danny surveyed the busy store. "You remember one guy from a few days ago? Don't get me wrong, I'm tickled you do. Just curious why."

Jesus pointed to the street corner. "Because the puta pissed on the wall outside. I threatened to call the cops if he didn't leave."

Angela cringed.

He's definitely off the reservation again.

"Any idea where he went?"

Jesus shook his head. "No. Just somewhere else." He peered over Angela's shoulder at the customers piling behind them. "Is that all? My boss'll chew my ass if I let the line get too long."

"No, that's it. Thanks."

Back out in the car, Danny crossed his arms. "Where to next?"

"No idea. This is the last place I can think to look."

Gunfire intruded into her melancholy as a man sped out of Thirsty's towards a car parked by the curb, pistol in one hand and a paper bag in the other. Danny had already scrambled out and taken a defensive position behind another car before Angela cleared her front fender.

"Police!" he yelled while Angela screamed, "FBI! Drop your weapon!"

They both dashed up in alternating cover and approach formation, but the man ignored them. He slid into his car as Danny sprung in front of him.

"Whatever's in that bag ain't worth it!" Danny yelled at him. "Don't make me shoot you!" The car engine roared to life, and Danny fired three shots into the man's chest, right through the windshield.

Angela only got off one shot through the passenger window into the man's side before he gunned the engine. "Danny!" she yelled.

Danny had the pale blue eyes of a *lupus*, and his face sported three-day-old stubble. The car thundered towards him, and he leaped onto the hood, springing off the roof and landing on the concrete behind. He spun around and sprinted two steps before he paused and snarled back at Angela, his heavy breathing producing clouds of misty breath in the chilly air. The untamed wild of his heritage twisted his face. He took three deep breaths and pulled the *renovatio* under control.

"Let's go!" he growled, racing for their car. His facial scruff had disappeared, but his eyes still glowed pale blue.

Tires squealed as Angela swerved onto the roadway.

Danny called in the chase. He glanced at Angela from the side, and she nodded curtly. He followed his report with,

"Suspect has assaulted a police officer. He is armed and dangerous." Every cop from miles around would join the pursuit now. "Did you see his eyes?"

"No!" She veered around a small foreign jalopy with its turn signal stuck in the on position.

"Soulless. Spooky."

"There he is!" she exclaimed, tilting her head up the road. Two Fort Worth Police Department black and whites skidded into pursuit. "Spooky, huh?"

"Yeah."

"He was dressed in a suit."

He glanced over at her. "*And* driving a Maserati."

"Gonna be hard to catch him in this."

"I shot three times!"

"I know. I shot once."

"I didn't miss."

"Neither did I. Could've had a bulletproof vest."

"Maybe…Uh, oh, watch out!"

A third black and white whipped on the road in front of the suspect and slid sideways, blocking the path of the escaping car. The Maz veered hard to the left, cut across opposing traffic, and dodged further to avoid a delivery truck. It vaulted off the curb and rammed into the corner of the Fort Worth Bank and Trust building, a man-sized chunk of early 20th century brickwork shattering in a blast of reddish dust. Police cars swarmed around the disabled vehicle, emptying of officers who were yelling for the suspect to put his hands on the steering wheel.

Danny radioed as they rolled up to the scene, "We need the suspect alive!"

The driver sprung from the car and staggered down the sidewalk, stumbled on the brick debris, and nose-dived to the ground. He tried to get up, but three police officers crowded around him and slammed him against the sidewalk.

Bad Girls! Bad Girls! As always, Angela couldn't stop the tune from running through her head along with the adrenaline of a chase.

She and Danny ran up, showing their badges. Angela dropped next to the suspect and put her thumb against the robber's neck. "No pulse!"

Danny ordered, "Turn him over!"

The driver's skin was flour-pale and his confused irises, white. She tapped his chest. "No vest!" she yelled, ripping his shirt open to inspect his wounds.

Abruptly, Angela transported back to her days at the Academy, standing over cadavers, sticking her fingers into bullet holes and knife wounds, and sniffing for different chemicals. The holes in the man's chest, as well as the pasty, dead-colored skin, reminded her of those classes. No blood oozed from them, but the bullets had clearly caused soft and hard tissue damage. She pinched his fingernails, checking for blood flow. They were already white.

The suspect struggled against the restraints.

Angela lurched up and backed away. "What the hell?!"

The cops all moved back with her, a mixture of surprise, fear, and disbelief on their faces. Two of them made the sign of the cross.

One of the cops handed the man's wallet to Danny.

"William Travolta." Danny let out a nervous chuckle. "Travolta? I'll be damned."

Another cop handed a paper bag full of cash to him.

Angela, though, continued studying the man. Other than tugging at his cuffs and looking around with those freaky, white eyes, he appeared…*well, dead, dammit!*

"What's that around his nose?" Danny knelt and scraped a sample of a yellowy powder into a small evidence baggie. "Smells like horse piss."

"Well, don't put it up to your nose!" Angela exclaimed.

"I don't have to put it up to my nose. It reeks." Danny abruptly shook his head, trying to fling off the stink his *lupus* nose was hanging on to.

Mr. Travolta closed his eyes.

A few minutes later, the ambulance arrived and took him to the hospital. As Angela and Danny followed it, the bad news came across the radio. Mr. Travolta had started bleeding while in the ambulance. In fact, indications were he'd come back to life. Heartbeat, color, everything. Then the bleeding stopped. And he died. Again.

Angela dropped her empty coffee cup into the trash and pulled out her keyboard. She typed in the facts of the case. No bleeding from gunshot wounds. The bleeding occurred later. White irises. No struggle once captured. Upper-middle-class. She pressed the *Search* button, sat back, and stared at the computer monitor.

While she waited for the results to show, she tried to decide whether to email her mother or phone her to tell her she couldn't find Chris. She was too chicken for *Option 3*, telling her in person. Watching her mother's heart break again was not easily added to the day's agenda. Her search finished, and its results filled her screen. With a moan, she promised herself she'd go over and deliver the news face-to-face…after she finished reviewing the…3,451 entries?

This might take a while.

She scanned a few random pages. It appeared the Task Force W archives concurred with her assessment. Zombies.

She punched in, "Substance: yellow powder. Location: upper lip."

The number plummeted to 19, all of them confirmed zombies. "That's better," she muttered with a happy lilt. Caribbean Santeria sects employed the yellow powder, assuming what she had was identical, to create a zombie-like trance.

Santerians in north Texas? Well, why not? We've got confirmed *zombies! Why not witch doctors?*

Ping, Ping! She grabbed her phone, and a message from the lab lit up the screen. "*Task Force W/Ft Worth - Unknown Yellow Substance 1. Order 87. Estimate: 6 weeks, 2 days.*"

"Dammit!" She typed back a lengthy response, densely populated with some rather choice words best reserved for sailors.

After mulling over it for a few moments, she slapped *Delete.*

She plucked a stick of gum from her pocket and shoved it into her mouth as she stormed down to Kent's office. "I need to register a Confidential Informant."

Kent glanced up from the folder he was reading. Disbelief painted his face in a rare display of emotion. "You've actually got a CI who can help with W cases?"

"She's more of a technical expert." She showed him the message from the crime lab.

He shook his head. "It was 50th in line this morning." He spun the folder he'd been reading around. "Three more cases have popped up in the Metroplex and two in Houston since yesterday."

"All got the yellow powder?"

He stared at her and nodded once.

She slipped her phone into her pocket. "Then we need

her. She's not really confidential, but I can't pay her without padding my expense report."

"Who is she?"

"Heather O'Leary. M.D. down at UT Southwestern Medical. Used to do research. Got tired of constantly begging for funds. Now she works the emergency room. Lives on adrenaline." Angela sat down on the edge of a chair. "She's already helped out a few times, analyzing things for me. That chupacabra blood?"

"I wondered how you managed to get the crime lab to vet those findings so fast." He leaned back in his chair and rested his interlaced fingers on his stomach. "I guess the fact I haven't seen her research on the blood in the papers answers the question as to whether she can keep her mouth shut."

"Yes, sir." She bit down on her gum. "But…she's got a thing for Danny."

"How big of a thing?" He caught his breath and raised his eyebrows. "Wait…can werewolves and humans…you know…?"

Angela nodded. "I checked—to make sure Heather didn't become infected. According to archives—" she pointed to the bottom of her fingernails "—little sacs of venom form here during the change. When they scratch someone, the venom is applied. Besides, I'm not sure I could stop them if I wanted. He isn't running away from her."

Kent let his breath whistle out through his teeth. "We know he can keep a secret."

Angela simply nodded at the unspoken, *"…so we don't have to worry about pillow talk on the nightly news."*

"Okay," he decided. "Let's not go the CI route though." He leaned forward and typed an email. "Laboratory Services should be contacting you. I have a small budget for hiring contractors and the like. Never use it. Hard to find civilians with all their marbles willing to help on cases, Wichita shamans and werewolves exempted, of course."

The aroma of roasting jalapenos, pepperoni, and cardboard pizza box made Angela's stomach growl. She pressed the doorbell button again. "Come on, Heather!" she yelled at the crack in the door. "I gotta pee, and my hands are full. I can't get the key!" She chewed hard on her gum, trying to forget about her angry bladder.

The door swung back, and Heather stood there in a bathrobe and hair mussed like she'd crawled out of bed.

Angela thrust the pizza box and a bottle of strawberry wine at her. "You sick or something? It's noon!"

"Wait," Heather exclaimed.

"I won't be long!" Angela hurried down the hallway, flew into the bathroom, and sat down on…nothing but toilet water. Then as she tried to extricate herself from the throne, the scene she ran past in the living room flashed through her head. Chinese food containers. Throw pillows next to the hearth. Cowboy boots in front of the couch. Snakeskin cowboy boots. She threw her gum into the trash, dropped the toilet seat a little too loudly, and did her business.

Cowboy boots? Who the hell wears snakesk…oh, hell!

Trying to harness her patience, she washed her hands a bit more vigorously than was necessary. Drying them on her pants as she stepped into the kitchen, she yelled, "You can come out, Danny!"

Her partner lumbered down the hall wearing his jeans and an unbuttoned shirt. She had to admit he kept himself in shape. And with his sleep-mangled hair…*no more cowboys!*

He paused at the entrance to the kitchen. "How did you

know?"

"Toilet seat." She pointed over at his boots. "And you wore them the day Chris got out of prison."

"Oh." His gaze drifted to the pizza box. "Smells good."

Angela ignored him. "In the middle of the day, guys?"

Heather giggled. "We just got to sleep." She pulled a corkscrew from a drawer. "That secret didn't last long." She peeked over at Danny, a snarky grin decorating her face.

Danny's ears had gone red, but it didn't stop him from taking a large bite of hot pizza. "She's is an FBI agent," he muffled. "They're smart that way." He quit chewing and stared at her. "Am I fired?"

Angela shook her head. "No."

Heather pulled the cork on the bottle of wine. "What gives, sister?"

"Nothing. Why?"

"You chew gum when you're pissed, you eat pizza when you're frustrated, and you drink wine or eat ice cream when you're fighting with the family. You came in grinding your gum like it was boot leather and—" she pointed at the wine and pizza. "I've got the trifectas of aneurysms here in my kitchen."

"Am I that easy to read?"

Danny and Heather nodded in unison, exchanging sharp, knowing looks.

Angela threw herself into a chair at the table. "I told Mom and Dad I couldn't find Chris."

"Oh." Heather poured three glasses and raised hers. "Here's to family. You can't choose 'em and…well, that's it. You can't choose 'em."

Angela took a deep drink from her glass as she dropped a folder of papers onto the table in front of her friend.

Heather slid paper plates in front of everyone and flipped the folder open. "What are these?"

Angela slipped two pieces of pizza onto her plate. "They're contractor sign-up forms. For you."

Heather's laughter filled the room. "You want me to be an FBI agent?" She made a pistol with her hands and stood in a perfect representation of the Shooter's Fighting Stance, evidence her Marine Corp General father had spent many hours with her in the shooter's box. "I get to crash through doors and shoot the bad guys?"

While Danny grinned around a cheese and tomato sauce mouth full of pizza, Angela laughed and shook her head. "No, I'm afraid not."

"Good. I don't want to break a nail." She leered at Danny. "I have special…uses for them."

Danny nearly choked on his pizza, and his ears went red again.

"TMI, Heather!" Angela cried.

"Okay, okay, what do you need me for then?"

"Your crack lab research skills. The FBI crime labs are a month behind on everything. And that's being nice to them."

"Okay." She flung her hair behind her shoulder. "Where do I sign?"

Her friend's flippant attitude took Angela back a bit. "You don't want to know the particulars? At least read them."

"Sister, if you were going to screw me over, you would have taken Danny here for yourself." After she signed everywhere Angela pointed, she held the stack vertical and aligned them, banging their edges on the table. "What's my first assignment, General?"

Angela pulled an evidence baggie out of her pocket. "I

need you to analyze this yellow powder." She eyed Danny. "And we have to hurry. Five more cases have been reported since yesterday."

Kent put Heather's report on the yellow powder on his desk. "Hammerhead worm?" He, Danny, and Angela were staring at a picture of a worm that appeared to be a cross between a hammerhead shark and a flattened worm with a racing stripe along its back. "How big do they get?"

Danny pointed out the highlighted section of text on the next page. "Six inches or so is the longest one recorded according to what I could find on the internet."

Kent set his cup of coffee down. "And Heather says this is what's causing these people to go crazy?"

"That she doesn't know. She only told us what's in the powder. Tetrodotoxin. It's a neurotoxin usually found in puffer fish. This particular strain comes from the worm, though." Angela picked the folder up and flipped to another page. "She also found traces of a species of Central and South American tree frog."

Danny slipped a printout of another Google search onto Kent's desk. "I did find this. It's the only thing that makes sense right now. The ingredients in the residue are nearly identical to the ingredients in what is commonly referred to as zombie powder. Used quite a bit in Haiti. And according to the archives, this is the same substance found in other cases. Close enough anyway."

"So, we're looking for someone who's importing hammerhead worms and/or—" he flipped another page up "—Osteopilus dominicensis…tree frogs…and using them to make zombies to rob liquor stores?"

"Yes, sir."

Kent's face remained neutral and his voice low. "You would think that after all these years, nothing would surprise me any longer."

Angela had a hard time distinguishing his 'surprised' look with his everyday 'dour' look.

Kent checked his tie's knot and stretched his chin up for a moment. He closed the folder and slid it across his desk. "Over the last week, we've received reports from Atlanta, LA, and Chicago. Find out who's making this shit and stop them. Use your W1 clearance if you have to. If that's not enough, come see me. I'll get whatever clearance you need."

Three days later, they still hadn't found any leads to who was manufacturing the powder. Everyone assumed the spree originated in the DFW area because they were the ones who'd figured it out. But when they scoured the archives, it appeared New Orleans was the most likely location as Suspect Zero showed up there first. The police interrupted Caleb Simoneaux robbing a bank. When he didn't respond to commands, they shot him. When he didn't drop, they shot him some more. When he took off down the street, everyone assumed he had a bulletproof vest on. Eventually, his foot slipped into a French drain, pinning him until the cops caught up with him. Soon after, he bled out and died. They took the yellow powder under his nose was some new form of PCP and closed the case.

Based on the new information, Kent assigned the entire Fort Worth Task Force W field office to going through import records and customs forms. He brought cots in for everyone, himself included. No one went home. Everyone worked. He assigned high priority for anything along the Gulf Coast. Angela had never combed through fertilizer receipts for anyone planning another Oklahoma City bombing, but what they were doing must have been close. No one had computerized the vast majority of the sales and transfer forms yet, and 5th-grade dropouts appeared to have filled them out; she didn't realize there were so many different ways to spell tree, frog, and worm.

Two days and nine hushed-up reported cases of "zombie attacks" later, they found what they were looking for. A self-proclaimed psychic in Mobile, Alabama, Madam Agatha, had ordered all the ingredients on the list, plus a few others everyone scratched their heads over.

FBI SWAT raided her house. She might have been psychic after all; she wasn't there. When all-clear rang out through their ear comms, Angela and Danny examined what could only be described as a voodoo laboratory the SWAT team had found in the attic. While the photographer took detailed pictures of all the items in the workbench refrigerator, Angela scanned the various containers, reading the names written on the sides.

"Toad teeth, hummingbird wings, werewolf fangs…"

Danny scooted over next to her when she'd read the latter aloud. "I wonder how she managed that!"

Angela ignored him and continued down the line. A plastic baggie containing a yellow powder labeled *coupe poudre*. "Zombie powder right here! And…bipalium secretions…Hey! I think this is it." She plucked a mason jar from the table and scraped the grime off the side. "There's close to a quart of the stuff here." She shook the jar, turning it sideways and back. "It's gooey."

The site forensics supervisor came over and gently pointed at the jar. "Agent, if that is indeed bipalium secretions, there's enough toxin in there to kill a small town. Please…carefully set it back on the bench."

Angela stared at the jar like she was holding a sleeping rattlesnake and set it down as if she might wake it up. "How much of that goo does one of those worms make?"

"If this is pure, she'd have needed to collect it from thousands of worms over a couple of years' time. An average four-inch specimen only secrets a few grams of the stuff every couple of days."

Danny was leaned over, hands on his knees, squinting at the jar. "Sweet! So where are all those worms…?"

The photographer interrupted them. "Agent Hollingsworth? I found something here. Looks like the deed to an old warehouse down on the riverfront."

Angela read the document. "So, it is. So, it is."

Angela stared at the blurry lines of the old, brick warehouse through the foggy night. Blacked out windows stretched along the top near the roof, while occasional flickers of light slipped out from around their edges. She flipped the wipers switch, squeegeeing mist from her windshield to show randomly working streetlights casting faded yellow splotches along the uninhabited sidewalks. Buoys from the waterfront chimed lonely clangs while the occasional ship's horn answered back with the same forlorn sadness. The stench of fish chafed against her, even through the closed windows. Two giant rats scurried into a drainage opening, dodging a Ford Pinto as it roared up the quiet street. It pulled to a stop next to the warehouse's side entrance.

Her ear comm relayed the message, "Grandmother has arrived."

She peered through the fog further down the street to the FBI team's tactical vehicle, disguised as a bread truck. There would be no SWAT tonight. They were a hammer. Considering the materials found in Madam Agatha's attic, Kent had decided discretion was needed rather than a shock and awe building clearing. He didn't want to risk the suspect contaminating the riverfront with whatever she was storing in the warehouse if cornered. Everyone had volunteered to enter, but he chose Angela and Danny. They'd caught the case.

"Grandmother has entered the cabin," Kent relayed. "You're up, Red Riding Hood."

"Roger, Wolf and Red are up," Angela said. She twisted her head to the side and shared a grin with Danny. She got to pick their call-signs for this operation.

They slipped out of their car and slinked along the sides of the buildings leading to the warehouse. The door was locked, but Danny came prepared; he pulled out a lock pick gun. Three seconds later, the doorknob clicked as the tumblers dropped into place. Brad and Bill, their backup, slid up next to them. They were to wait at the door until called.

Angela swung the door in while Danny covered her. He nodded once, and they stepped into a long hallway, the beams from their flashlights disappearing into the murkiness. The floor was wet and slimy in places where it had sunk lower than the rest. It reeked of mildew and mold. Incandescent bulbs hanging by their power cables flickered on and off sporadically, transforming their shadows into moving apparitions. They followed the hallway to the right and came to a stairway on the left.

Danny tapped her shoulder. He pointed to his ear and upstairs.

Angela's heartbeat pounded in her chest as she nodded her head. She licked her lips and took the lead, slowly climbing the stairway. Shuffling noises drifted down to her the higher she went. One step before reaching the top, she glimpsed back to verify Dany was in position. Behind him, the hallway looked like a black hole with the occasional glimmer of flickering lights giving the impression of a lightning storm. She took the remaining steps, her head breaching the edge of the loft's floor.

Flickering candles turned the vast, shadowy space ominous. In the center of the smoky room sat a large black cauldron on a grate above a brick fire pit.

Someone's gone full Grimm's Fairy Tale.

An electric vent, mounted in the roof, vented the smoke from the fire. She ran up the remaining three steps so Danny could join her. A long table sat on their right with a gruesome hoard of jars and pails, candles and Bunsen burners, powders and liquids scattered along it. There was even a human skull with a melting candle on top of it.

As Danny stepped from the stairway, an old woman with frizzy grey hair and wearing a 40-year-old sundress, Madam Agatha if the driver's license photo was to be believed, elbowed aside a curtain dividing off part of the loft into a back room and headed towards the cauldron. Her skin hung in flaps and wrinkles. She looked like she was melting too.

She was focused on the contents of the wicker basket she carried, so she gave a little lurch when Danny erupted with, "Get down, police!"

Angela moved alongside him. "FBI! Drop it! Drop it! On the floor!"

Madam Agatha held up one hand to block Angela's flashlight glare and spit to the side, toppling the basket at their feet as she did so. The floor turned slick as human body parts scattered all around them. Angela and Danny pulled up short and stepped carefully.

Angela glanced sideways at Danny as he growled. His eyes were pale blue. She figured the scent of fresh death had tickled his *lupus*.

Madam Agatha recited passages in an unknown language. Electricity charged the air, and the hair on Angela's body stood up.

Danny didn't wait for her to finish whatever spell she was casting. He squeezed his trigger as Madam Agatha swept her arm to the side. His hands swung wide in response.

The witch cackled as his bullets splintered the wall to her left.

A ruffling noise from behind her. Angela spun around. "Jee-zus!" she cried out. A hammerhead worm, man-size, slithered towards her out from under a pile of mildewed straw and old rags.

So much for six inches! Guys can't measure shit!

"Danny, I've got a problem!" she yelled, up on her toes as she skipped and skidded backwards.

The worm continued sliding towards her but stopped when it got to some of the body parts lying on the floor. It engulfed a leg, and the acid from its embrace melted the foot and calf as it worked its way up to the thigh.

She took a step back. Fired a triple shot. The bullets spawned no damage.

No meat. Too much goo.

A hunch. She kicked the remaining body parts into the far corner. The worm followed them.

A loud growl snatched her attention, and she spun back to Danny and the hag. He'd performed his *renovatio* and was in full *lupus* form, ripping himself free of clothes.

"*Lupus Sapiens!*" the old crone screeched. "*Frenator*, too!"

She pulled a silver dagger from under her dress, flipped the hilt open, and took a deep snort from it. She shook her head and dropped into a knife fighter's pose. Knees bent. Weight on the balls of her feet. Her eyes flashed with vigor. The grip on her dagger, firm, sure. "Now be still! I need your blood!"

Danny dropped to all fours and raised his snout to the ceiling, loosing a howl. Dust shook from the timbers in the old warehouse's ceiling. The windows rattled and threatened to shatter.

Chill bumps ran the length of Angela's spine. This wasn't her first wolf fight though. She fired three shots but missed as her pistol jumped sideways in response to the witch whipping her hand about again.

Madam Agatha showed no fear. She put her hand into a pocket, and yanked it out, throwing a yellowish powder at Danny as he took his first menacing steps towards her.

He stiffened in his tracks.

Oh, shit!

A garish laugh erupted victoriously from the hag's toothless craw.

Angela took another step back from the worm and yelled, "Danny! Get your shit together!"

His eyes turned bloodshot.

He sneezed. Once. Twice. Three times.

With slow deliberation, he raised his gaze to the old woman. A deep, rumbling growl rose from his feet, through his musclebound midsection, and wove through his teeth and past his lips.

"Fuckin' *Frenatus*!" the crone screeched with her whole body. She gripped her dagger tighter and rushed the werewolf.

More shuffling from behind. Angela spun around. The

191

worm had finished the last of its meal. She climbed up onto the workbench.

Gotta be something she's using to control the fucker!

Her gaze landed on a large plastic bottle with a rubber hose and a sprayer hanging from its side. Two empty salt boxes sat next to it. A dark grin crossed her face as she remembered when she and Chris used to sprinkle salt on the snails in the backyard. She rapidly pumped the handle on the top of the tank while Danny and the witch growled and screeched at each other.

As the gooey fiend glided towards her, she pointed the nozzle at its head and pressed the trigger. Faster than she thought it could move, it scampered for the corner, curling up in a ball when it ran out of space. She walked hunched over down the workbench, following it, continuing to shoot a steady stream of saltwater over its body. Large pieces of translucent flesh sloughed off and plopped onto the wooden floor.

She slipped down off the bench as the crone and Danny circled each other. Blood ran freely from her partner's arms where the silver dagger had repeatedly found its mark. The witch was unharmed.

Moving too fast for Danny to catch, the hag leaped and spider-crawled up the wall to the ceiling. Her toenails elongated, digging into the wood, and she hung from the bottom of a rafter like a bat. She was a demon possessed as she slashed at Danny. He dodged the silver weapon hack after hack.

The old woman screeched, "Be still dammit!" and held her arms out to her sides.

Danny seized the advantage. He swung a massive arm back into the crone's head, knocking her off her bat-perch.

She dropped back to the floor but landed on her feet with a twist a cat would be proud of. Ducking a double swipe of werewolf claw, she pressed in again, fast and agile, scoring another gash on his chest.

Angela took aim at the old woman's center mass. And waited.

Danny was tiring. *The silver?* He backed into a corner. Too late, the witch realized the feint as she showed her back to Angela.

Three silver, 9mm slugs found their marks in the old hag's back, staggering her, but not dropping her.

She spun on Angela, face twisted with hate. "You're next, bitch!"

The crone saw the shock on Angela's face as Danny leaned down, but she dodged to the side too late. His great maw bit through her skull, popping it like a torpid grape.

"Red Riding Hood, we're coming up!" Brad relayed over the radio.

"Stand by!" she responded. Then, "Danny, get out of here!" she yelled off-mic.

Danny sniffed her foot and leaped through the curtain, leaving Madam Agatha's mangled body behind him.

"Stairwell clear!" Angela announced.

Brad and Bill ran up in classic cover formation. They scanned the scene, saw the old woman's headless body on the floor, and took up covering positions in different corners.

"Where's Officer McIver?" Brad asked.

"Back here!" a weak voice called out. Danny stumbled through the curtains, blood running from his arms and stomach to the floor. "Ange—" Her name cut off as he fell against the wall.

Angela keyed her mic as she rushed over. "Agent Down! We need medical services up here. Now!"

She cradled his head while Bill applied pressure to his wounds. "What happened to his clothes?" he muttered as he eyed their ripped remains.

Danny raised his head. "Tell Heather—"

"Shut up, redneck! You ain't dying today!"

Brad, his face white, joined them after clearing the back room. "Good God, who are these people?" Then, seeing Danny's condition, regained control, and ripped his shirt off for a make-shift bandage to staunch the flow of blood.

Danny's face turned pale. He was on the cusp of passing out.

"I can't stop the bleeding!" Bill exclaimed.

Angela slapped Danny's face. "Wake up! How do we stop the bleeding?"

Danny's eyes rolled open. "Wolf...wolfsbane."

Brad and Bill both stared hard at her with faces closed.

"He's a werewolf, guys," she confessed to them with a long breath.

They blinked, and Brad smiled.

"Well, shit!" Bill said. "Why didn't you say so!"

"Yeah," Brad added. "That explains some things."

Danny drooled but nodded his head. "Tablespoon. Quart...water. Rub..."

Angela pointed her head at the workbench. "Brad!"

He dashed over. "What am I looking for? Wolfsbane?"

"Danny!" Angela cried, "Wake up! Stay with us!"

"Found it!" Brad exclaimed. By the time he'd made the concoction, Danny's pulse was weak and rapid. As soon as they rubbed the mixture into his wounds though, the bleeding slowed. Angela hoped it was the mixture working and not him dying.

"How much of this are we supposed to use?" Bill asked.

"No idea," Angela muttered. "Use it all."

For the next few moments, none of them spoke a word as they rubbed their bloody hands over Danny wounds. By the time they'd poured out the dregs of the mixture, Danny's breathing had steadied, and his pulse had strengthened.

"Hang in there, partner," she said, running her hand over his forehead.

The steady beeping from the monitors intruded into Angela's sleep. It's what allowed her to relax, though. A quick squeeze of Danny's hand gave her the reassurances she looked for. Warm. Calm. He was alive. Her partner was alive. That's all that mattered. She'd dozed on and off throughout the night, the chair in his ICU room not comfortable enough for real sleep. But sleep was what she needed. The last 24 hours had taken its toll, and when she came down off her adrenaline rush, her body decided a square chair was comfort enough.

She peeked up from her uneasy sleep when Heather ruffled through some charts. Sometime in the night, she'd arrived in Mobile as promised. It comforted Angela knowing that Heather was on the scene and doing her thing. She took his pulse—regardless of what the machines told her—and checked his pupils. The reason Angela and Heather got along so well was when things turned south, they both kept their shit in one sock.

"Morning." Angela relished her stiff yawn and lazy stretch. "How'd you get here so fast?"

"Daddy."

"Oh." Angela forgot at times that a United States Marine

Corps general had perks. Like getting your daughter the doctor a seat on one of the military's *Air Mobility Command* flights. Anytime. Anywhere. "They put you over him?" She pointed her head at Danny.

Heather peeked over her shoulder at the door. "I exerted my 'family physician' privilege."

"How's he doing?"

"Good," Heather said with a smile. "Too good actually, but I'm not complaining." She straightened his sheets. "Eighty-four stitches on fourteen different cuts. Why the hell didn't he shoot the fucker with the knife?"

Danny mumbled, "Because chicks dig scars."

Angela jumped to her feet. "He lives!"

Heather's eye's sparkled with joy as she leaned down to give him a hug.

"Yow!" Danny protested. "Watch it…wait…not there either…Is this what passes for bedside manner for city folk?"

"Shut up," Heather cried with a pillow-muffled voice. "You're lucky I don't kill you."

A nurse came in with a tray of fresh bandages and broke up the reunion. "It's time to change his dressings, doctor."

Heather stood and wiped the tears from her cheeks with the sleeve of her jacket. "Good. Make sure it hurts."

Episode 6: Morstat

"**. . .H**appy birthday, Dear Ben. Happy birthday to you!"

Ben blew out the candles on his double-decker, chocolate sour cream cake.

"I thought I was gonna have to pull out the water hose!" Anne exclaimed.

"Glad we didn't need it!" Ben's old boss, Allen, quipped. "If the house burns down, he'll have to come out of retirement. I don't wanna see that grumpy old fart's face every morning again."

Allen's wife, Cindy, slapped her husband on the arm. "Allen, that wasn't nice!"

"Don't you worry none, Cindy," Ben said. "The feeling's mutual. I would've belly-flopped on the cake first to keep that from happening."

While everyone fanned the smoke out of their faces and laughed, Ben cut the cake, serving Allen and Cindy first, followed by a few of the neighbors who'd showed up for the party. Heather stood up from Danny's knee and took over with a quick hug. "Happy Birthday, Mr. H!"

"Thanks, Heather." His appreciative smile turned sad as he licked the sugary frosting off his fingers. Quickly though, he put up a happy front. "With you here, we've almost the whole damned family together!"

Anne stiffened for a moment while she shot Angela a hurried glance, but no one else brought up anything about Chris's absence. Other than missing him, it was a perfect, happy family gathering. She continued to sit quietly in the corner, eating her cake, while everyone else made small talk and enjoyed each other's company.

She'd finished scraping the last of her crumbs from her plate when Anne made eye contact with her and pointed her head towards the kitchen. They stood at the sink, looking into the backyard, while Anne twisted a dishrag in her hand. "Heard anything about Chris?"

"No, ma'am." Angela washed her plate and fork and put them in the drainer. Danny stood in the middle of the backyard, looking at the trees. "I've looked everywhere. His P.O. held off as long as he could, but he's had to list him as 'Missed Appointed, Pick Up.'"

Anne leaned on the edge of the counter with both hands and bowed her head. A single sob wracked her shoulders.

Angela put her arm around her mother's waist. "I don't know what else to do."

Anne spun on Angela. "It ain't your fault, you know. Your pa and I blamed you for Chris's problems. That wasn't fair. He's the one got the problems. Testifying against him, I know it was to protect us. Get him some help. We knew it. Didn't wanna accept it. Forgive us?"

Tears stung Angela's eyes as she wrapped her mother in a ferocious hug. "Th…there's nothing to forgive, Mama."

Dad had told them numerous times he'd done his part, and it was their job to continue the family line. People often thought he was kidding in his 'family line' banter, but Angela knew the pain he hid from the world. Through years of prolonged sicknesses and short tragedy, he was now the last Hollingsworth from his line and only wanted the family name carried on. That was the big responsibility and one only Chris could uphold. Sadly, Angela knew Chris didn't take it seriously. Maybe it's why she was always protective of him, even taking the blame sometimes as kids for things he did. She didn't want him to let their dad down. Was it better their parents had finally faced the truth about him? Was it better he'd fallen from grace in their eyes? As she and her mother continued the hug in front of the sink, the cop in her knew it was the right thing. The big sister hated it.

After a few minutes, they broke the embrace and wiped away their tears with smiles.

Her mother gently caressed Angela's cheek. "This new job of yours agrees with you. You look younger."

Angela stiffened for a moment and then relaxed. "Thanks," was all she could muster.

Anne looked out the back window. "Danny doesn't like cake? He's still fiddling around out in the yard. Sounds like Mrs. Shoemaker's angry about something, too."

"I'll go check." She passed through the dining room on the way outside, and her dad winked at her for the first time since the day of Chris's trial. She smiled back as a loving warmth spread throughout her chest.

Danny was still standing in the middle of the backyard, staring off into the woods when she got out there.

She peered over at a corner of the backyard to where her dad's first pick-up truck sat on cinder blocks—*and people wonder why I hate the country*. Mrs. Shoemaker's caterwauls came from under the rusted-out shell. "You picking on my mom's cat?"

"Huh?" A sardonic smile crossed his face. "Oh. Maybe a little."

Angela snickered a bit. "Well, she's kinda cocky. 'Bout time she met her match."

"Allow me," he said with a grin. His eyes turned pale blue, and he growled lowly, not much, but enough to let Mrs.

199

Shoemaker know cat might be on the menu if she didn't behave herself.

Message received, the bushes rattling as she disappeared into the woods behind the yard.

Angela's snicker turned into a laugh. Finally, she asked, "What are you doing out here? Cake's almost gone!"

He looked at his feet and kicked a small stick. "Nothin'."

She chided him. "Come on, partner. I know bullshit when I hear it."

"You've got a good life, Ang."

First time he's called me that.

"I think all lives look good from the outside."

"Right." He nudged the stick again. "Did you know it's my dad's birthday, too? He ran off when I was nine. We didn't celebrate many of 'em. Left my mother and me alone. If it weren't for the pack, we'd've never made it."

"Why'd he leave?"

"Don't know. Some say he killed my Uncle Job for sniffing around mom. Couldn't ever find a body though. And the both of them just up and disappeared. I never accepted the fact my dad would kill his own brother. I don't remember much, but I remember them being close."

"You know we have a thing called an FBI...we could run a search, see if we can find him."

Danny looked embarrassed. "I already did. No joy. Doesn't surprise me, though. Any werewolf who wants to hide, can."

"Hey!" Heather's call came from behind them. "What are y'all doing out here?"

"Fresh air," Danny said, a shy, country-boy smile showing up on his face at the sight of Heather. "I can't believe you didn't bring me any cake. What kind of girlfriend are you?"

"The feminist type." She poked him in the ribs. "Get used to it."

Garry McNeil, FBI Assistant Director in charge of Task Force W, stood up at the large podium. "Can everyone take their seats now, please?"

Angela sat down next to Danny and scanned the crowded room. Twenty-two FBI agents and two consultants: five from Fort Worth plus Danny; four from Chicago; six from New York; seven from LA plus someone who looked more like a yogi than a law enforcement officer. These men and women constituted the entirety of Task Force W. And they were all in Quantico, Virginia for the first time anyone could remember, for a meeting on the findings from the Mobile, Alabama warehouse and Madam Agatha.

"Thank you, everyone, for making the trip out here today. I'll get right to it. Congratulations to the Fort Worth team. They found our proverbial Rosetta Stone linking a series of events that have been occurring around the world. What everyone here may not know is that each office has been involved in its own cases that, on the surface, appeared to be isolated. Here at Quantico though, we've seen patterns."

The agents stirred in the seats, sitting up a little straighter. A few of them looked over to Angela and her colleagues, giving them slight nods of acknowledgment.

"We haven't been sure what those patterns were telling us. However, after going through this—" he held up a large book with raised, astrological-looking symbols on it "—we're fairly certain we know what's going on now."

He scanned the room, making sure he had everyone's attention.

"The information in this book describes an alternate

theory for déjà vu. If we are to believe what's in here, individuals experience déjà vu as two dimensions come into contact with each other. Like two soap bubbles, when they touch, where they touch, looks the same, smells the same, tastes the same, everything. In reality, they are the same. This is why people think they've seen or done something before. They are experiencing it twice, once in our dimension and once in the other dimension.

"There's some math in the book—the techs are calling it N-Dimensional Quasi-Physics—that proves where these two soap bubbles touch, the dimensional rift is weakest."

One of the LA crew spoke up. "Quasi? Fake?"

"Yes. Only in this case, hell, I don't know either. I just know that's what they're calling it. Could be all bullshit, but the techs don't think so. In either case, we have reason to believe that the Forsaken Dweller, whoever, and whatever that is, plans to transition into our dimension through one of these weakened rifts. Why it wants Earth and not some other planet billions of light years away is still a mystery. Maybe Earth is the center of the universe after all. Or maybe we happen to be lucky enough to have the only cultists in this universe stupid enough to want that to happen.

"In either case, if you'll follow along with me in the attached agenda on page two, I'll walk everyone through the different cases and how they relate."

Angela sat back in her chair and listened to the rest of the briefing. As promised, Assistant Director McNeill went through the catalog of cases, Angela's and Danny's included. Strange books. Cryptozoology that included chupacabras, a unicorn, a winged lizard, and merfolk. Cultists in abandoned subway tunnels. Talking rocks. Crystal necklaces that turned the women who wore them into Stepford Wives—which she figured should have been advertised in *Redneck Times* instead of on a television shopping network. And last, but not least, the one case that tied them all together, the raid on the voodoo shop in Mobile, Alabama.

Near the end of the lecture, he threw up some digital scans from the book on an overhead projector. Angela nearly fainted. In the margins of some of the pages were English translation scribblings. "The translations stopped here—" He pointed to the last sheet in the series. "Looks like Fort Worth's raid interrupted the process."

The back of her throat filled with bile. She reached for a stick of gum.

Danny must have sensed something was wrong because he leaned over. "You okay?"

Part of her, Chris's twin sister, shook her head at her partner. The FBI agent in her scrawled a note on the gum wrapper. The twin tried to rip it up. The agent handed it over. Danny looked confused but accepted the gum wrapper and untwisted the foil. If he was working on his poker face, he sure wasn't doing a great job of it. Reading Angela's scrawl made his face drain of all color. He looked up at the projector, down at the wrapper, and back up at the projector. Angela caught his attention again and widened her eyes, jerking her head in Kent's direction. Danny slowly passed the note on while still staring at Angela.

She looked back at the projections, not because she was trying to pay attention, but because she was trying to keep from looking at Danny and Kent. Still, she sensed, more than saw her boss stiffen. He snapped his gaze between her and the wrapper, between her and the note, *Chris's handwriting. Margins.* Finally, he put the wrapper in his sports coat pocket and ignored her for the rest of the briefing.

What the hell are you doing in this book, oh twin brother of mine? How was she going to tell their parents the reason she couldn't find her brother in Texas was because he was now part of some modern-day Mississippi Cthulhu cult? Assuming she could even explain what Cthulhu was to them. The worse part? This dropped the burden on her shoulders to carry the family's DNA to the next generation.

Wait, what the hell am I worried about having babies for? My brother is trying to destroy the fricking planet! Let's grab a bit of perspective here, shall we?

Once, he'd hid her backpack their first morning of high school. He'd held his pinky to his mouth, elbow out high. With his head shaved for football season, he was the perfect caricature of Dr. Evil. "I'll return it for...one million dollars." In her mind's eye, she pictured him in a catacomb somewhere, laughing maniacally, holding the Earth hostage for the price of a dark red high school backpack. She stifled a chuckle-snort. He transformed into a Knight of Ni from *Monty Python and the Holy Grail* and demanded a shrubbery.... Her imagination degraded from there.

By the time a dozen different scenarios had run through her head on what it meant for Chris's handwriting on the FBI's Task Force W Come-to-Jesus Meeting wall, McNeill had finished his presentation. Kent, Danny, and she requested a private meeting with him as soon as he adjourned and everyone else had left the room.

"We'd like to examine the book," Angela said. "I think I recognize the handwriting."

"Absolutely," he said, as he shut down the projector. "By the way, Officer McIver." He stepped up to Danny and offered a handshake. "I'm aware of your *lupus* heritage. I'll admit, I had my reservations about signing Hollingsworth's request, but I'm glad I did. Your performance has been exemplary."

Danny's ears turned red as he accepted the offer. "Thank you, sir. I've enjoyed the assignment."

Angela wanted to mock his aw-shucks attitude, but she wanted to get her hands on the book even more. She let him have his moment. McNeill led them through an inner door behind the projector screen and nodded to the agents posted inside. Angela immediately took the lead, putting on a pair of evidence gloves, and slowly flipping pages until she got to the notes in the margins. She turned to Danny. "What do you think?"

Danny leaned over the book and took a deep sniff. "I think it's him. Faint. It was windy the day he got out of prison."

"Who?" McNeill asked.

Angela let out a deep sigh. "My brother." She slowly closed the book.

She hadn't realized it, but McNeill had been holding his breath, too. "Agent, you don't know how happy I am to hear you say that."

She spun on the assistant director. "You knew?"

"Yes. His fingerprints were on the pages." He placed a folder next to the book.

Kent straightened his back in agitation. "This was a setup," he said in the level timbre Angela had come to recognize as pointed agitation.

McNeill matched Kent's gaze less than apologetically. "Yes."

Angela took her gloves off. "You were looking to see if I was in cahoots with Chris." She nodded. "I would have done the same thing, boss."

"Irrelevant," Kent said, "I would have, too." He turned his icy glare on McNeill. "If there's an operation involving my office, I want to know about it from now on."

McNeill raised his eyebrows at Danny.

Danny nodded. "You know us better than I thought."

Kent looked at both of them. "Danny works for me. You got a problem, you talk to me."

"I would've picked up your nervousness," Danny told Kent. "And you," he said to McNeill, "were testing me, too."

Kent looked off to the side and back again. Angela swore his scowl dropped the temperature in the office by ten degrees. "Again, irrelevant."

McNeill returned the scowl, degree for degree. "Your whole office is an incubator for this type of consulting arrangement. We haven't had the time to properly implement controls to handle the possibility of a catastrophic or even a partial *lupus* virus infection. You're under a microscope, and you'll remain under a microscope." He relaxed his shoulders but held Kent's eyes. "However, you are now let in on the situation. You wouldn't be if I didn't have faith in your abilities."

Kent took the offhand praise as it was intended, as a truce. He too backed down.

Crisis averted.

McNeill smiled and nodded and put the book in a large, leather messenger bag. He handed it to Kent. "Your next assignment is to investigate Dr. Stan Drapper."

"Who's that?" Angela asked.

"There's a reference to him in the book. Supposedly working on parallel dimensions. See why he's in the book and if he's responsible for the math."

Angela and Danny walked into Kent's office. "Hey, boss," Angela said. "Good weekend?"

Kent sipped his coffee. "I worked." He looked at a rolled-up paper in Angela's hand. "A supermarket tabloid, Agent Hollingsworth?"

"Yes, sir," she said, holding it up. The first blushes of embarrassment washed across her face.

Shit. Maybe not a good idea after all.

She handed it to him. "I'd like permission to investigate this while we're in Houston."

"Roman Numeral Stalker Takes his 12th Victim," he read aloud. He looked up at her with sincere concern apparent in his wrinkled eyes. After a few moments, he shifted to Danny. Without a smile, he said, "I assume there's a punchline here, Officer McIver."

Danny shrugged. "She's serious."

Kent gazed at her for a moment and opened the magazine to page two. Refusing to let the rag touch his desk, he read the article silently to himself. "What am I missing?"

Angela sighed with the same exasperation she used when Danny called her nuts. "Twelve disappearances? That's a high number even for gossip-mongers. Nine of them went missing in the downtown Houston area. The rest, just outside that. The article even lists names."

"Are you getting your intel from the tabloids now, Agent Hollingsworth?" Kent asked.

"No, sir. But this one piqued my interest while I waited in the grocery line for a sweet, old lady to count out exact change in nickels and pennies."

Danny leaned forward and pointed to the list of people in the article. "We ran these names. All of them have less than stellar reputations."

Kent sat up a little straighter in his chair. "These people really exist?"

Angela smiled. "Yep!"

"Last knowns are old," Danny said. "Houston cops aren't interested in finding them. Bad guys disappearing? Not exactly showing up on the nightly blotter."

"What makes you think this a Task Force W case?" Kent asked, skimming the article again.

"Three of the names," Danny answered, "are known *lupus*. Known to me, anyway. Earl Campbell, Joe Dan Wood, and Eugene Miller. Could be more than those three. Campbell there, when he'd come through Redstick, we'd run him off down the street as soon as we got his scent. Big troublemaker."

Angela flashed back to the revealing conversation she'd had with Redstick Police Chief Wilcox. "*We keep our territory clean*," he'd said. "Well?" she asked Kent.

"Someone kills some bad guys. Three of them are werewolves. I'll need a little more than that."

Danny scratched his jaw. "If someone's running around killing *lupus*, a war might break out. Maybe between the clans if it's a *lupus* doing the killing. Maybe between humans and *lupus*. In either case, we need to find out about it. If we're on the brink of war, we need to stop it."

Danny crossed his legs and rested his elbow on Detective Billy Alvarez's desk. Angela stood by the window sipping a cup of coffee.

"The reports vary from person to person," Alvarez said. "The most trustworthy one I've got—" he read from his computer screen "—is some guy showed up, asked for a cigarette, and as soon as he took his first puff, the power went out in the area. It's wasn't quite pitch black, but all the witnesses agreed it was darker than it should have been. No one knew what was happening. And…when the power came back on, the victim and the cigarette puffer were gone. This is all that was left—" He turned his monitor around.

Angela stepped a little closer while Danny leaned in. On the screen was a series of pictures. All of them were of Roman numerals on sidewalks, floors, and chairs.

"They look burned in," Danny said.

Alvarez nodded. "They are." He turned the monitor back around and read some more. "Suspect is of an indeterminate race, black hair, tall, stooped shoulders. Two people reported hearing what sounded like a Harley riding away."

Angela took a sip from her cup. "How scattered about in time are they?"

Alvarez grabbed a pencil and wrote while he flipped through the screens. "You know, we didn't purposely ignore these." His eyes jumped to Angela a few times. "The cases are still open. We're just overworked these days." He finished writing and handed the sheet to her.

Angela looked at the dates. "Once a month. Roughly." She handed the sheet to Danny. "Full moons?"

Danny shook his head. "No. Just the opposite. New moons. Darkest night of the month."

Alvarez laughed as he looked at the dates on the screen again. "So…what? We got a guy who thinks he's a werewolf, but can't read a calendar?"

"Looks like," Angela said, grinning. Danny wasn't smiling, though. In fact, he'd pressed his lips together and tugged at his earlobe.

Later, when they pulled out of the police station, she asked. "What's on your mind?"

"Morstat."

"What?"

"Not what. Who." He picked the sheet of paper back up and looked at it. "It's our bogeyman. What mothers tell little wildling children to watch out for."

"You mean a Fector? One of those werewolf-hunting Catholic priests?"

He shook his head at her. "No. We worried about them all the time. Morstat comes after bad little werewolves."

"What is a bad werewolf?" she asked. "You forget to howl at the moon or something?"

"We have our own laws," he snapped. "They keep us hidden. Safe."

"Sorry," she said. "What kind of laws?"

"We call it The Pact. All *Frenatus* swear to uphold it. For instance, we aren't allowed to kill another *lupus* without the consent of *Lupus Rex*."

"You aren't allowed to kill each other, but you can kill humans with impunity?"

"We aren't allowed to piss off the humans either. Killing one? That would do it."

Angela shifted from one foot to the other. "Killing humans that wander into your territory doesn't violate that law?"

"Redstick's on a state highway, for Christ's sake," he exclaimed. "We *are* part of the community, you know. We only take care of the bad guys when they come around looking to start some shit."

Lupus society made a bit more sense to Angela. "All right. I can see how violation of either one would lead to war." She stopped at a red light. "So, this Morstat comes after *lupis* who violate the Pact?"

"Maybe. The legend says he comes after the bad little boys and girls. Not adults. Cuts off their heads. Feeds 'em to his horse."

"Jesus Christ, Danny! Werewolf fairy tales are hardcore."

"Yeah, I guess so." He looked thoughtful. "In any case, he comes every 13 years for 13 heads. He only takes the heads on the new moon. And the victim must be in *lupus* form. But the count? The Roman numerals? The new moon? Too damned coincidental for me."

"Me, too," she said. "Thirteen, huh?"

"Right."

"Just our luck."

"Right."

"When's the next new moon?" she asked.

"Three nights from now."

"Well," she said, "Drapper's out of the country until after that. Might as well do some good."

Angela and Danny were sitting in their car in Sunnyside, probably the most decrepit area in downtown Houston. Danny insisted the area was crawling with *lupis*, and when pressured for more information, he confessed it was only hearsay on his part. According to rumors, there was a whole *lupis* underground who sold their sexual services to the depraved: men who wanted to screw a *lupa*, women who wanted to screw a *lupus*, and everything in between.

"This, um, takes bestiality to a whole new level," she muttered.

"Yeah," he agreed, looking up the street to the blinking traffic lights. "I wonder if Task Force W doesn't need a vice squad."

"So, you believe this Morstat is real, don't you?" she

asked, eager to change the subject.

"I'm not sure." He shrugged. "I will say that most of the legends we've grown up with have more or less turned out to be true."

"Yeah, well, after some of the weird shit I've seen on this job, you'll have to convince me it does *not* exist."

He turned and gave her a sideways smirk as their radio squawked, "Power outage reported. Wilmington and Cullen."

"Gotcha," Danny murmured as he pressed the "GPS" button on their computer screen. "Hell, that's only four blocks over. Hit it!"

Angela pulled out into the street, tires screeching, lights flashing, and siren blaring. As they neared the intersection, Danny rolled down the window and sampled the night air. Angela slowed and turned the siren off. The roads were mostly deserted.

"Ahead!" Danny shouted. "I hear something in the loading alley behind that strip mall."

Angela sped up and took the turn around the corner of the building. She braked when her headlights showed a tall, lanky man swing a long sword at the neck of…a werewolf. They were all the way at the other end of the alley.

"Don't lose him!" Danny growled as Sword-Man climbed aboard a motorcycle and rode off.

As they passed the headless werewolf body, Angela peeked out her window. The body turned to dust under a slight breeze and 'XIII' remained there, etched into the concrete. When she looked back out her windshield, the road ahead had disappeared in a thick wall of fog. Peeking at her in the distance was the taillight of a motorcycle. "Danny?"

"Just keep going…" He said. He'd hung his head out his window and was squinting through the fog. "I don't think…I don't think we're in Kansas anymore."

Angela slowed down as the fog grew thicker.

"Don't stop! Catch the fucker!" His eyes had turned pale blue.

"Get yourself under control, Officer!" she ordered.

What the hell am I supposed to do if he changes and I'm driving?

"I'm under contr—"

The motorcycle rider had stopped and was setting his foot on the ground. Angela pulled up short. The dim headlights were good enough to show the man to be well over six and a half feet tall. He wore black jeans and jacket without any patches she could see. If he was outlaw, he wasn't affiliated. The skin on his face was shrunken, pale, and his eyes, dead.

This was not a live person.

Angela and Danny got out. She pulled her weapon but held it down at the ready.

He just cut the head off a werewolf, for fuck's sake! Tough sonuvabitch. I don't think silver's gonna do shit to him.

The biker took two steps towards Danny. "If you follow me any farther, *lupus*, you will be unable to return. I have no need of you. Turn back now."

Danny took two steps forwards himself. He'd clenched his fists. The growl of his other nature rumbled in her ears. "Why did you take my dad, Morstat?"

Morstat stared at Danny and spoke in level tones, almost matter-of-factly. "I did not harvest Robert McIver. Job McIver killed him. I harvested him, the murderer."

"Uncle Job killed my dad? That's bullshit!"

Morstat snapped his fingers, and his bike rolled up. In the place where there should have been a gas tank sat a head, barely human, barely *lupus*, wires and flexible, translucent hoses pumping viscous fluids of assorted colors through them. Some went into the head, some came out. "Speak!"

"Hello, Danny-Boy," the disembodied head said.

Danny cried out, "Uncle Job!"

"Yes." The crackly voice sounded like it was talking with half its mouth in water. "Morstat speaks the truth. I killed your dad."

Danny's eyes widened, and his mouth hung open. He clenched and unclenched his fists and walked up stiff-legged. "Uncle Job? I don't understand! Why?!"

"I wanted what was his."

Danny paused for a moment. "My mom?"

"Yes. My brother, your dad, he…he was a good man. Undeserving of the death I wrought. I now serve *Statera Mortis*."

"Are you satisfied?" Morstat asked. "Will you turn back now?"

Danny dropped to his knees and stared off into the distance.

Morstat lifted his leg over the seat of his bike while Angela holstered her weapon and rushed to Danny's side

"How long will Uncle Job serve you?" he asked.

"As long as Robert McIver remains dead by his hand. Though I feel that may not be long."

Angela helped Danny to his feet but addressed Morstat. She had a hundred questions. Well, start with the basics. "Who…or what…are you?

"I am the Balancer of Deaths," Morstat said. He pushed a button, and his motorcycle started up. It wasn't quite as loud as a Harley-Davidson, but it thundered. "I was born of Julius Caesar's blood the day Marcus Junius Brutus, a man who swore to die before he let Caesar do so, spilled it upon the

Senate floor." He revved the throttle, and the face mounted between his knees screamed in pain with a thousand voices. "I balance the scales between betrayal and honor."

"You're done for another thirteen years," she asked, "right?"

"No," he answered with a slow, sad shake of his head. "The scales remain unbalanced by an unwieldy amount. Such is life. Such is death. With the Forsaken Dweller near, I must work to fulfill my destiny and restore the equilibrium before the end." He shifted his bike into gear and rode off. The mist evaporated as the sound of his motorcycle grew dim.

"No, ma'am, we aren't building an interdimensional portal," Dr. Drapper said. Angela could tell he wanted to laugh, but the FBI badge seemed to have removed any humor from the question. "We don't build things here. We're theoretical physicists." He let out a nervous chuckle instead. "My wife would tell you that I can't change a light bulb."

"So, this theory about opening portals where two universes touch is just so much hoopla?"

"Absolutely not!" Drapper gave her a look as if she'd called his baby ugly. "It's all math at this point, but…wait, you know about the theory?" He looked at his whiteboard. To Angela, it was a cornucopia of letters, numbers, and Greek symbols reminiscent of what a crossword puzzle written for Azathoth, H.P. Lovecraft's god of chaos, would have looked like.

"It's…come up in one of our cases," Danny said.

He sighed and shook his head. "As I said, it's only math at this point. We're decades away from building anything."

Angela shared a look of approval with Danny, and he pulled out copies of the pages from the Spationomicon. His name, not hers. He spoke Latin, and *Spatium* was the closest word he could come up with meaning 'another, all-encompassing place.'

"Do these formulae mean anything to you?" Angela asked.

Dr. Drapper read the first page of math as someone else might read a novel. A blood vessel pulsed in his right temple. "Stinking internet. They even got my name here!" He shook his head and finished reading it. He flipped back and forth a few pages and underlined a few sections. He muttered, "No way."

"Problems?" Danny asked.

"Can I put this into the computer and run it? Some of this doesn't make sense to me. I want to verify some things."

Angela and Danny shrugged to each other. "Sure," she said.

"Thanks. Shouldn't take long."

She and Danny went through two cups of coffee, two large unsweet teas, two waters, two Subway sandwiches, and three potty breaks over an agonizing eight hours. About the time she was ready to storm the lab with gun and badge flashing, Dr. Drapper called them in. "The model's finished. You want to see it?"

Angela choked on her tea. "You built it?"

"Built…?" He paused for a moment before he chuckled. "No, I didn't build anything in the sense you're thinking. I modeled the math." He pointed to a series of computer monitors.

Angela and Danny watched the video. Two bubbly clouds circled each other.

"This—" Drapper said, pointing to the one on the left "—represents our universe. The other represents another one. This is the math I've been working on. However—" he punched a key on the keyboard "—this is where the other math picks up." The two bubble-clouds moved closer together and touched. "When I zoom in, you'll see how they interact with each other. Where the bubbles from the two different dimensions intersect, nothing spectacular happens. However, if two bubbles share more than an intersection, energy is transferred between them."

"Could something from one universe move into the other universe?" Angela asked.

"Of course." He took his glasses off and started cleaning them. "Energy. I thought I explained that."

"No, I mean like a person or something?"

"Well, we're made up of energy. $E=MC^2$. I suppose if someone was converted into pure energy, they could make the trip."

Danny grinned. "Like in Star Trek?"

"Yeah, I suppose."

Angela stared at the cookbook on how to bring something over to chow down on Earth.

"I'm actually kind of miffed," Drapper said.

"Why's that?" Angela asked.

"Someone's already figured it all out. This research was supposed to keep me busy for a decade. I published a paper a few years ago that theorized this. And now to find it already done? Pah!" He looked at the sheets. "Who's the scientist who solved it?"

"We don't know."

"What?" Drapper's eyes bulged. "This is Nobel-level work." He paused a moment and smirked. "Matt Damon been solving problems on chalkboards again?"

"No…" Angela tilted her head to the side as one of the

bubble-clouds consumed the other. She pointed at the screen. "What just happened?"

Dr. Drapper ran the simulation backwards for a few seconds and watched the conclusion. "Oh. Yeah, that was something I didn't take into account but found fascinating." He pointed to a section of math on one of the sheets that he'd underlined. "This part right here. If enough of the bubbles line up and the energy transfer is high enough, the receiving universe will start absorbing the source universe. Picture a siphon. The lower end of the hose pulls the fuel from the higher end; once the transfer starts, the lower energy state will pull the higher state with it."

"Wait," she said. "You're saying that one universe eats the other?"

"Eat implies an active decision. I'm not sure that applies here. More likely, anything at the source location would convert to energy and be absorbed by the parasite universe."

"How long would it take to finish the transfer?"

"That's a good question." Drapper interlaced his finger and tapped his thumbs together while he considered it. "It's a function of the dimensional surface tension and energy differential. It could take as little as a thousand years to ten billion years to absorb a solar system."

"It couldn't be done faster than that?"

Drapper looked at Danny with curiosity. "Well, I suppose if there was an intelligence at the receiving side, the other universe, controlling the transfer from our universe, it could be done faster. But spontaneous absorption? A Big Bang-sized boom. A Big Pucker." He chuckled again at his own joke.

"How would you stop it?" Danny asked.

"You are asking a bunch of questions for something

that's highly theoretical," Drapper said. "What's going on here?"

Angela stepped up. "We've got a cult who thinks they can trigger this manually."

"Impossible with today's technology," Dr. Drapper proclaimed.

"That may be but knowing the process will help us track them down."

"Of course," he agreed. "Hmm. How to stop it. Well, stop the transfer early enough, or increase the energy level on the other side. Lift the hose, in other words."

Although the good doctor was relaying the information in layman's terms, and she understood it as far as he was explaining it, something didn't make sense. The Forsaken Dweller was supposed to be the one doing the eating. In Lovecraft's world, the elder gods took eons to do things.

Do we really have anything to worry about? We're talking billions of years here.

Artemis hinted the danger was more imminent.

"Doctor," she asked, "Let's assume there is an intelligence controlling the transfer. What would something like that look like?"

Dr. Drapper frowned in deep concentration and looked to his keyboard. He punched a few keys, and two large bubbles appeared on the screen. He pushed another button, and they superimposed themselves on each other. "The entire universe would have to be under control."

When the simulation finished, a mathematical formula appeared on the screen. The letters and symbols literally meant nothing to Angela, but with a little imagination, they looked like…"Doctor," she asked, "What do those symbols mean?"

"That's the formula that describes the receiving universe…if it were to control a spontaneous absorption."

"Do they look like anything? Like maybe two words?"

He tilted his head up and rubbed his chin, looking at the symbols. "Why, yes. They look like they spell 'Forsaken Dweller.'" He tapped his thumbs together again. "Wait. That's…that's impossible."

Angela and Danny both raised their eyebrows and crossed their arms.

"If I understand this correctly, that formula means spontaneous absorption could only occur if the intelligence was the size of an entire universe." He stuck a finger in the air. "No, wait, that's not right. The universe would have to be the, well, it would have to be the intelligence itself. A living being. The universe would have to be a living being!" He slowly picked up the pages of the Spationomicon. "Where did you find these?"

"Danny, you're the storyteller," she said. "I've got to go to the ladies' room. Again."

Episode 7: Responsibility

Angela stood in the middle of the field and stared across the gently rolling hills to a stand of trees. Bluebonnets were in full bloom, and the knolls looked like someone had colored them by tapping a blue crayon on the landscape. A slight breeze kicked up and blew her hair into her eyes. She reached up and pulled it behind her ear.

"We're in position," her ear comm sounded.

She knelt down and opened a long, wooden box. Inside, nestled in velvet, was the arrow Artemis had given her months ago. She gently lifted it from the box, and with a shrug, snapped it in half over her knee. "Stand by," she relayed.

Which is what she did for ten minutes.

"Maybe she knows you're hiding in the woods."

"You got friends around here somewhere?" a woman's voice asked from behind.

Angela spun around with a startled movement. "Yes, but it's not a trap!" she sputtered. Artemis stood there with a wide, genuine, friendly smile. Today, she was dressed in black leather. Everywhere.

Lord, she's hot!

"I was beginning to think you wouldn't show."

"Yeah, sorry about that," Artemis said. "I was arguing with Apollo. He wanted me to ignore the summons."

Angela moaned and shook her head in disgust. "Di, don't take this the wrong way, but your brother, he's a dick."

Artemis laughed. "You didn't grow up with him. He's a

good ally, though. Tough when he needs to be. He's just used to doing things his way." She adjusted the bow on her back and stepped forward. She offered her arms out for a sisterly embrace.

Angela didn't hesitate to return it. The two-week vacation she'd spent with her had forged a deep friendship. It seemed like a faraway dream but being in front of her brought it all back. "It's good to see you, Di."

"And you, Ang." Artemis stepped back, but they continued to hold each other's wrists. It's been too long.

Angela blushed. "You only gave me one arrow."

"True. We'll have to do something about that." They fully broke the embrace. "So, why have you called me?"

"We're fumbling in the dark here," Angela confessed. "We need help. All kinds. Tactical, strategic, logistical…Moving in and out of places like you do, that's handy."

Artemis rubbed her forearms. She stared at the ground before she looked back up. "I'll ask again, but they still want something in return. You're one planet in an entire universe."

Angela handed her a thumb drive along with a folder containing a briefing of the stored information. "This contains all the intelligence we have on the Forsaken Dweller. We recovered a book that contains a whole slew of math and physics that explains exactly how the dweller is supposed to do what it does."

Artemis tilted her head up a smidge but stared at the items. She took the folder and read through the briefing with lightning speed. As she did so, the expression on her face transformed from borderline interest to outright surprise. "The Forsaken Dweller is a living universe?" She wandered in circles for a few moments. "This does explain some things! No wonder we've never found the beast. We couldn't see the forest for the trees."

"Will you help us?" Angela asked.

"I'll take this information back. I make no promises. But if what's in here pans out, it will help our case."

Angela was pleased she said 'our case' and not 'your case.'

"Hollingsworth," Angela gasped out. Answering the phone was the last thing she wanted to do right as she tried to balance two armloads of files and hold the phone to her ear at the same time.

There was a slight chuckle on the other end, and a friendly voice asked, "Apart from being sexy, what do you do for a living where you have to answer your phone with your last name?"

"Randy?" A flush warmed her neck. Angela found herself giggling at the lame one-liner.

Did I just giggle?

She couldn't recall the last time she'd giggled.

Oh, yeah. I remember now. The night before I caught Karl in bed with the cheerleader.

In either case, girls giggle. Girls with crushes on boys. Not FBI agents talking to contacts.

"Yes, ma'am," he said. "Who else? Wait! Have I got competition on who's allowed to call you sexy?"

"I don't give up my secrets that easily," she teased, dropping the files on Danny's desk. "What are you doing?"

"Working on wiping out illiteracy," Randy bragged with exasperation in his voice. "It's a full-time job."

"Well, you keep giving books away, you won't be able to afford to fund that project." She sat down at her desk, the files forgotten.

"I only give books away to people I like. And those I trap under avalanches of shelves."

She giggled again and looked up over her desk. Danny caught her eyes and chuckled.

Oh, shit, he can hear the whole conversation.

"Okay, Casanova," she said, "that's enough."

"Well, I've never!" Randy said, mock-insulted. "And here I was, doing you a favor."

"What kind of favor is that?"

"Someone came to the store this morning and bought some H.P. Lovecraft. I asked him if he'd ever heard of the Forsaken Dweller. He claimed he didn't, but he got really nervous after that."

Angela sat a little straighter. "I'll be right over," she said and hung up.

Later, as they drove up Interstate 30, Danny asked, "Who's Randy? And why does he call you sexy and good-looking and sound like he's laying the Don Juan on as thick as maple syrup on Sunday morning pancakes?"

"The owner of the Dusty Spine Bookstore. Strictly research on the Forsaken Dweller."

"Uh huh," he said.

"He's nice," she insisted. "Sweet daughter. Clumsy, though."

"If you say so, Scooter."

They drove the rest of the trip in silence, but whenever Angela managed to catch a glimpse of Danny's face, he had a smirk.

When she opened the store's door, she had to pull a little harder than normal. "Hey!" she said as she stepped in, "you finally put a hydraulic closer on this death trap."

Randy came from around the counter, a big smile on his

face. "Yeah, I got tired of replacing the window." He looked over her shoulder when Danny came in, and his smile faltered to nosy. "Hi, I'm Randy Tracer."

"Randy," Angela said, "This is Officer Danny McIver, my partner."

The smile disappeared completely. "Partner?"

She blinked a couple of times as his question registered. "Oh, my gosh!" she exclaimed. "Work partner! I'm, uh," she stammered, "I'm an agent for the Bederal—"

"*Bed*eral?" Danny snickered, tilting his head and rubbing his grinning mouth.

"—shut up, Danny," she snapped. "I'm an FBI agent. I work with him!"

Randy stared at both of them for a couple of heartbeats as his smile slowly returned. "FBI Agent?" He blinked again. "So, all this time, I've been an unpaid informant?"

"Um, no. Yes. Not really. A case we're working on. People think they're living in a Lovecraftian world. I had to read up on it. I never thought I'd enjoy the stories." She smiled and put her hand on his arm. "Sorry, Randy. I didn't mean to keep anything from you. Not on purpose, anyway."

"No problemo!" he confessed. "I'm a bit surprised, though. You don't seem old enough to be an FBI agent. I figured you to be a college student."

Angela's face blushed hotly at the compliment.

Danny piped in. "You really thought she was that young?" He looked at her with the studious eye of a man evaluating an earthworm for fishability. "Yeah, I guess so. Maybe."

Angela elbowed him in the ribs without taking her eyes off Randy. "Good genes, I guess. I'm surprised you remembered our Forsaken Dweller conversation."

"What can I say? You leave an impression every time you come in here." He smiled and held his hands out to his sides. "You aren't my typical horror junkie. I think you've read every Lovecraft book I've got."

Danny had walked farther into the store and was reading the titles on the New Releases table. He cracked a grin over Randy's shoulder and shook his head.

Angela ignored him. "I'm glad you got a good memory," she said. "So, tell me about your customer."

"No one's known about anything called the Forsaken Dweller. Not until today anyway. As soon as I asked, he got all nervous like, said no, dropped a twenty on the counter, and left without getting his change."

"Any idea what his name was?"

"No. First time here that I recall. What is it anyway?"

"Cult leader," Danny interjected, saving Angela the need to lie to Randy.

Thanks, partner!

"That's what he calls himself," Danny continued. "Can you describe him?"

"No. But…" He pointed over his shoulder to a small security camera. "Not every part-time employee we hire is as honest as they want to be. That helps them stay that way. I bet I got a picture of him."

"That would be awesome!" Angela said.

As soon as Randy turned around, Danny threw a questioning glance at Angela and mouthed, "Awesome?" To top it off, he put his hands on his cheeks.

She gave him a *Go To Hell* look.

A few minutes later, they were looking at a low-resolution printout of a short, skinny rat-man with mussed hair and clothes that were too big for him. Danny blurted out, "Well if it ain't Marion Dinkleton, a.k.a. Speed."

"Yeah," Angela growled, "I've been looking forward to meeting that little bastard again."

"I take it he's a bad guy?" Randy asked.

"Not really," Angela said. "Just a wannabe."

"Hmm. Not that I'm greedy or anything, but is there, uh, you know, a reward for his capture? College tuition soon."

Danny pulled out his phone and scrolled through the Wanted Fugitive list. "In fact, there is. $2,000."

While Danny took down Randy's contact information, Angela put in a request to get a warrant to acquire all the traffic cams pictures and videos in the area.

As they pulled out of the parking lot, Danny said, "That man has got the hots for you, you know that, right?"

"No, he doesn't."

"Angela, you forget about this nose," he said, tapping it. "I can smell attraction. And unless I'm mistaken, he triggers a case of the Itchy Britches in you, too."

"Shut up, Officer McIver."

"I never took you for a tattoo fan."

"It's a long walk to Fort Worth, Officer McIver."

Danny laughed. "Yes, ma'am, it is."

Angela stepped into the rundown single-story house and wrinkled her nose after *Clear* had sounded. "Dammit, Speed, if you're going to hide out in a shit hole, have the common decency to at least live like a human being?"

SWAT had him on his knees, hands behind his head.

"Front toilet's backed up," he said.

Danny pinched his nose between his thumb and forefinger for a moment before blowing out a long breath. "Shoulda called a plumber."

The SWAT team members appeared oblivious through their air masks.

"How'd you find me?"

"We put the word out that we were looking for a Rat Man," Angela said, "and the tips came pouring in."

Speed bit down on his lower lip and slumped over. One of his front teeth had disappeared since their last meeting. It gave him an "All I want for Chrithmath ith my two front teeth" lisp.

"What? Did you honestly think I wouldn't find you?" She looked around the room and found some newspaper. "Didn't your daddy ever teach you that you never chase someone?" She pulled a chair from the kitchen and set it in front of him. "Paths will cross eventually." Covering the seat with the newspaper, she sat down. "And when they do, deal with them then. FBI agents cross many paths, Speed."

"Okay. I can tell. Yep. You're pithed at me."

Angela was not amused but couldn't help sneering and snorting at Speed's ridiculous new speech impediment. As if he needed anything else to make him appear dumber. And when the snort turned into an edgy laugh, she didn't realize how horrifying she could be. "Still pissed? Why would I be pissed, Speed? Because you left me at the hands of a smelly biker with a perky tit fetish?" When his eyes drifted to her breasts, she leaned forward and slapped him across the face. "Up here, shithead."

Danny cleared his throat and looked at the SWAT team. "Why don't you guys wait in the hallway. I think the agent has this interrogation under control."

They all chuckled but did as he asked.

"Yeah. Still pithed," he said. "I'm sure there's something I can do, right? I mean, I'm a businessman. I know how to work deals."

"Do you now?" She stood up. The blood pounded in her ears. Speed's eyes widened as she handed her pistol and her badge to Danny. "Hold this, Officer?"

Interrogations work best when the suspect doesn't know it's an interrogation. *Angela's Interrogation Tome, page 9*.

"I got a deal for you, Speed. You tell me everything I want to know, and I won't shove your head in that stopped up shitter of yours."

Danny took her items of commission and cleared his throat again. "Agent Hollingsworth? Maybe we should take him downtown."

"Yeah!" Speed agreed. "Downtown!"

"Nooo," she said lightly shaking her head. "I think this place is just right." She brushed off her sleeves and pant legs. "So, Speed. You want to help us or should I start looking for that bathroom of yours?"

"I don't know nothin'!" Speed insisted. "Now get me my damned lawyer!"

"Okay, Speed, I'll get you a lawyer," Danny said. "But I got one question first. Are you on drugs? Is that why you can't see what's about to happen?"

"Whadda you mean?"

"While we're waiting on your lawyer, this agent is gonna kick your ass. I'm not gonna be able to stop her. I'm a cop. She's a federal agent. She overrules me."

"No, I'm not gonna kick his ass," Angela said. "I ain't got the time to fuck with that." She turned to Danny and winked. "Bite him."

Speed shifted his eyes back and forth between the two of them. "Bite me?"

Danny grimaced and sighed. "Well, since you asked so

nicely, Speed." He looked down at the floor for a moment. When he looked up, his eyes had turned pale blue. Agony rippled across his face as his cheekbones rearranged themselves, extended his mouth out into a snout. Hair sprouted, Ears moved up and out. He snarled, licked his lips, and took a step forward.

Speed screamed out, "Get the fuck back! Christ! A fuckin' werewolf? Help me in here!"

Angela put a hand on Danny's shoulder. "Hold on a sec. I think Speed here wants to help out our case. Right, Speed?"

"Yeah! Yeah! Just get that fucker away from me!"

Danny backed off into a corner and changed back to human. "Damn," he growled. "I was looking forward to some rat this afternoon."

Angela wasn't sure how much was acting and how much wasn't.

"Christ on a Crutch," Speed whispered. "I thought those guys were making shit up. You really are a fuckin' werewolf."

Angela sat down again. "I'm not sure I can hold him back again." She raised her eyebrows questioningly. "Understand what I'm saying here?"

Speed licked his lips and nodded but kept his eyes on Danny. "Yeah, but know I was just scared, okay? I act out when I'm scared."

"What are you afraid of, Speed?" Angela asked.

He glanced back and forth between them. "Those crazy dweller cult fuckers, that's who!"

"Why are they after you?"

"Cause I tried to sell them an old textile mill."

Angela let the surprise shine through on her face. Sometimes it paid to pretend you were behind the eight ball. It was easy when you really were. "You own a textile mill?"

"Yes. Well, not really. Won a property deed in a poker game. When the sale went through, turned out the property deed was forged." He grimaced. "Let me tell you, those fuckers are not very forgiving."

"I thought you were a wrench, not a confidence man. You've impressed me, Speed!"

Speed puffed his chest out. "I'm a businessman."

Ego massages, free for the asking! *Angela's Interrogation Tome, page 5.*

"What did they need a textile mill for?"

"Needed a place to perform some ritual. Something about the timing and opening the hole. They needed a place out of the way."

Angela sat back in her chair and crossed her arms.

She grinned. "Do you think it's all bunk?" she asked.

"I don't know." He shrugged.

"Hmm." Angela nodded. "So…where do you think they're gonna have this ritual at?"

"I don't know, Agent Hollingsworth," he shook his head. "If I knew, I'd tell you."

Speed jumped back when Danny stepped up. "How do you get this information?"

"I hear things."

"Have you heard anything else?"

Speed shifted around on his knees and bit his lip. "Well," he said, staring into Angela's eyes, "I heard that your brother was helping them. And that they want you too. Something about twins."

"Twins?!" Angela blurted out. "What about twins?!" She stood up and grabbed him by the collar. Her mouth went dry.

Danny took a step forward.

"I...I don't know, Agent Hollingsworth! Honest! That's all I know!"

She released his collar and frowned at Danny. Concern clouded his features. She stood quietly for a few moments as a chill scurried up her back. Danny's heavy breathing was apparent.

She shook off the chill and reached for Speed's arm. "Well, we're going to put you in 'protective custody,'" she said. "We don't want some mean ol' cultists to kill you, now do we?"

"Maybe that's for the best," he said. "I'm tired of hiding. Can I go to the bathroom first?"

Danny tilted his head to the side. "Yeah." He stepped into the hallway. "Commander, will you check the bathroom, please?"

While Speed did his business, Danny huddled with Angela at the front door and away from the smell. "You think he's telling the truth? About the ritual coming up soon? About them being after you?"

"I don't know." She shook her head. "I have absolutely no clue what I bring to the table."

"Speed mentioned it. There's no way he could have known you had a twin and that he was working with them. I think the intel's good."

"Yeah." Angela pursed her lips and nodded reluctantly. "The doormen seem to like experimenting on them." She looked down the hallway at the commander.

He shrugged his shoulders.

Angela yelled down the hallway. "Hurry up, Marion!" She leveled a sardonic at Danny.

No answer.

Danny rushed down the hallway and knocked on the

door. "Pinch it off, Speed! Time to go!"

Still no answer other than Disturbed playing on a boom box.

They looked at each other and pulled their pistols.

"Speed! Open up!" Angela ordered as she wiggled the locked doorknob.

When silence echoed back at them, Danny kicked the door in.

Speed had pushed the toilet into a false wall. Disappearing into the spot where it should have been was a man-sized hole. They both peered over the edge. It dropped straight down about eight feet and turned north into a tunnel.

Danny took a sniff. "I don't smell him over the sewage."

"You fucking bowlegged crotch-scratching cockroach!" Angela yelled down the hole. "Keep looking over your shoulder for me, shithead!"

Danny stood back. "Wow. Somewhere there's a sailor whose tattoo just blushed."

After calls from local and state police asking why one of his agents was calling up and demanding a full man-hunt mobilization for Speed, Kent told Angela to take the day off. And more if she needed it.

The look in his eyes left no doubt it was a non-negotiable suggestion.

Angela didn't know what to do with nearly a whole day to herself. She was on paid leave, but unable to investigate anything. Heather was at work. Her parents were in Houston visiting her Uncle Bill.

"Hot tea and a book," she grumbled. "Yeah, I'd much rather do that than go shoot a bad guy." She flopped face down on the couch. "Not."

Her phone rang, and she snatched it up. "Hollingsworth! What?"

"Oh, wow," the friendly voice said. "A two-word greeting today."

"Randy?" She sat up and pulled her feet under her. "Hi! Everything okay?"

"Yeah. I, um, wanted to…I wanted to see how the book was coming along." He paused. "Sounds like you're busy though."

"Actually, I'm not. That's the problem."

"Good!" he exclaimed. "I've got you all to myself."

"I guess you do!" She giggled.

The hell with it!

She giggled again. "The book's exciting!"

That time, he giggled. "Exciting? Lovecraft?"

"Yeah, Lovecraft." Giggle.

Oh, Lord, what have I gotten myself into?

Tiffany yelled in the background. "Dad, ask her!"

Her heart fluttered. "Ask me what?"

Randy took a deep breath. "Would you be interested in, well, seeing, you know, a movie? *The Necronomicon* is playing at the dollar theater."

"A movie?"

"And dinner!" Tiffany shouted in the background.

"Only if you take me to dinner first," Angela said, her mood shooting for orbit as Speed all but disappeared from her thoughts.

"And dinner," he added. His voice got distant. "I can handle it, Tif!"

"Dinner and a movie!" Angela cooed. "Hmm. A real date. I haven't been on one of those since—"

Angela's door crashed in. Four men in black ski masks ran through the doorway and across the dining room. She jumped up and glanced with chagrin at her pistol. Five running steps around the couch and to the breakfast bar stood between her and dead bad guys.

She lifted her phone to her face. "Randy, call Danny!" She took a step backwards and yelled into the phone, "Four of you to take down little ol' me? Ski season ain't for another few months!"

The adrenaline pumping through her veins slowed everything down. The carpeting massaged the soles of feet.

The men no longer ran. They seemed to be walking as they moved into the living room.

She turned away from them and shoved her phone down her pants.

Maybe they won't raid the cash register.

She took one step around her couch as she grabbed two pillows. Threw them at her closest attacker.

"Ha! A couple of throw pillows, jerkwad!"

Her assailant spent two heartbeats ducking instinctively. She used those beats to dash farther around the couch. Towards her pistol.

The carpet jumped up towards her face.

That's weird!

Her arms refused to protect her from it. It hit her in the nose.

Shit! Taser!

A black bag slipped over her head. Four sets of arms each grabbed a limb.

Ew, an octopus.

Wait! Fish smell.

She yelled, "They ate fish!" but all she managed was

235

"Furbble" and a stream of drool.

A muffled voice. "You didn't think we forgot about you, did you?"

A sharp pain in her upper arm.

The world went even darker.

*clink. *clank. *brrzzap*

Drills. Yeah. Drills. That's it. Drilling my head. They're turning me into Frankenstein's Monster. To hell with the Bride shit. Even God screwed up the first time. That's why he made woman. We're perfect. Except for that stinking chocolate addiction. And Italian food. Damn, I love Italian food. And cowboys.

Angela fluttered her eyelids a couple of times. When the light didn't scorch her brain, she left them open. She tried to raise her hand to wipe the hair out of her face. Both arms were tied down. Tightly. Legs, too. She shook her hair out of her face instead and looked around. The last time she'd been in a lab like this, it had been a dusty barn. Or a moldy, church basement. This place was high-tech....

Other than the metal gurney I'm strapped into.

Linoleum floors. White walls. Fluorescent ceiling lights. One door in the far corner. She couldn't see if one was behind her. An IV tube dangled from her hand, neatly taped.

They've stepped up their game. This is bad.

She pulled against her restraints again. Flat screen monitors hung along the walls as well as some new-fangled, transparent models.

The movies! Randy! Crap! I hope he's not pissed. Ha! I hope he called Danny.

A doorman walked into her view, it's tri-fold mouth closed and squelchy skin roiling over wiry muscles. *Oh, fuck!* Her heart rate jumped. It ignored her and disappeared from her view.

Dozens of men and women were busy typing in commands on the computer keyboards arranged in a circular NASA control center layout. She sat in the middle. She strained her neck to look around. One other gurney sat close. Empty.

"Hey, Ang," Chris's voice called from her side.

"Chris?" she exclaimed as he stepped into her view, wearing jeans and an AC/DC t-shirt. "Fuck! Really?" She looked at his arms, at the fresh track marks. "Shit! You're shooting up again?"

The smile on his face vanished. He crossed his arms to hide the needle scabs and stared at his feet. Still, her FBI agent's analytical eye told her he was relaxed. Confident, even.

"Dammit, Chris!" she said, shaking her head and pursing her lips. "I'd heard you were messed up with these fuckers, but I didn't believe it!"

He looked up at her with glassy eyes and dilated pupils. "Wow, man! You knew?"

"Of course, I knew, you little shit! You left your fingerprints all over the math book. Doesn't make it any less surprising to see your ass walking around here like you own the place."

He blinked a few times and looked over to a doorman monitoring a security camera feed. He spoke a few sentences in some foreign language, and it responded back with an apparent negative.

A chill rattled her shoulders at the sight of its mouth rolling open. "Lithuanian?" she asked, trying to keep sane.

"Yeah. Older dialect though. Really old. Ancient, in fact." He indicated the doorman with a dull wave of his arm. "It's their native language."

"Chris, how the fuck did you get mixed up with these guys?"

He shrugged. "They found me. One of their guys works at the FBI."

Drones in the FBI?

"He read a report about the time I translated that notebook for you. They offered me a chance to redeem myself."

"Redeem yourself?"

"Yeah. I read those reports, your notes, my psych evals." He worked hard to stare at her with a steady eye. "Your concerns about me."

Angela did her best to maintain a neutral expression.

Must be someone high up to have of access to that information.

"I don't understand the science," he said, "but..." He stopped for a moment and looked around in short, jerky movements. "Wow! I'm sorry, Ang, are you thirsty?"

"Yeah, a little. Headache, too." She wasn't lying. Her head throbbed with her heartbeat.

"I'll be right back." He rushed away, stumbling once, as a man came up and checked her blood pressure.

"Agent Hollingsworth," the man said. "I'm Dr. Connors. You should know the Forsaken Dweller asked for you specifically. You've kept it entertained since your encounter with Lilith."

"Me?" Conrad Sabine and the picture of her and Heather with the writing on the back came to mind. "Why is he interested in me?"

"You are the only human to have put all the pieces together." Connors looked over his shoulder. "And with a twin brother? Oh, we simply had to have him, too."

"Wait," Angela said. "You recruited him because of me?"

Dr. Connors smiled and collected his tools. "Recruit implies a concerted effort. Once he found out he could have all the heroin he wanted, he begged to work for us."

"You sonuvabitch!" Angela growled. "He was clean!"

"Now, now, Agent Hollingsworth," Dr. Connors cooed. "There's no reason to get upset. We've given him purpose and a chance at redemption. Something you couldn't do."

Angela struggled against the restraints as Connors walked off behind her.

A few moments later, Chris showed up with a glass of water and a folding straw. He pushed a button on the side, and the gurney rotated to a near-vertical position. "Sorry, I can't let you go. Here." He held up two aspirin. "Open up."

She took the proffered pills with just enough water to swallow them and sate her thirst; who knew when she'd get to pee again? Being strapped to a gurney was no way to experience the pleasure of a full bladder. "Chris, why are you mixed up with these guys?"

"It's my chance to do good. Like you.

"What do you mean 'do good?'"

He put the cup down and pulled up a chair. His face fell, and he chewed his inner lip. "You've always been the smart one. The good one. Everything you touch turns to gold. Me? Everything I touch turns to shit."

"That's bullshit, and you know it."

"No, Ang. Look at how many children you saved working for the FBI." He stared down at his feet. "You're as close to being a superhero as anyone I know. Mom, Dad, I know they're disappointed in me. And that's just with the stuff they know about." He raised his gaze back up to her. "If they knew all my shit that you'd hid from them?" He shook his head. "I didn't realize I was such a burden on you until I read those evals."

Angela let him talk and occasionally glanced over his shoulder to the security station and studied the camera screen.

"You were right to send me to jail." A tear rolled down his cheek. "What kind of son beats the shit out of his dad?"

She wished she had a piece of gum. "You're better now. That therapy did you good." She wiggled against her restraints. "You've had a little setback. We can fix it. Let me free. We can still go home. Mom and Dad are worried about you. You missed Dad's birthday, you know. Double-decker, chocolate sour cream cake."

"I'm not going home until I've fixed myself." He waved his arm in an arc, indicating the lab. "That's what all this is."

"What is?"

"It's a grand experiment. They're going to merge us. Make us one."

She gasped, and her mouth fell open. "What?"

"They have this serum, see. I get the serum. It changes me somehow. Then I infect you, like with a scratch. We become truly identical at that point. More than clones, they say. Then—" he pointed to the large postmodern Frankenstein-type Tesla coils mounted around the gurneys "—they hit us with some electricity. Then we'll be one."

Angela leaned forward as much as the restraints let her as four drones rolled up pallets with flesh pods on them. They weren't pulsing like the other ones from Hallsville, but they were larger and more robust. Their blue veins bulged out along their sides like a plaster cast of the Mississippi Valley. Her skin tingled at their sight. "Why would you want to do that, Chris?"

Chris shrugged. "We've always been better together. This is my chance to make right everything I've done fucked up." He looked back at the floor. "This'll be the last time you gotta help me."

Angela clenched her fists. A junkie will believe anything you tell him if it means a guaranteed fix. "Chris, it doesn't work that way!"

He stood up in a flash. "We were one once." He pointed his finger at her. "A mistake of nature split us apart in the womb. We're only setting things back."

"No...I don't think you understand. You aren't thinking straight. It's the drugs, Chris!" She looked around the room. "Think! All of this? It's not for you or for me. They're trying to destroy Earth."

"No, they ain't." Chris gave a slight, half-smirk and subtly wiggled his head, not quite a shake. "You can't destroy a planet." He gazed at the flesh pods out of the corner of his eye. "Not really."

A shred of doubt. "The Forsaken Dweller? I'm sure you read about it in that book, right?"

"Yeah, what about it?"

"What do you think it is?"

"Oh! He's someone they're bringing in from a parallel dimension. He controls the process." He laughed. "Forgot to mention him."

"No, Chris," she said in a near whisper. "The Forsaken Dweller *is* the universe. It's going to convert Earth into energy like black tar heroin on a spoon and suck it up like a syringe."

"What?"

"That's right! They need our blood for the ritual, to open the portal—" she looked around "—probably right here in this fucking room." His eyes met hers. She knew he was having second thoughts. Twins can't lie to each other. His drugged mind was foggy, though. "We sent that large book from the warehouse to experts. They've verified the math."

Chris licked his lips and looked around. "No, way! An intelligent universe? Woah! Now that's a trip!"

Two men in white lab coats walked up to Chris. "We're ready to start the procedure, Mr. Hollingsworth." One of them set a shiny, metallic case down on the table.

One of them stepped around to her side. He held a syringe up and pressed the plunger until a clear fluid shot out. "This is the catalyst, Agent Hollingsworth."

"Catalyst? Catalyst for what?" She struggled against the restraints.

"You shouldn't feel any discomfort, but if you continue to resist, you might injure yourself."

She knew he was right. The IV tube was too long to deter the injection. The fluid disappeared from the syringe and into her hand. As soon as the chilly liquid hit her vein, a strong sense of déjà vu struck her. Hard. Harder than in the church basement. This was it. The end. The two universes were touching right there in that room. She looked at Chris. The other drone had done the same thing to him.

"Please lay back onto the gurney, Mr. Hollingsworth."

Chris slowly stepped over and did as he was asked.

"Chris…" Angela whined.

"This is gonna work, right guys?" Chris asked. His voice shook.

"Of course, Mr. Hollingsworth," the empty-handed drone said. He gently strapped Chris's left arm down.

Chris looked at it. "Are the straps necessary?"

"Of course, they are, Mr. Hollingsworth," the drone with

the syringe said. "We've discussed this many times. The serum will wring changes from your body that could be violent. This is for your protection, as well as ours."

"Chris!" Angela screamed. "Don't let them do this to us!"

"Is what she's saying true? About Earth?"

"Of course, Mr. Hollingsworth. But that won't happen right away. It will take thousands of your years."

"We'll still be one though, right?"

"Of course, Mr. Hollingsworth."

"No," she murmured. She peeked over to the doorman monitoring the security screen. It was studying her. She was certain the look on its face was one of victory. She glanced down at the monitor when it blanked out as a bright flash of light lit up the alley. When it cleared, the SWAT entry team stood ready with Artemis, Apollo, and Danny standing center and proud in front of them.

Relief washed through her, turning her stomach into quivering jelly. She worked hard to suppress a joyous giggle. She didn't realize how alone she was until she saw them. She was even glad Apollo the Turd had shown up.

They immediately moved into action around the door and ran off the screen. A loud explosion blew the door and wall in the far corner to splinters. Dusty drywall powder clouded the area. Everyone in the room, including the two drones tending to Chris, looked up as the flash bangs bounced across the floor.

Angela closed her eyes and opened her mouth. It was the best defense against them.

Unfortunately, the room was too large to contain the compression blasts, and as one, every drone in the place ran to intercept the SWAT team as they stormed out of the cloud in single file. Arrows flew past them, skewering drones and doormen alike.

"Hang on, Chris! Help's here!"

"Wait…what…how did they find us?" he screeched. "Are you lo-jacked?"

"Yes, I am, you little shit!" she screamed as she jerked at her restraints. As if to confirm that statement, her phone starting playing a muffled Disturbed ringtone from within her pants. "Now get me out of this!"

Chris scrambled to untie the single restraint holding him down. Knots flexed on the side of his face. "You don't understand!" His neck muscles corded up. "I need this! I need to be perfect like you!"

"I'm not perfect, Chris! You're fuckin' stoned! Now let's go home, dammit!"

"They don't love me! They love you!" He stood up, unrestrained, his tennis shoes squeaking on the shiny floor. "But I'm going to change that!" He spun and ran towards the workstation nearest the closest flesh pod. He typed a few quick commands and turned to watch the pods as they swelled and pulsated. He pointed to one of the doormen on the other side of the room, and it shoved an electrical breaker closed. Lightning bolts shot across the room with loud crackles of discharge. He shined a dark, grinly face at her. "You'll see!"

Angela looked past him. While a doorman shot acid webbing at her rescuers, two of the SWAT team fired on full-auto at it. The lightning bolts healed it, though.

She jerked at her cuffs and looked back at Chris. He flipped open the top of the small, metallic case and withdrew a syringe. Pus-yellow fluid sloshed in the tube. "I'm scared, Kis," she said softly as he put the needle to his arm. "I won't be able to catch you."

As the point pressed into his skin next to the multitude of old needle scars and even newer scabs, he stopped and looked up at her. For a moment, a bare moment, he was that little boy standing on top of the TV, scared out of his mind but determined to get his prize. Then he shook his head, inserted the needle, and pushed the plunger down. He screamed in hellish agony and fell to his knees, the syringe still in his arm.

"Angela!" a voice called from across the room. Lightning and rapid-fire machine guns deafened her, but the sound of her name wormed through the explosions. To her left. Danny was tearing his clothes off. She looked back at Chris. Hair sprouted from his arms.

She struggled against the shackles, and her right arm popped loose. "Hurry, Danny!"

Schlorping from her left. One pod down. Three to go. SWAT must have been briefed on hers and Danny's last encounter. They were shooting the pods and ignoring the doormen. They were also falling like flies cocooned in spider webbing. Webbing coated in battery acid.

The world turned blue as one of the lightning bolts struck her metal gurney. She'd never been kicked by a mule, but when her chest constricted, she figured she had. She slammed back against the gurney. Her tongue was thick. *Copper pennies. Yuck!*

She wasn't sure where the thought came from, but her training on tasers kicked in. She laid back. Heather's voice said, "Enjoy the ride, sister. Don't force it. Let it happen." Heather, the drug coach. *Ah, college.*

A howl broke her taser trip.

She was familiar with Danny's howl. This was not his. She flopped her head to the side. Chris squatted on all fours.

Muscles ripped through his shirt and jeans. His tennis shoes split along their soles.

Oh, no! "Dannah!" she yelled with a taser-thick tongue. "Dannah! Danny!"

A growl on her left. She flopped her head again. Danny stood above her. He slashed at her restraints, and an electrical bolt shot from the gurney to his hand. It knocked him down.

She forced her way through the effects of her electroshock therapy. She reached over and unstrapped her left arm.

Chris stood up and stretched. He was a Hulk version of Danny. Overdeveloped muscles bulged. Two feet taller. No forehead to speak of. Low eyebrow ridges. Shorter snout. Two rows of fangs. And three times as pissed.

She sat up. Keeping one eye on Chris-Monster, she made a quick tactical appraisal. More SWAT lay on the floor. Two more pods destroyed. Two doormen guarded the last one while drones rushed the machine guns.

Chris-Monster turned his head and stared at her. Insanity burned in his eyes. This was not Chris. This was not a *Frenator*. And it was not strapped to the gurney.

Danny growled and stood up.

Chris-Monster took one giant step towards her. Claws out. Snout snarling. Slaver dripping.

Muscles pulled and corded along her arms and legs as she frantically strained and struggled against the restraints holding her legs.

Danny's claws dug into the linoleum. He took off like a shot, putting himself between the twins. If Chris-Monster managed to scratch her, to transfer that fucked up pseudo-*lupus* virus….

Angela's FBI analysis training took over again; her mind sped up, slowing the events around her, giving her time to evaluate all threats. She scrutinized Chris-Monster. He was a beast, raw savagery, half again larger than Danny, ruthless in his single-minded pursuit of infecting her. She compared that with what she knew of Danny. He too was a beast, but there was a modicum of civilization there. This was not the time to be civil. Danny was not going to win this dogfight. And he was the only thing between her and her brother. Only one thing could save her. Save Chris. Hell, save planet Earth if you believed that shit.

"Danny!" she yelled. "Scratch me!"

Danny leaped towards the monster facing him and swung his claws. He alternated between right and left, right and left. The monster's chest opened up into deep furrows.

The smell of wet dog and blood reached her.

Chris-Monster screamed in pain and anger. He twisted to the side and unwound, clobbering Danny in the head, sending him across the room to land next to Angela's gurney.

"Danny! Do it! Do it now!"

Danny crawled to his feet and met Angela's gaze with glassy eyes. He looked down at his claws, the claws they both knew he had to use on her. Then a deep, rumbling roar came from behind him followed by an outstretched claw. It raked her partner across the back. His sadness turned to pain. He fell forwards on her. Chris-Monster grabbed him by the neck and pulled him away as one would pick up a rag doll. Chris-Monster's gaze never left Angela.

"Now, Danny!"

As Chris-Monster yanked her partner away, claws raked down her left shoulder to her breast and her stomach.

Angela screams as fire roars through her scratches. It spreads out from them. It covers her whole body. Every strand of hair turns into a white-hot icepick and jabs her skin. Her clothes rub her raw. The gunfire pounds her skull. The hum of the electronics makes her teeth ache. Man-smells—fear, anger, determination—make her stomach growl with hunger.

A smell. Woman. Strong woman. Shooting arrows. Angela loves her. Would do anything for her.

And the smell of her brother, Chris. Strong. *Lupus* strong. It's not right, though. Not natural.

He's fighting Danny. Why are they fighting? That's right! Chris did something bad. That's why. What was it? Fuzzy. She only knows she needs to punish him. He's always getting in trouble. Pissing the pack off.

She tries to get up. Her feet are tied down.

She howls in anger.

She jerks at the leather straps.

She slashes at them, and they come apart.

Panting, she jumps up. Her clothes still rub her. They burn. She rips them, shreds them, lets them fall to the floor…

…and rushes Chris. She has to punish him.

Danny. Bleeding. Still fighting. Falling.

Chris stands two heads taller than her. She rushes in, slash after slash. She backs up. Crouches. Danny shambles to Chris's other side. Instinct. Bracket the prey.

She wipes her snout. Blood lands on her tongue. Her brain turns to a buzzing fire. Her nipples tingle. Other places do too. Love, lust, addiction. She needs more. She licks her claws. The muscles in her arms, her legs, her back, warm and relax. She quivers.

The fire doesn't bother her any longer.

Chris rushes Angela, snarling. Almost catches her off-guard. She pounces the same time Danny does. He lands on Chris's back. Danny buries his fangs in Chris's neck. Chris roars in agony.

Angela veers left. Chris swings his hand at her. She catches his wrist in between her own fangs. She slashes out with her right hand and rakes her talons across his stomach. He shakes his arm, tries to shake her off. She flops. Her neck hurts. Instinct tells her not to let go. She bites harder.

She reaches out with both hands and grabs a double handful of spine and ribs. Chris screeches even louder and slashes at her with his free hand. Danny's arms wrap around Chris's chest and the same arm Angela is chewing into. He's trying to hold on too. His claws dig into Chris's chest and plow deep furrows. Ribs pop out.

The smell of blood overwhelms her. She will do anything to have it.

Chris drops to his knees. His free arm slashing. First at Angela. Next at Danny. He gives a final, bubbly growl and drops face-first to the floor.

Angela scrambles to the side. Her throat is scratchy. Vision blurred. Cold. She feels sad but doesn't know why. She skitters up and pokes Chris. Her brother. He's dead. She wails until stars dot her vision.

She stands and licks the blood from her talons. The blood on her tongue is hot. The heat spreads through her body. She's not cold any longer.

Heartbeats slam her ears. Prey across the room. The pounding gunfire is coming from them. She rushes them. **"You hurt my ears!"** she growls and dashes for them.

"No! Let them be!" Danny growls at her.

A shiver runs down her spine. Her ears fall to the sides. She needs the control. She wants to be told what to do. She drops to the floor and stares up at Danny.

He blinks and sprints across the room. There is a creature. Not human. Not tasty. She knows. Danny smells of anger and desperation. She follows him. They must kill the not-human.

It doesn't run from them. It doesn't smell like food. Its smell burns her nose when she concentrates on it. She sneezes as she and Danny both leap at the not-human. Bullets tear into its flesh as they bury their claws in its guts. Its hand slaps a big, black button on the control console. Bolts of lightning erupt from the walls, the ceiling, the floor, and the machinery, striking her, Danny, and the not-human. She loses control of her muscles. The light gets brighter and then fades to black.

She falls to the floor, but she knows she did something good. And she knows she did something bad. She can't tell the difference, though.

Drills. Yeah. Drills. That's it. Drilling my head. They're turning me into Frankenstein's Monster. To hell with the Bride shit. Even God screwed up the first time. That's why he made woman. We're perfect. Except for that stinking chocolate addiction. And Italian food. Damn, I love Italian food. I love its smell, the meat, the pasta. The medicine. Medicine? Lots of it. And blood and guts and chlorine. And cowboys.

Angela fluttered her eyelids a couple of times, and when the light didn't scorch her brain, she left them open. She tried to raise her hand to wipe the hair out of her face, but both arms were tied down. Tightly. Legs, too. She shook her hair out of her face instead and looked around.

Wow. What a dream.

She expected a laboratory, not the inside of an ambulance. An IV tube dangled from her left hand, neatly taped. She pulled against her restraints again.

"Hello?"

Danny opened the back doors of the ambulance and stuck his head in. "Hey."

"Hey, yourself," she said. "What's going on?" She lifted an arm and rattled the straps.

He didn't answer her. Instead, he crawled up inside and sat down next to her. "How do you feel?"

"Fine," she said. "Now let me out of these!"

He placed a hand on her shoulder. "Give me a few minutes first, okay, partner?" The look on his face told her she needed to shut up and listen.

Damn, he smells good. Wild. Woah, slow down, girl!

She nodded her head. "I remember waking up in a doorman lab, tied to a metal gurney." She relaxed for a few minutes. "Chris was there. And a bunch of doormen." Then…"Oh, crap! He wanted to turn me into one of those weird-ass werewolves!" Memories flooded her brain. Danny raking his claws across her shoulder. She tried to reach up and pull the gown from her shoulder.

"Here," Danny said. "Let me." He lifted the fabric and looked off to the side, giving her a bit of privacy.

There on her shoulder and down across her breast, four scars told her the nightmare flooding her mind had been real. She let her head drop back to the pillow. Her stomach rolled, and her heart beat in her chest like a baseball bat on a 55-gallon barrel. *Monster!* She looked around, seeking a way to escape. Not enough air. "I have to get out of here! I can't breathe!"

Danny scooted towards her and talked in level tones.

"Angela, I need you to take slow, deep breaths. You know about *lupis*. There's no need to be scared. But you do have to realize that you are one now."

She gently pulled on her restraints. "Can you…" Her lips were dry. "Can you let me out of here?" The inside of the ambulance was stifling. "I have to get out!"

"No, Angela. What you have to do is take control." Danny ran his hand over her forehead. "If you don't, you'll change. You'll break out of here and kill a bunch of people. And if you're lucky, real lucky, you might survive another day. Because once the word gets out that a *lupa* has gone on a feeding spree, the Fectors will come for you."

She raised her head and looked out the back of the ambulance. Green fields. Blue sky. She tried the restraints again.

I want to run! To hunt! Danny's blood tickled her nose.

She forced herself to take steady breaths, to lick her lips. "You call that a pep talk?"

He smiled at her. "That's good," he said after a few moments. "That's real good." When she'd finally got her breathing under control, he said, "Most people either pass out or perform a *renovatio* when they find out. I guess being around a werewolf kinda prepped you."

"I don't know why I was surprised. I asked you to do it."

"True. But knowing it and understanding it are two different things." He reached down and pressed the up button on her gurney to lift her into a sitting position.

"Did we win?" she asked.

"It depends on what you call winning," he said. "We lost 12 SWAT, seven injured. Two Task Force agents, Brad and one from Chicago. Arnold Verstat. Kent's lost a leg. That acid webbing burned it off clean right above the knee. He might lose an eye. Don't know yet."

"Any bad guys left?"

"No. Six doormen dead. Untold numbers of drones have died all around the world too. Seems they were all connected somehow to something in the lab. Their brains melted right inside their skulls."

She stared out the back of the ambulance.

He leaned back. "And I'm no longer *lupus*."

She snapped her head around. "What?" She blinked a few times. "I thought there wasn't a cure."

"Me, too." His eyes softened, and he closed his mouth.

"Oh, hell, Danny. I'm sorry."

He shrugged. "I don't know how humans go through life with their senses dulled like this."

"You get used to it," she said.

He smiled. "I want you to remember that when you start going through sensory storms. You will come out the other si—"

"Oh, shit!" she exclaimed. "Chris!" Her eyes turned hot, her vision, watery.

"Yes." He unstrapped her arms and legs.

"I tried to save him." A sob rattled her chest. "I did, Danny. What do I tell Mom and Daddy?"

He didn't say anything. He sat there and let her cry on his shoulder.

Angela stood by the graveside, her arm linked with Randy's while her mom and dad stood on her other side. Heather and Danny were across from them, her mother and the general standing next to each other.

The reverend droned on about life and death. Life and death. Life and death.

Why couldn't they ever talk about the fun times? I guess that's what wakes are for.

Somber. Cheerful. Life and death. The happy part before the sad part. Until you're actually dead, and they have the fun part. Maybe people should have more fun before they die. Then the funerals would be a formality. A quick, "Adios, Amigo!" She squeezed Randy's arm a little tighter.

Afterwards, she walked arm in arm with her mother to the limousine. Randy and her dad followed them. "Mom," she said, stopping and looking her in the eyes. "Chris was trying to better himself at the end."

"He was?" She stood a little straighter and stopped her sniffling for a moment.

"Yes, ma'am."

"Well, he wasn't that bad. He was a good boy. Life cut too short." She laid her head on Angela's shoulder. "I'm glad you got the people who killed him."

"Me, too."

"You always were the responsible one."

Angela knocked on Kent's door.

"Come."

She and Danny stepped into the office. Garry McNeil sat at Kent's desk. "You wanted us, sir?"

"Yes, I did," he confirmed. "Please sit down. I've read your report in great detail along with the debriefings from all other personnel at the doormen laboratory." He patted a tall stack of folders. "Well done. Both of you." He looked at Danny in particular.

"Are we still being tested?" he asked, not without a bit of sarcasm in his voice.

"Of course. Every agent, every day."

"We stopped the Forsaken Dweller." She was ready to get back to work. Convalescent leave was over. "What next?"

"To start with, the Diutinus. Thanks to our success and the intelligence we gave them, they've moved on to another planet. They'll visit from time to time to check on us, though."

"I'm going to miss Artemis, but I think that's great news," Angela said. "If they feel confident enough to leave, they think our world is safe."

"Indeed," Garry said, nodding. "You two saved mankind. I going to hate losing you."

"Sir?"

"You're a werewolf now. And Danny here isn't." He sat back up and pulled a red file folder from inside the stack. "It says here, 'Senior Special Agent Hollingsworth has yet to control the change from human to *Lupus sapiens*. She is what the *lupus* community refers to as a *Defrenator* or a wildling. As the description indicates, she is wild, uncontrolled. It is the judgment of this medical board that she remains on medical leave until such time as she learns to *Frenis* or control the change.'" He flipped the cover closed.

Angela knew this was coming. The only reason Danny qualified as a full-time consultant was because he was a *Frenator*. Now he wasn't even a werewolf any longer. Everyone's best guess is Chris's pseudo-*lupus* virus combined with the electrical shock killed the real virus in his system. He's even immune now. She, however, was not. The catalyst the drones injected her with appeared to have protected the *lupus* virus in her system. It's also why she transformed as soon as the virus hit her bloodstream instead of waiting for the next full moon.

Lucky me.

"Well, sir, I would like to remain on duty. I feel I can keep it under con—"

"Not according to Danny's report—" he flipped open another file "— 'She's not going to be able to control it under high-stress situations. And I'm not going to be able to tamp down on her. I'm no longer *lupus*.'"

Angela snapped her head around and stared hard at her partner. He was looking at his hands. She couldn't blame him even though she wanted to. "Well…shit."

"Yeah, a real bitch, huh?" Garry pursed his lips, stood, and stared out the window. "Agent, you have entirely too much experience for me to let you work on your tan. And Danny has told us that if he can't work with you, he's going back to Redstick." He turned around and stared at them. "For all intents and purposes, I would be losing two agents for the price of one." He cocked a sideways grin. "It's been a while since grade school, but I can still cipher. That doesn't add up for me."

Angela's heart pounded in her chest. Excitement. Not anger. She was learning what emotions triggered a *renovatio*. Excitement could, but rarely.

"So, Agent Hollingsworth, I'm assigning you to restricted duty until you learn to—"

He opened another folder, but Danny interrupted him. "*Frenis*."

"Yes, until you learn to *Frenis*. In fact, it's going to be boring. I'm assigning you to follow-up investigations. Making sure paperwork is complete. You might get to consult with other agents. You will not be participating in raids. I've even debated confiscating your sidearm. However, I would prefer it be handy should the situation arise versus having you fall back on the alternative." He sat back down in his chair and neatly arranged all the folders again. "And if you think we were testing and watching you two before, it's nothing compared to the scrutiny you'll be facing going forward.

"Bill, I believe, has been loading up your desk with follow-ups. I'm sure you'll enjoy the change of pace. Dismissed."

Tom Bont

Latin to English Translations

To assist the reader, below are English translations of the Latin phrases and words used throughout this tome. Translations and pronunciations may not be exact, but this is how the Race has handed them down from generation to generation; as with any language, there is drift in meaning and pronunciation.

Defrenator / Defrenatus
Noun: dē-frə-nā'-tôr/dē-frə-nā'-tus

1. A *lupus* who has not learned to control his or her emotions or make conscious decisions while transformed.
2. Slang: Wildling, Unbridled.
3. Plural: *Defrenatus*.

Frenator / Frenatus
Noun: fren'-ə-tôr/fren-ät'-tus

1. A *lupus* who has learned to control his or her emotions and make conscious decisions while transformed.
2. Slang: Bridled.
3. Plural: *Frenatus*.

Frenis
Verb: fren'-is

1. To control one's emotions and make conscious decisions while transformed.

2. Bridle, control, restrain.

Interfectore

Noun: in-tər-fek-tôr'-ə

1. Killer.
2. Murderer.
3. Slang: Fector. A member of *Lucerna Veritatis*.

Lucerna Veritatis

Noun, Phrase: lü-ser'-nə()**ver-i-tā'-tis**

1. Lamp of Truth.
2. Ancient order of priests formed to fight *Lupus sapiens*.

Luna Amator

Noun, Phrase: lü'-nə()ä-mä-tôr'

1. Moon lover.
2. Clan Name.
3. The *Luna Amator* Clan originates from the northeastern portion of North America.

Lupa/Lupas

Noun: lü'-pə/lü'-pəz

1. Slang for female *Lupus sapiens*.
2. *Lupas*, the plural form, is used when referring to multiple females.

Lupus/Lupis

Noun: lü'-pəs/lü'-pis

1. Slang for male *Lupus sapiens*. May refer to males or

females.

2. *Lupis*, the plural form, is used when referring to multiple males or males and females together. Does not typically refer to the individuals of the entire Race.

Lupus Rex

Noun, Phrase: lü'-pəs()reks

1. Wolf King.

Lupus/Lupis sapiens

Noun, Phrase: lü'-pəs/lü'-pis()sā'-pē-ənz

1. Wise wolf.
2. Scientific name for the werewolf species.
3. Used when referencing the entire Race as a whole.
4. *Lupis*, the plural form, is typically used when referring to the group of individuals comprising the entire Race.
5. Slang: Howler, Race, werewolf, *lupus, lupa*.

Lupus (Lupis)(Lupa)(Lupas) solitarius

Noun, Phrase: lü'-pəs()sä-lə-ter'-rē-əs

1. Lone or solitary Wolf.
2. A *lupus* who has been shunned by the Race, or one who is not recognized by the Race.

Renovatio/Innovationes

Noun: re-nə-vä'-tē-ō/in-ə-vä'-shən-əs

1. Rebirth, rejuvenate, or renewal.
2. The transformation from human to *lupus*.

3. Plural: *Innovationes.*

Sans Peur

Noun, Phrase: sänz()pyür

1. Without fear.
2. Clan Name.
3. The *Sans Peur* Clan originates from the British Isles.

Vagor

Noun: vā'-gor

1. A howl, typically a commandant.

Viatorius/Viator

Noun, Phrase: (v)(w)ē-ə-tôr'-ə-us/(v)(w)ē'-ə-tôr

1. Traveler.
2. Ancient times: a *lupus* tasked with spreading *Lupus Rex's* decrees
3. Modern times: a *lupus* given free reign to go where and when he wants to.
4. A non-shunned *Lupus solitarius.*

Viam Lupus

Noun, Phrase: (v)(w)ē'-əm()lü'-pəs

1. The Way of the Wolf.

If you liked *Hollingsworth*, then you'll like
Howlers: Lupus Rex

Other Works by Tom Bont

Howlers: Lupus Rex universe

- *Howlers: Lupus Rex*
- Father Jake Chronicles
  - *Howlers: Candle in the Night* (novelette)
  - *Howlers: The Eye of God's Wrath* (novelette)

No Bullshit Stories

- *Transplanted Yankee: Lest All My Balderdash Be Forgotten*

With Alan O'Brien

- *Iron Broderick*
  - TWB Press

Young Adult Southern Humor

- Big Game (working title)

Short Stories

- "Redstick"
  - *Roadkill: Texas Horror by Texas Authors*, Eakin Press
- "Concerning the Affairs of Jeremiah James"
  - http://moonmagazine.org/
  - http://jumbelbook.com/wordpress/
- "Free Range"
  - http://www.theflashfictionpress.org
- "Liars' Club"
  - *Locked In*, Horrified Press
- "Mhuld'enda of the Deep"
  - *Lovecraftiana, Walpurgisnacht 2018,* Rogue Planet Press
- "Conrad Usry's Estate"
  - *Rabbit Hole*, Writers' Co-op
- "That Kind of Magic"
  - TWB Press

- "Rocket Fuel"
  - http://jumbelbook.com/wordpress/

Short Stories - Upcoming
- "Merry-Go-Round"
  - *Twisted Time*, Horrified Press
- "Cotton Candy"
  - *Bought and Sold*, Horrified Press

Tom Bont

About the Author

Tom is a United States Navy veteran, has a degree in computer science from Louisiana Tech University, is a licensed pilot, and is a competitive dancer. He lives in North Texas with his family. Married since 1992, he still spends as many hours as he can on the dance floor with his wife.

You can catch him at:

- www.TomBont.com
- Facebook: @AuthorTomBont
- Twitter @TomBont
- DFW Writers' Workshop